THE OTHER

THE OTHER

Matthew Buscemi

Published by Matthew Buscemi, 2020
Seattle, Washington USA

ISBN 978-1-62802-020-5

Typeset by Matthew Buscemi in Eloquence with Helvetica Neue display

This is a work of fiction. All of the characters, organizations, and events portrayed in this
novel are products of the author's imagination. Any similarity to real events or people,
living or dead, is entirely coincidental.

to Alex
for helping me remember why

TABLE OF CONTENTS

ASURA
Year 91

Citrine
Cynine
Deniz Bay
Adamantine
Asym Valley
Bengine
Barne
Bekel Plains
Dazine
Adrine
PORTAL CITY
Exenine
Besserine
Eline
Enim Valley
Enerine
Eser Coast

KILOMETERS
0   50   100   150   200

N
W   E
S

● The Reclamation
■ Nanite-Bodied Cities

PART I

Walls

"Why are you here, Charles?"

"I don't remember."

"Don't be smart with me, Charles."

"I'm not trying to be smart with you."

"What is your purpose in the Reclamation?"

"I don't remember."

"What are your objectives?"

"I want to talk to Dr. Ekeer."

"Don't be smart with me, Charles."

"..."

"Do you want to destroy the walls?"

"No."

"Do you want to transmit information back to the deranged?"

"No."

"Do you want to help the government derange everyone in the Reclamation?"

"No."

"What are the government's plans for deranging everyone in the Reclamation?"

"I don't know of any such plan, and based on what I do know, it's unlikely that such a plan exists. Dr. Ekeer said that most of the stuff you tell yourselves in the spokes is flat out misinfo—"

"Don't be smart with me, Charles."

"If I'm not that smart, why are you interrogating me? If you won't believe anything I say, why ask questions?"

"We love the Reclamation, Charles. We're going to protect it, with or without your help."

"I want to talk to Dr. Ekeer."

"That's not possible, Charles. He and his party are seditious. They are endangering the Reclamation."

"That's not what it looks like to me."

"Tell us, then. Tell us all about your time with Dr. Ekeer. Start from the beginning. Tell us what they're planning in the seditious cities."

"You know when you call them that, all it does is reinforce—"

"Tell us everything that happened to you from the time you woke up inside the walls."

"... Okay. Fine."

The auditorium was one of those spaces that seemed poorly lit on purpose. Pragati Una stood under a beam of light at the center of the stage, over a thousand of her supporters enshrouded in near blackness around her.

Sahaan wondered at that, all the focus on the candidate, and yet the people who would vote for her couldn't see one another. They still cheered for her at all the right moments though. Every beat he'd written into the speech caused a small laugh or cheer or applause to go up from the assembled crowd.

He stood in a room with glass walls, far back and suspended over the rear of the auditorium. To his left, in an adjacent room were the media folks, whose background chatter was more interesting than the speech itself.

Bharo stood next to him, his hands stuffed in his pockets. "I don't know why we even bother at this point."

"It does seem kind of pointless in Adamantine."

Bharo shrugged. "Pointless anywhere, if you ask me."

Sahaan shook his head. He, like the rest of the cabinet staff, had watched the polling data attentively for the past nine months. Una had it in the bag. Always had. But that was just data. Something about the whole situation didn't feel right. "I don't know about that."

Bharo turned his head just enough so that Sahaan could see his raised eyebrow. "You still taking that trip to Citrine?"

"Yeah."

"You sure you don't want to come back to the capitol instead?"

"The acceptance speech is already done."

"There's talk about getting a bigger space for the election night party. We could use your help."

That caused Sahaan to raise an eyebrow. "There's a bigger space than Portal City Convention Center?"

"The arena."

"No kidding." A thought jumped to his mind. He'd briefly dated a theater major in college, one who'd taught him he was never to wish luck upon an actor before their performance, but should instead tell them to 'break a leg.' He wondered if perhaps Una wasn't rushing her assumptions.

Both of them paused to watch how the crowd would respond to a particular beat in the speech—one about finding ways to work together with their political opponents. The crowd clapped. Funny how that worked with this side and not the other.

Bharo, seeming to sense Sahaan's unease, added, "we're getting a good deal on the space rental, and there has been demand for more tickets."

"All the more reason for me to go to Citrine."

Bharo shook his head. "All the data says that's a lost cause."

"Sometimes you don't do a thing because of the data."

Another beat in the speech. That one didn't go over quite as well as Sahaan had hoped but it had managed to garner some applause. He'd have to think about how to present infrastructure maintenance. In a civilization that depended on four-nine's integrity of quantum field-generating walls, the cost of infrastructure was a touchy subject for both political parties. Except, of course, for Una's idiot opponent, who wanted to build six hundred fifty kilometers more of them at a time when they were barely managing to maintain the walls they already had.

Bharo cast him a skeptical side-glance, hands still shoved in pockets. "Why do you do it, then?"

Sahaan shook his head slowly. "Because the spokes matter."

Sahaan and Bharo stayed on until the end of the speech, and even a little later still. Una smiled graciously at the end, then waved as she walked offstage. She had good presence, her delivery of the speech had been near-flawless, and the crowd adored her, but there was something Sahaan couldn't quite place about this entire campaign cycle, something he especially sensed when he watched the chatter from the other side on the media. Now that he was thinking about this, he realized, it wasn't so much the chatter on the other side that bothered him, but the way his colleagues *ignored* what the other side was saying. That and the growing sense that the other side was ignoring them, too.

The assembled crowd dispersed slowly through the auditorium exits while Sahaan and Bharo checked the email and news on their handhelds. Initial media reports confirmed Sahaan's sense that Una's speech had gone over well.

"Is Una still heading back to Portal City tonight?" Sahaan asked.

Bharo looked up from his handheld. "That's the plan. We still on for dinner?"

Sahaan nodded.

Once the crowd had gone, they hailed a cab and went to their favorite restaurant in Adamantine, The Hedgerow. Hedgerows, a particularly rare ancient flora, had been re-cultivated from ancient biomatter preserved in the former scientific and military bunker that the city of Adamantine had been built on top of, which, before the founding of the Reclamation, had been called merely 'A2.' Those hedgerows now lined the entire restaurant front and were a distinguishing feature of the large public gardens adjacent to it.

Bharo talked almost exclusively about their post-election plans, mostly all the different ways that they were going to try to establish relations with the nanite-bodied, who lived beyond the Reclamation's walls.

He remembered the first time, as a child, when his father had shown him the satellite images. Portal City and all the hub cities were swathed in green. Brown roads stuck out from them, reaching out to little dots of green on the periphery. Beyond them, for thousands of miles in all directions, the ground was red-brown with splotches of silver. And then there were the cities of the nanite-bodied, spiky pinnacles of serrated metal.

It was time to figure out what was going on out there, but Sahaan maintained a mild concern that some of his colleagues were jumping to the conclusion that the nanite-bodied would not threaten them again. Especially in Sahaan's family, no one could forget the fact that barely more than a century ago, the expressed goal of the nanite-bodied had been to mutate all of humanity into their idea of 'perfect.'

"Is Una still planning on dinner with the Alterran prime minister tomorrow?" Sahaan asked.

Bharo smiled as he chewed his salad.

"Is there a story there?"

"Just rumors," Bharo said. "It seems that they don't like each other much. I think the only thing they have in common is complete revulsion toward Gadh."

That was Una's opponent in the election.

"Maybe they can spend the whole dinner talking about him, then."

Bharo chortled. "Maybe."

"I wonder though..." Sahaan was immediately sorry he'd given voice to his wandering thoughts.

"What's that?"

"Oh, nothing."

The expression on Bharo's face told him he wouldn't be getting away with that. What are best friends for, anyway?

"I just wonder... Clearly Gadh is resonating with people in the spokes. Take, for example, the walls. He wants to expand the Reclamation to include the Asym Valley, the Eser Coast, the Esim Valley, and the Bekel Plains. Now, adding, let alone maintaining that much more wall would devastate the economy and be a maintenance liability. And, of course, it would leave us vulnerable to attack. But to them, it would make them safer. Citrine, Bengine, Exenine, and Enerine would effectively become 'outer hub' cities."

Bharo had stopped eating his salad and was now looking at Sahaan as though there were food on his face.

"They want what we get to take for granted. A feeling of safety."

"You've read the same reports I have, right? The ones that explain how it doesn't matter if you're in Portal City or a hub city or a spoke city? How, if a hostile nanite-bodied could actually get through, all parts of the Reclamation would instantly become insecure."

"Yes."

"So?"

"They don't read government reports out in the hub."

"Why not? They're not classified or anything. This government has gone out of its way to be transparent about our security risks and our security strategy. Establishing contact is part of that."

How could Sahaan explain? "It has to feel that way to them."

Bharo chortled in that dismissive way he sometimes did. His dismissiveness of the spokes was one of Sahaan's least favorite qualities in him, but Sahaan checked his irritation straight away.

"I prefer to operate on facts," Bharo said.

Sahaan let the topic drop and took a few bites of his

salad before turning the conversation to the details of Una's election party.

That night, back in his hotel room, Sahaan wasted no time dialing his home on the handheld and linking into the room's holography.

His son appeared on the line. "Hey, Dad!"

"Heya, Jaan. How are you doing?"

"Good! I drew a map of the Reclamation at school and Mr. Drid said it was the best one."

"Great job! Do you have it at home?"

"Sure, just a sec." Jaan's hologram moved away, dissipating in Sahaan's room as his son moved out of the scanning area. His form rematerialized momentarily, holding a rendering of the Reclamation coastline, complete with dots for all twelve Reclamation cities, excepting Portal City, where he'd drawn a star instead. He'd even done the wallroutes, too, which he'd highlighted in bright yellow.

"That's really good work, Jaan. Do you like drawing?"

"Yeah, it's all right. I think I like math better. Or maybe reading. I'm not sure."

Sahaan smiled. Both a reader and an artist and a mathematician. Whatever his son ended up doing, Sahaan was sure it was going to be amazing.

"Are you coming home soon?"

The question stung. "Soon. Two more days. I'm going to Citrine tomorrow morning. I have to host a town hall meeting. Then I'm going to come straight back home on the train. You have any plans for this weekend?"

"I was maybe going to sleep over at Rahan's."

Sahaan had been planning him a surprise trip to the next Quantums game. He could easily get two more tickets, he thought. He'd call Rahan's father and see if they both wanted to join them. With the election nearly over, this coming weekend would be a brief lull in between large workloads.

"Sounds like fun," Sahaan said. "Is your mom there?"

Jaan nodded.

"Can you get her for me?"

"Sure."

"Love you."

"Love you, too," Jaan said as he scampered off.

Before long, Lachel shimmered into appearance in his room.

"How is everything?" Sahaan asked.

"Pretty well. This is the last stop on your campaign, right?"

"Not quite. One more town hall in Citrine."

Lachel's smile dropped.

"It's only two more days."

"I should know how these election cycles work by now. Once the election's over, you'll be tied up for three months at a minimum."

"That's why I'm taking Jaan to a Quantums game this weekend. But don't tell him. I still have to see if Mein and Rahan can go."

"Even if they can't, you should take him anyway."

"Oh?"

"He talks about you constantly. He can spend any weekend with Rahan. He won't even let me tell the story. He says it has to be you."

Sahaan quirked a smile. "I'm worried that story is going to his head."

"I think he just likes hearing stories. Probably any

story would do, as long as it came from you."

"And what would *you* like to do on our one weekend alone?"

"Well, I did have a big stack of papers to grade, and I can't think of anything else to do with Jaan at his friend's."

"Nothing comes to mind?" Sahaan grinned.

Lachel winked. "Just the papers."

"If I were to make dinner..."

"Sounds perfect."

"See you then."

Lachel's smile turned inquisitive. "Did you say Citrine?"

"Yeah."

"I heard they're voting Gadh. Hard. Not even remotely swing."

"That's right."

A moment's awkward silence.

"I'll be home soon. I've got the whole weekend."

Lachel's smile returned. "See you then."

"Love you."

"Love you, too."

The hologram fizzled away.

Sahaan threw himself down on the bed and stared at the blank, white ceiling. Just what did he think he was going to accomplish in Citrine, anyway?

Bharo leaned over, nudged Sahaan's arm, and whispered, "What'd you think of her argument?"

The two of them sat in the expansive, insulated basement room of Thiksay Hall. Chairs, perhaps a hundred of them, were arranged in rows before a podium. At the podium stood a woman with red hair, though Sahaan's attention had been entirely focused on the black-haired woman sitting two rows in front of him. Her name was Lachel, she was in his rhetoric class, she had two sisters (she'd mentioned it in class while answering a question), her dorm was in Choglamsar Hall (he'd overheard her talking about it with one of her friends after class), and Sahaan was wondering how he could possibly get a chance to talk to her. Perhaps if he paid more attention in rhetoric class.

"Well?" Bharo asked.

"Um, pretty good. Her presentation could use some work, though."

"You even paying attention?" He followed Sahaan's eyes. "Oooh. Got it." Another nudge in the arm. He lowered his voice even further. "You know her name yet?"

"Yeah. She's in rhetoric."

"What are you going to talk to her about?"

"No idea."

"Well, she's here, isn't she? Maybe pay attention to the speakers and see if she'll talk politics later."

Sahaan had to admit, his best friend's logic was so simple it might actually work. He paid careful attention to the next two speakers, evaluating their arguments. He didn't like the first. It was a young man he recognized from a couple of classes but had never talked to. Sahaan didn't like when members of Reconciliation, the political party of his affiliation, drifted toward implying that the nanite-bodied were actually superior to humans. The nanite-bodied, when they had controlled the majority of Asura's surface, had referred to themselves as *homo sapiens superus*, and to normal humans as *homo sapiens in-*

ferus. No one talked about that much these days. In some quarters of the Reconciliation party, mentioning it was even taboo, but so far as Sahaan could tell, it was the truth that all the history books had confirmed, not to mention the stories his grandmother had told about Sahaan's great grandfather.

Everyone clapped for the final speaker, whose speech, Sahaan decided, hadn't been bad, and he told Bharo as much. After a few closing words from the event's host, one of the university's political science professors, everyone clapped again and then began filtering out of the door at the far end of the basement. A couple of students from the Reconciliation student caucus began taking down the large white sign suspended from the ceiling over the podium, bearing the emblem of a podium, Reconciliation's ubiquitous icon.

Sahaan and Bharo struck up a conversation about the last speaker, whose presentation had been about the ways in which they might safely establish communication with the nanite-bodied. Lots of people had ideas, and various Reconciliation governments had tried a number of them out over the years, but none had yet been successful. From the lands of the nanite-bodied came only satellite imagery and silence.

"Hey, check out the deranged-lovers," jeered a male student standing just outside Thiksay hall. He had a muscular build, beady eyes, and a face full of cruelty. "Can't wait for the next Guardian government to send them all outside the walls."

"That's not funny!" A female voice from the crowd, one that caught Sahaan's attention— Oh, no, Lachel. Don't engage with the brute. Sahaan instinctively moved toward them.

"Hey!" Bharo called out.

"You're right," the man said. "It won't be funny when it happens. It'll be a relief. Good riddance to all of you."

"Why do you think Reconciliation wants reconciliation?" Lachel was leaning toward him now. "For our own amusement?"

"No. Because you're a bunch of dipshits."

Sahaan realized the man's eyes were red, and some of his friends were wobbling on their feet. They were clearly drunk. The crowd of students was looking at them now, more apprehensive or put-off, while Sahaan was desperately trying to push through them to reach Lachel.

"We're doing it because it will protect us a hell of a lot better than building more walls!"

"I'll bet the Vedans said that, too."

"You're entitled to your opinion, but that's no reason to berate people attending a political rally. We all love the Reclamation—"

He had begun laughing at her mid-sentence, and Lachel stopped, hands balling up, face red with fury. Sahaan had almost reached them.

One of the brute's troglodyte friends reached out and grasped Lachel by the arm. She shrieked and tried to pull away. Now the Reconciliationists were turning, and some were shouting at the man to let her go.

Sahaan's world was a blur. He'd never been a particularly physical person, and he'd avoided sports in high school. He'd certainly never been in a fight. All the same, he found himself hurtling toward the man with his hand on Lachel's arm and a lecherous look on his face, roaring, "Get your hands off her!"

His fist went flying through the air, all around were other people, a blur, stifling the air, an impact in his gut, then noises, perhaps voices, but he couldn't understand any of them. He found he was lying on the grass. A face hovered into view, and he smiled. It was Lachel's face, her dark hair hanging down in brilliant strands, the lamp by the path illuminating them into millions of lines of light.

"That was really stupid," she said. "But thank you all the same."

All of a sudden, he realized she was reaching out a hand toward him. He grabbed it, and she pulled him up. His head spun, and he stumbled, feeling off-balance. His gut ached terribly, and he reeled momentarily, but then felt a hand on his shoulder steadying him. Her hand, he realized. His pain was forgotten. The spinning became a kind of giddiness, and his stomach quaked, because Lachel was talking to him or perhaps because of the punch he'd absorbed, he wasn't sure.

"What's your name?"

"Sahaan."

"I'm Lachel."

"Nice to meet you."

"Same."

Sahaan blinked. "Where'd they go?"

"The bullies? A group of Reconciliation caucus members started moving toward them, and they ran off. One of them told me he got a picture of them grabbing me and asked if he could report to the campus police. I told him he could."

Sahaan felt momentarily worthless, but then he smiled, because he was talking to Lachel.

"Are you in the caucus?" she asked.

"No, I'm a poli-sci major," he said. "I always go to these."

"Do you just jump in like that every time you see trouble?"

"I don't know," Sahaan said, quite honestly. "I just didn't like the idea of those guys... assaulting you like that."

"They're bullies," she said, fidgeting, and looking off in the direction of the crowd. "Most of the time you can get bullies to back down if you stand up to them. It's because they're insecure. Apparently that doesn't work when they're drunk."

Sahaan realized she probably had somewhere to be. "Can I walk you back to your dorm?"

Lachel smiled. "Sure. If you're feeling up to it."

"I couldn't be better."

Citrine Central Station was shabbier than its hub city counterparts. The infrastructure in all the spoke cities felt that way. It wasn't for lack of government funding, certainly. It was for lack of people, which diminished their overall tax revenue. Government reports had made the fact clear for the last four decades—the Reclamation's population was migrating away from the spokes and into the hub. Anyone who could was getting out of the spoke cities. Despite the other reports, the ones that explained that the spoke cities weren't any more dangerous to live in than the hub cities, it simply felt safer to have fully reclaimed land outside the city limits. The spoke cities, to contrast, possessed a single wallroute connecting them to the hub. Besides that, it was nanite-bodied territory everywhere outside their city limits.

Sahaan exited the train station and hailed a cab, giving the driver the address of the venue. It was still early in the morning, and it was a bright, gorgeous, early summer day. He watched the streets as he went past. Half the storefronts were boarded up in the commercial district, and several houses in the residential district looked vacant, too.

Citrine had a city hall at the edge of the business district, but Sahaan had chosen a park at the city limits for his town hall meeting. He wanted the location itself to underscore the message of his presentation.

First of all, he wanted to drive home the point that the Reconciliation party's primary mandate was in fact the maintenance of the existing walls. No contact would ever be possible without adequate protection against the worst. The Reconciliation leadership understood this, despite what fringe members of their party might say.

The second element the venue highlighted was related to the park itself. Greenery was uncommon in the Reclamation. Most of the plants they had were imports from Alterra, the parallel world accessible via the portal in Portal City. However, there were also some native flora. The modern cities had all been built upon ancient defensive outposts, most of which had also been research laboratories, and some of those had preserved Asura's original flora through the dark years. Citrine's Orchard Park was also a literal orchard, one of the biggest of the Reclamation's ecological achievements. Sahaan wanted to show them that Reconciliation recognized that accomplishment.

He had a beautiful day for it. They reached the granite gates of the park, and he instructed the cab driver to drop him off at the great amphitheater at the park's rear, the one up against the metallic wall slabs, beyond which lay nanite-bodied territory.

He rolled his suitcase behind the amphitheater and parked it there, then walked up to the podium at the center of the stage. The chairs had been set out, and he saw a few of the park staff lingering in a nearby park shelter. He waved to them, and they waved back.

No one had prepared a banner or any kind of sign with the Reconciliation logo on it, he noticed. It was probably better that way. Let the park and the walls send their message.

Just before noon, Citrine citizens started to filter in and fill the chairs. The turn out wasn't amazing. He had perhaps a hundred people, about a third of the available chairs remaining empty. It reminded him of the student caucus political rallies he'd attended as an undergraduate. Too many people with 'more important things to do.' But it was a substantial group, he reminded himself. He could honestly tell Lachel and Jaan that he hadn't come for nothing.

'You're here to keep the dialogue going across the aisle,' he reminded himself. It was as important for the MPs to do that with their colleagues as it was for those in his position to make time for constituents of all varieties.

At five after twelve, he decided not to wait any longer and to get things started.

"Good afternoon," he said, and the mumbling of the audience dissipated. "My name is Dr. Sahaan Ekeer. I'm the Senior Consul to President Aavee, though that's just a fancy way of saying I advise him on what's going on in the country and help arrange things when he has to give a speech or host a formal dinner. Thank you for having me here, and especially for allowing me to host this event in Orchard Park, where you have all these beautiful fruit trees, some of which are the only of their kind in the entire Reclamation. I don't have anything else in the way of a speech. I wanted to use this time to hear your concerns and questions."

Hands shot up immediately.

"Yes," Sahaan pointed. "There in the blue shirt."

A middle-aged man stood up, and a park service person passed him a special handheld that was connected to the amphitheater speaker system. "Hello, Dr. Ekeer. I am very concerned that we will continue to have a Reconciliation government after this election. We are out here all alone, and if Reconciliation makes contact, we will be the first to go. That's why I support the Guardian party."

About half the audience clapped at the man's statement, while the other half remained awkwardly silent and looked embarrassedly toward the amphitheater's edge.

Sahaan nodded very slowly. "I hear that you're concerned about what Reconciliation governments will do to ensure your safety, and about what will happen if we establish contact with the nanite-bodied. I share your concerns, and so does everyone in the party leadership. The first priority of both Reconciliation and Guardian is the maintenance of our existing walls. The Aavee government has fully funded wall upkeep and an Una government would be no different in that regard. As to the threat level to Citrine in particular, it is a threat level that you share with the rest of the Reclamation. No one place in the Reclamation is more vulnerable than any other.

The perimeter monitoring software in Citrine is the same as the monitoring software in all eleven other cities. Now, about contact. I know this can seem particularly worrisome. I want to assure you that contact with the nanite-bodied is a *defensive* strategy. We have not had any communication with the nanite-bodied for over a century. For having shared this world with them for all that time, our information about them is shockingly limited. Satellite scans show us the locations and configurations of their cities, and that is the entirety of information about them. Establishing their intentions is, in my opinion, the best way to defend ourselves against them, if they indeed remain hostile."

More hands. "Yes, with the red hat."

An elderly woman stood, was passed the microphone handheld, her hands shaking as she spoke. "We want more wallroutes out of Citrine. Why won't Reconciliation build more wallroutes?"

"Great question. There are a number of problems with building more wallroutes right now. The biggest problem is production. Wall slabs need heavy exposure to a metaxic field for over a decade in order to work. Right now, we only have the one permanent portal to Alterra. A plan to open others is in the works, but until that happens, we can only generate about twenty wall slabs per year. Right now, we need twelve wall slabs per year in order to maintain all the walls we've got. Building a new wallroute would increase the number of wallslabs we need for maintenance, which would put our ability to maintain the walls at risk. And if there were an emergency, we could end up in a situation where more of our wall slabs fail in a year than we would be able to replace.

This would leave us open to attack.

"But there's another problem, too. Remember that we know nothing about the nanite-bodied right now. If we build new wallroutes, that act in itself might be perceived as an attack. For that matter, *anything* we do might be perceived as aggressive. We simply don't know. Knowing more will help us defend ourselves better. And the only way to know more is to start talking to them."

Sahaan noticed that some of the audience members who had clapped after the first question were now stroking their chins, or looking away pensively. He smiled inside, but didn't dare let it show on his face. Moments like these made his job feel worthwhile.

He pointed to a man in the back.

The man snatched up the handheld and spat as he spoke. "Why you callin' them 'nanite-bodied' instead of 'deranged' like they should be called."

Multiple members of the audience winced at his use of the slur, especially those who had not clapped.

"If we go back in our history, we come to a time one hundred and twenty-one years ago, the dark period, before the Reclamation existed, before our contact with Alterra. Shelters had to be covered with nanite defense perimeters, which guzzled energy and required both artificial and enhanced human intelligences to keep up with the nanite-bodied's attacks. That term you have used comes from that time, when we were under constant attack and rightly worried that our species would be eradicated.

"That time is past. Our walls have kept us safe for over a century, and all indications are that they will do so for many more centuries to come. If we are to further ensure our own safety, we should not use that term to describe them. No one would broker a treaty with a person who names them with an insult. And again, a treaty, if handled correctly, would not be a sign of weakness, but a step toward true security."

No hands went up.

"Next?" Sahaan asked.

The assembled crowd seemed fixated on him, and they all just stared. Even the park attendant who had been running the handheld around was just staring at him.

Sahaan furrowed his brow. It had been a long time since he'd found reading an audience to be a challenge. "Are there really no more questions?" The last question had been awkward, but he thought he'd handled it well enough. What was wrong with them?

It was then that he realized that the assembled crowd was not looking directly at him, but slightly to his right, just off the edge of the amphitheater. Sahaan hesitated, then brought himself to walk down off the stage and peer around the amphitheater edge. The Citrine citizens behind him began screaming, at first one, then many more. He heard the sounds of a stampede—chairs toppling, shrieks of pain from the trampled, but his eyes remained fixed on the wall. One of the slabs was glowing bright red. It had started a dull red but was increasing in luminosity by the moment.

Sahaan stumbled backward but was unable to take his eyes off the wall slab. He stumbled over a fallen chair, fell, and righted himself, all the while staring at the wall slab, which had now moved from bright red to bright orange, then a brighter yellow-orange.

He stuffed his hands into his pockets and pulled out his handheld. He dialed the emergency number, and a voice began speaking, but he yelled over them, "Code 1! Code 1, Code 1! Citrine! Orchard Park! Amphitheater!"

All at once, the yellow, coruscating wall slab condensed, collapsing in on itself into the shape of a person, a person perhaps ten or twelve years old. It remained glowing yellow, but that yellow was becoming orange, then red. Features began to emerge, a face, eyes, hands, feet—a boy.

The red diminished to the gray sheen of metal, metallic everything, skin, hair, eyes and all. The boy seemed to be looking around, gaining purchase of his surroundings. Sahaan remained transfixed on him. He could just hear police sirens wailing in the distance.

All at once, the boy's metallic skin began oozing skin-colored pigmentation, a light brown. His eyes gained the appearance of human eyes, and his hair turned black. Despite being naked, he now looked rather ordinarily human. He certainly would have passed for human if he hadn't just metamorphosed out of a slab of metaxically-treated wall paneling. He stood now in the gap where the panel had been.

Sahaan redialed the emergency number.

"Yes?" the voice said this time.

"There is now a gap in Citrine's defenses. We need to get a replacement panel to Citrine *now*."

"How was the panel destroyed?"

"It turned into a boy."

"Sorry, we must have misheard that."

Sahaan repeated the sentence, but he was drowned out by the sirens of the twenty-odd police cars that were screeching to a halt behind the mess of chairs he was standing in. When the last siren had been turned off, he said again, "the panel turned into a boy."

"What kind of boy?"

"He looks..." Sahaan decided to finish the sentence. "He looks *human*."

The path from Thiksay Hall to Choglamsar Hall ran around the periphery of the campus, skirting the edge of a pond. Maple and oak trees lined the other side of the path. The sun had fully sunk and light posts now provided the sole illumination.

All Sahaan could think about was not stuffing his hands in his pockets, looking forward, speaking confidently, all the stuff they'd been teaching him in the social science portion of his studies. That, and trying his best not to smile too much.

"Where are you from?" Lachel asked him. Most of the students at Portal City University were from other Reclamation cities. The university prided itself on diversity.

"I grew up in Eline. Most of my family's there. How about you?"

"Besserine."

Sahaan smiled. Besserine was famous for having set wall slabs into the ocean floor, with a second set on buoys. Besserine possessed the Reclamation's only beach. But there was something about the way she'd said it that made Sahaan hesitant to ask more about that.

"What made you choose poli-sci?" she asked.

Sahaan hesitated. That topic would open up a million issues he didn't want to talk about yet. How to proceed?

"I've seen a lot of political disagreements. And, I admit

that I don't understand it all— no, more like I see a lot of conflicting data. I guess, I kind of want to make sense of it all. Put it all together in a way that's coherent. I'm not making much sense right now, am I?"

She shook her head.

He supposed he'd have to broach the subject sooner or later. Might as well be sooner if she decided to hold it against him. "I'm talking about my family. My last name is Ekeer." And with that, she would instantly recognize the other half of his family.

"Oh." Lachel's eyes widened slightly. "Your grand-mother is very brave. I'm very proud of how she handled things in parliament."

"My family doesn't talk about that much."

Lachel nodded, seeming to understand. "Do you have to live in the shadow of that? Of everyone recognizing your family when they hear your name?"

"Yeah." He didn't realize until she'd said it aloud just how much he envied the way everyone else could just be themselves, they didn't have a 'name' or a world-famous great-great-grandfather.

"Then the next time you need someone to treat you as you and not as some extension of your family, come find me."

Sahaan would later identify that moment as when his crush started to bloom into love.

At first, no one moved. Sahaan stood in the sea of wrecked chairs, and the police took up positions behind their car doors, pointing their guns at the boy. The boy just looked around.

"He said that a wall slab turned into a boy that looks

human," the voice from his handheld was distant, speaking somewhere away from the receiver. The voice seemed to move back toward it. "What's the boy doing now?"

"Just looking around."

"What's behind the hole in the wall? Is anything coming through?"

"Not that I can see. It's just red earth and... I think I can see the silver on the ground in the distance, but that could just be the heat. We're running nanogenic scans on the park, right?"

"I'm not authorized to share that—"

"This is Sahaan Ekeer."

"Right. Yes, sir. We're just getting back a scan now... Forty-two seconds ago there was no nanite activity anywhere in the park. We're running another now."

That got his mind spinning. How could that have been possible? If nanites hadn't done this, then what had? What else besides nanotechnology could have possibly rearranged the molecules of a wall slab into a boy?

The boy took a few steps forward, and this caused the police to all immediately begin shouting for him to halt and charging their guns, in a cacophony of screaming and buzzing. The boy shrieked, and stumbled backward, wrapping his hands around his head and huddling on the ground.

Sahaan's protection instinct surged. He turned and held up a flat palm toward the policeman. He made the motion for verbal silence, then the motion that indicated he would be going in, and to cover him. He had absolutely hated the training he'd taken when he'd first arrived in government, particularly the course about interacting with the police. How glad he now was that he'd forced himself to pay attention.

Convinced that he'd gotten the police on board with his plan, at least for now, he turned back toward the boy, who remained huddled on the ground, shuddering. Sahaan stepped carefully through the toppled chairs, trying to make as little noise as possible.

"Still no nanite activity," the voice on his handheld announced.

"Thank you, I'm going to need to call back later."

"Wait, sir—"

Sahaan had already hit the disconnect button on his handheld, just as he reached the far shore of the sea of chairs. He walked slowly towards the edge of the amphitheater. Now he could really see out through the gap in the wall beyond where the boy stood. Red hills rolled away into the distance, mountains a vague shimmer beyond them. All at once, one of those hills burst and began deflating like a balloon, flattening itself out into nothing. Those were the nanites of the nanite-bodied, which covered the surface of the entire planet, constantly reshaping it, attempting to perfect it. Everywhere except in the Reclamation.

Sahaan was close to the dangerous gap now, as close as he would dare come. The boy huddled, just inside it, perhaps five or six meters away. Sahaan adopted the calmest voice he could muster. "Hello? Can you hear me?"

The boy looked slowly up. He looked so very afraid.

"Do you understand me?"

The boy nodded slightly.

"I'm Dr. Sahaan Ekeer. What's your name?"

"Charles."

Charles? It barely sounded like a real word, let alone a

name.

"Do you know where you are?"

Charles shook his head.

"You're in a place called the Reclamation."

Charles didn't respond to that one.

"Do you know how you got here?"

Another head shake.

"Do you remember anything from before you... arrived here just now?"

Charles looked up. His eyes seemed vacant for a moment. He started to shake his head. "Lights. I think. And voices." He furrowed his brow. "I understood them then, I think, but I don't now." His utter fear had seemed to morph into dire confusion.

"What do you want to do now, Charles?"

"I want the men with the guns to go away. And some clothes would be nice. You all have clothes and I don't. I should have clothes." Interesting. He didn't seem humiliated by his nakedness, as Sahaan would expect. It was more like Charles recognized that it was simply the way things were supposed to be.

"I can't make the men with the guns go away, but I can get you some clothes. I'm going to go do that now, all right?"

Charles nodded. "Thank you... Dr. Ekeer." He gave Sahaan a slight smile, one touched with trepidation.

Sahaan turned and walked around the sea of chairs, scanning the police regiment until his eyes spotted the officer who was in charge. Sahaan approached her, and she lowered her gun, though the rest of her squad kept their gazes fixed on Charles.

"Good afternoon, sir." Did Sahaan detect a hint of

irony in her voice?

"Good afternoon, sergeant."

"Did it say what it wants?"

Sahaan nodded.

"And?"

"He wants your squad to put their guns down, and he wants clothes. I told him he could have clothes."

The sergeant stared at him blankly for many seconds.

"Can we get him some clothes?"

"Yes, sir. I'll get right on that."

She turned to her second in command and ordered him to put in a request. Sahaan crossed his arms and looked out over the amphitheater, the chairs, and through the hole in their wall. One hundred and twenty-one years. The nanite-bodied had been unable to even come near a shield wall for one hundred and twenty-one years, let alone breach one, and now this.

It hit him all at once—the election, Una and Gadh. Oh, no. No, no, no. Gadh could *not* become president. Especially not now.

He grabbed up his handheld and dialed his office in Parliament.

"Sir!" the voice on the other end struck a note of shock. "You're all right!"

"That remains to be seen. Tell me the polling numbers."

"We have to run a full report. Sometimes the instant polling data is inaccurate, especially in a situation like this—"

"What is the instant data?"

"Besserine, Adamantine, Eline, and Barine have all flipped Gadh. That would give him the election. But, sir, we still need to run more data—"

His aide continued speaking, but Sahaan had stopped listening. His gaze was focused on the small, naked boy, who'd returned to huddling and shivering before the landscape of self-sculpting red hills beyond their walls.

Lachel sat across from the table staring at him intently, the conundrum within her mind twisting up her beautiful features. She didn't seem angry, exactly. More perplexed than anything else.

The table was in a small cafe in Dazine, where the two of them had retreated, in order to get some time to themselves away from their history classmates. They had been dating for about a year, now both in their third year of university. The Dazine trip was to visit the ruins of the old base D3, from which Stok Thiksay had recovered the access codes to open what was then the sealed metaxic portal. There was nothing left of the building now—the nanite-bodied had devoured the ruins after Stok's team had retrieved the access codes. A park, a memorial statue, and a museum now stood at that spot.

"Stok was a pacifist," Lachel insisted.

Sahaan nodded. "A pacifist who picked up a gun when he saw one of the bases being overrun and the horrific enforced transformations of the people there."

"But your grandmother..."

"I agree with her."

"And your great uncle...?"

"He's not *wrong*."

"Then what is he?"

"Not right." Sahaan shook his head. "In history classes, we're so focused on Reclamation history, starting with the incorporation of Portal City. I've always found Alterran history much more interesting."

Lachel seemed to be searching her memory for something about it. "What about it?"

"The history of the Institute."

Lachel furrowed her brow. "The Alterran university?"

Sahaan nodded. "When Stok and Le were our age, there was no Institute. Instead, they had two schools: the Monastery and the University. Students had to choose. Learn about history and literature, or learn about math and science. You couldn't choose an integrated curriculum like you can now in either Alterra or the Reclamation. And mom's always insisted on this when she tells the story: people in Alterra couldn't even *conceive* of integrating them. You might as well have suggested mixing oil and water. And this led to the creation of two political parties, two sides that grew progressively more hostile toward one another."

Lachel nodded. "You see the same thing happening now, with Reconciliation and Guardian."

"Yes."

"But what Guardian wants—"

"Isn't insane. To the extent that we need to be able to defend ourselves. Have you ever seen out over the walls?"

"My father took me up the Tower once." She referred to Outlook Tower in Eline, the second tallest structure in the Reclamation, which provided a spectacular and frightening view of the Enim Valley, its ever-shifting hills and blotches of metallic grass.

"The walls keep us safe, but they also make us blind. I get the feeling that, in Reconciliation, people sometimes forget how perilous our world really is. They're too quick to assume that if we just approach the nanite-bodied with open arms, they'll be our best buddies. And don't get me started on the fringe groups that think we've 'oppressed' them. They were trying to murder us."

Lachel jolted to a stance.

Sahaan knew immediately that he'd gone too far.

"Lachel." He put a hand on her shoulder.

She removed it. "Don't follow me." She stormed gracefully out of the cafe and walked away down the streets of Dazine.

Sahaan slumped back into his seat and gulped, wondering what he'd say to her next. He considered texting her an apology on his handheld. He'd summoned up the courage to do just that when the waiter arrived with both of their plates. Sahaan gave him a weak smile, and the waiter returned a knowing look, set down both plates, and retreated into the kitchen.

Once the initial shock of Charles's appearance had passed, Sahaan found himself gazing out through the gap in the wall, silent and transfixed, a cold, dark terror crawling up over him, smothering all action. It felt unreal. There had never been a gap in the walls.

One missing slab in and of itself wasn't dangerous. The wall slabs' efficacy came from the quantum field they generated. If they had simply been slabs of iron, then the nanites would simply climb up and over them. But these were not simply physical walls. Each slab had been exposed to an open metaxic portal for sixteen years or more and had thus gained a quantum field that let large bodies pass through, but repelled microscopic ones—ones like nanites.

It would take four consecutive missing segments to let the nanites through. Everyone knew that. With only one, two, or even three missing segments, the fields would overlap enough to keep the nanites out. But not four.

Even knowing that they remained relatively safe from the nanites beyond the walls, the horror of that vacancy stifled all Sahaan's thoughts. He could only stare at the gap, through to the silver-laced hills beyond. The police around him still stood, their weapons pointed at Charles. The boy sat on the ground, cross-legged, his hands wrapped around his head.

An officer emerged from the group, breaking Sahaan's trance. He carried a pile of clothing in his arms. He stepped carefully through the wreck of the chairs, set the clothing down a few meters in front of Charles, then retreated, backwards toward his contingent, tripping every few steps over chairs.

Sahaan took a deep breath and willed himself to take action. The first thought that came to his mind was Jaan, Lachel following immediately in his wake. He fumbled for his handheld and dialed home.

Lachel answered, breathless. "Tell me you're all right."

"I'm fine."

A long silence. She must have been so relieved. "They're saying... the news says... there's a hole in the wall."

"Yes. There's a hole. It's just one panel. But it's a hole."

"Sahaan... what's happening?"

He bit his lip, but only for a moment. She was tough. He didn't need to cover anything up for her, but anything he did share would be mere speculation. "I don't know."

"Will you be able to come home?"

"I don't know. The police are here. The rest of the local government will be arriving soon, I'd expect."

"On the news, they're also saying..." A gulp. "That Gadh's going to win."

"He does want to build more walls, after all."

A weak laugh. "Are you sure you're not in any danger?"

Now he really bit his lip. "I'll be home as soon as I can."

"Stay safe."

"I will. Love you."

"Love you, too."

Sahaan ended the call.

Charles was now fumbling with the clothing, a T-shirt and shorts, which were a bit too big on him. He looked almost comical, a tacky, red shirt and shorts with a pair of beaten up hiking boots. And the way he moved. It was almost as if having a body, or rather *this* body, was a new experience for him. When he moved, he threw his limbs about with too much force, as though he was accustomed to moving a much larger and heavier frame.

The nanite-bodied averaged five or six meters tall, their forms densely packed with muscle, all of their organs suspended in a cloud of nanite activity. Sahaan wondered if Charles had been such a being until recently.

"Dr. Ekeer?"

Sahaan turned. Behind him stood a well-dressed man in his sixties. Some ways behind the police cars, just at the edge of the amphitheater parking lot, sat a contingent of six black cars with tinted windows. Sahaan recognized him as the mayor of Citrine, but it took him a few moments to recall his name.

"Mayor Samaapt." Sahaan managed. "It's too bad

we've had to meet under such circumstances."

The mayor nodded morosely. He was staunchly Guardian, if Sahaan recalled correctly. The mayor twisted his lips around, then said, "What is the situation?"

"I know it sounds ridiculous, but that boy over there—" Sahaan turned and pointed; Charles, now fully clothed, had returned to sitting on the ground with his hands wrapped around his head. "Well, the wall panel turned into him."

The mayor was silent for many moments, his expression blank. "No," he finally stated. "The nanites can't get near the wall, let alone touch it, let alone change its molecular structure. That can't have been what happened."

"That's what I saw."

The mayor sighed.

"There is no nanite activity in the park. We've confirmed that."

"Indeed. But walls do not just turn into boys."

"I suppose not."

"What do you suppose he is?"

Sahaan's eyes widened. "We have to suppose he's human until we prove otherwise."

"Do we?"

"I think we do. I insist we do."

The mayor shot him a dangerous look. "Are you proposing he *stay*?"

"What are you proposing?"

"That we wall him out, of course."

Sahaan's mouth hung agape only momentarily. "We're not doing that. It's inhuman."

"He's not human. He's one of them."

"We don't know anything about him."

"Wall panels do not just turn into boys."

"No, they don't."

"When that wall slab arrives, I want him walled out—"

Sahaan straightened his back and locked his gaze with the mayor's. "That wall slab is federal property. If you want it installed, you will install it with every human and presumed human *inside* Citrine. Is that clear?"

The mayor nodded. "It is. We'll play it your way, doctor." He turned to walk away, then added, head turned over his shoulder. "This is why we vote Guardian out here in the spokes. Because, at the end of the day, it's clear whose side you're all really on."

Sahaan shook his head. "You're lashing out because you want safety and security. I'm trying to give it to you."

"That's not what it looks like."

The mayor turned his back to Sahaan and walked back to his black car.

During their final year at university, Sahaan and Lachel both got absorbed in their respective majors. Lachel applied to law schools while Sahaan applied for internships with Reconciliation. Their weekdays became a flurry of classes, papers, exams, and applications, leaving only a few scant hours on the weekend to spend time together, but they made time for each other. Every Seventhday without fail, they looked up a new recipe on the net, tried it out, ate together, and watched a movie. The food and the films ranged in quality, but regardless of how their experiments turned out, Sahaan enjoyed himself.

One evening, after a particularly good dinner and a particularly good movie, they found themselves talking about what their lives would be like after graduation.

"It doesn't seem real yet," Lachel observed.

"I don't think it will until it happens."

She paused then and looked at him. She leaned closer to him, putting her elbows on her knees. "How do you want it all to go?"

"What? Life?"

She nodded.

"How do you mean exactly?"

"What do you want to accomplish? What do you want it all to be like?"

Sahaan thought for many moments. Finally, he said, "When I was in high school, I remember this time in my first public speaking class. We got assigned to random groups of four, and the teacher asked us to choose one person in each group who would be the spokesperson for that group for the rest of that activity. In other words, the leader. And everyone, like always, looked at me. And I remember feeling, for the first time, as though this was becoming a pattern, a thing that kept happening in these kinds of situations, and so I asked them, why me? What about me made them want me to do this? And they just sort of shrugged and said it seemed like my kind of thing, and I clearly enjoyed it, so it just seemed natural that I do that. I realized I had the power to inspire others to follow my direction, and, being sixteen, completely overconfident, I proceeded to lead my group into bombing the activity. I realized then that it wasn't enough to just have this charisma I never asked for. I had to learn voraciously, and that I had to *really* listen, and not just assume I know better. And that it would be so very possible for me to mess things up. So, I guess I want to inspire others, and not make a mess of things. I want to see everyone around me be their best. And when I look at all of the Reclamation, I see us... kind of... moving apart, if that makes sense. I want us to move together for once. I don't know about all the details, but if I can just make things a little better rather than a little or a lot worse, I'll take that as a victory. Does that make sense?"

She nodded.

"And you?"

"I want to keep people safe. When the government went Guardian ten years ago, they changed the work-force laws, and dad's company was able to force him into a lower pay grade. They said it had nothing to do with him taking all the time off when my mom was ill, but he didn't believe them. Then medical plans got restructured—Guardian government—and we had to pay for all of mom's funeral out of the money that we'd put aside for Nishkap and my education. If Reconciliation hadn't come back into office and passed all those education reforms, I wouldn't be here, and Nishkap wouldn't be starting pre-med right now. And I guess... I just want to make sure... Because you should know that I want to fight their idiotic, backward policies with all my heart. I don't want to find a way to work with them. Every time they come into office, they divert everything into the military and wall technology research, and everyone suffers. I don't want any of that anymore."

Sahaan reached out and clasped her hands in his own. He released a deep sigh. "It's time I told you about my grandmother."

"Doesn't everyone know—?"

He shook his head. "They know the official story. In the family... Well, it's best if I just explain. The official story that everyone knows is that my grandmother and her brother both went into politics, both became MPs, and that their public argument in the senate reorganized what were then five political parties into the two that we have now. What most people don't know is that their rivalry had deeper origins. Their father... you realize who that would be...?"

Lachel walked it back in her mind. "Mox Thiksay, right?"

Sahaan nodded. "He was wild. Even as an adult. He was constantly pitting my grandmother and her brother in competition against one another. He was trying to drive them to solve hard problems through conflict, but it messed up their relationship. He couldn't have known that they would diverge ideologically so far, but they did, and they just kept fighting one another, competing with each other for their father's approval. I don't think I even know the full scope of everything that happened between them. Dad kept as much of it from me as he could."

"Your family... blames Mox... for Guardian and Reconciliation existing?"

Sahaan nodded.

"And you think... that it's up to you to fix it? To put them back together?"

"That's one way of putting it. You won't tell anyone?"

"I won't."

"Thank you."

She clasped his hand tighter. "You can't make yourself responsible for putting the hearts and minds of eight hundred thousand people together. But if it will help put your heart at ease, I will do my best to see what you see in Guardian. Even if I still fight with every last iota of energy against their unjust policies. But I will see. And who knows? Maybe I'll change. Just a little." She said this with that beautiful quirk of a smile at the side of her mouth.

Sahaan smiled, too.

It was less than a week before he'd work up the courage to ask her to marry him.

Sahaan watched the mayor and his entourage retreat. As soon as they were gone, he pulled out his handheld and dialed Bharo. He didn't answer at first. When his voicemail kicked in, Sahaan redialed.

Bharo answered that time. "You all right?"

"More or less. Where you at?"

"The office. Everyone's basically gone insane, as you can probably imagine. I'm trying to hold everything together. Sorry I didn't answer at first."

"They're going to have to do without you for a while. I need you in Citrine with a full hazmat team, our best nanogenics experts, and, come to think of it, a psychologist might not be a bad idea, too."

"I take it you mean to interrogate the kid and figure out what his purpose here is."

"Damn right I do. This could be it. Contact. I mean, never in a million years would I have guessed that this is how they would do it—"

"There are a couple of problems with your plan. First of all, Adamantine has sealed their end of the wallroute to Citrine."

"That's a protocol violation, unless there's a nanite

breach I don't know about. Order them to open it up again."

"Sure. What about facilities? Does Citrine even have a secure place we can put him?"

"Leave that to me."

"I just think we'd be better off bringing him back to Portal City. We're better equipped here."

"And that will just reinforce two stories the people in Citrine and the other spokes are telling themselves: one, that they don't matter enough for important things to be handled in their city; two, that their federal government is conspiring against them with the nanite-bodied. I want to do this here, and I want to give the local government full transparency into what we're doing."

"I'll let you know when I've got Adamantine figured out and the team ready. Might take a day or two with everything going on. Have you thought about what you're going to do with him until then?"

"No," Sahaan said, but his mind was already roiling with possibilities. "Actually, I think I just had an idea for that."

All twelve cities of the Reclamation were built on top of the remains of former military bases, the ones that had held the nanite-bodied at bay before they'd gotten the wall technology from Alterra. The bases had combated the nanites of their enemies with nanites of their own. It was effective, but there were a number of problems. First and foremost was the energy expenditure. Only a small area could be defended. Second was the phenomenal rate at which the programming of nanite-bodied adapted, a problem which required them to maintain an army of artificial and biological intelligence defenses. The walls had solved both of these problems. They required no energy, and it didn't matter how adaptive their enemy's programming was—the walls simply repelled nanites regardless of the code running them.

Now that they had walls, the old bases had been converted into memorial centers, such as the one in Dazine that Sahaan and Lachel had visited during university. While Dazine's base had been reduced to scrap by the nanite-bodied, Citrine's base, called C8, had not. It had been subject to a particularly bad assault, but from what Sahaan remembered, C8's infrastructure had not been touched.

A few calls to local authorities later, and Sahaan had confirmed that the nanite defenses around the base could be brought online within half an hour, and there were plenty of software engineers willing to drop everything and do the job.

Sahaan consulted with the police chief again and had her organize her people to prepare Charles for transportation. The armored transportation van arrived an hour later, followed by an enormous, flat-bed semi carrying a replacement wall slab.

Charles still sat on the ground, just inside the gap in the wall, his arms wrapped over his head.

Sahaan identified himself to the drivers of both vehicles and explained that he would be bringing Charles to the van. The wall panel installation was to wait until that had been accomplished.

Both the wall engineers and the Citrine security detail operating the van seemed skeptical of this plan, but they voiced no concern. Sahaan asked himself in that moment how certain he was of Charles. How much was he willing to wager that the nanite-bodied were trying to communicate with them, that this wasn't some kind of plot to bring down the walls from the inside? He looked at Charles, who was hunched over himself and shuddering intermittently. Sahaan decided to take this chance.

He walked through the sea of chairs, to Charles, and sat on the grass before him.

"Hi, Charles. It's me. Dr. Ekeer."

"Hi."

"I'd like to ask you something. Could you look up?"

Charles slowly sat up. His red face and terror-filled eyes activated every last one of Sahaan's paternal protective drives, which he immediately tempered by reminding himself that Charles's intentions were far from clear.

"Yes?" Charles asked.

"I'd like you to come with me."

Charles looked over Sahaan's shoulder. "Where to?"

"There's a place. It's in this city. It will be underground. A facility. We'll make it as comfortable as we can." Sahaan wasn't sure how else to sell it.

Charles looked behind himself. "I could go back out there, you know."

"We don't know what would happen to you if you did that."

"I'd be fine. It's just not what I'm supposed to do. I think."

That struck a chord of unease in Sahaan. "How do you know that?"

Charles shrugged and frowned, seeming genuinely perplexed himself as to the source of his knowledge.

"Do you know what would happen to me if I did that?" Sahaan asked.

Charles made wide eyes, continued frowning, and nodded slightly. Charles, it seemed, did have some relatively accurate idea.

"I'm not supposed to go outside, though," Charles said. "I'm supposed to stay here. It's, like... there are all these memories I've got, and I don't remember exactly who was in them and none of the conversations make sense when I try to think about what I was talking about, but there's some stuff that just... it just makes sense. Anyway, I hope you're not going to ask me to get in that ugly gray van while all those people in purple uniforms point weapons at me. If that's how it's going to be, I'd rather go outside."

It was at that moment that Sahaan realized he wasn't quite talking to a boy. Whoever Charles was, he had the form of a boy, and perhaps some of the emotions of a boy, but in other ways, he was a social and intellectual force to be reckoned with. The way he had wielded power just now had been unlike anything Sahaan had ever seen in a child. Most adults weren't even capable of that kind of political savvy—he'd identified something Sahaan wanted from him and navigated his context into a political advantage.

"I can get them to lower their weapons," Sahaan said. "But I'm afraid it will have to be the gray van. All our gray vans are ugly, I'm afraid."

Charles's frown flattened out, just a bit. "Will you go with me?"

Sahaan nodded. "Yes."

"I also remember... there will be people here who want to hurt me. Will there be any of those in this place we're going?"

"No."

Charles seemed to mull that over. "How can I be certain?"

"I'll be there," Sahaan said instinctively, then regretted that maneuver the moment it was out, but out it was. He'd have some explaining to do to Lachel and Jaan.

Charles nodded a few times. "Okay."

"Okay?"

Charles stood up, his movements still jerky and awkward. Sahaan stood, too.

"Let's go," Charles said.

The interior of the van was no less ugly and gray than its exterior, and the suspension seemed to absorb none of the shocks of Citrine's dilapidated roads. They jolted upwards at every pothole, all six of them, Sahaan, Charles, and four heavily armored, masked guards holding rifles at the ready.

They sat in silence.

Sahaan wondered what President Aavee must be thinking right now. Sahaan would have to talk to him, too, soon. Mostly, though, he thought of Lachel and Jaan, and whether he'd done the right thing by keeping Charles inside the walls. He had had to. He couldn't live with what the alternative would have made him. And yet, there were close to a million other people to consider inside the Reclamation's walls.

After what seemed like an eternity of pothole jolts and swift turns, the van finally came to a halt and the hum of its engine petered out. The back doors opened, and the guards escorted Charles out into a dimly lit concrete cavern studded with stone beams at even intervals. Piles of rock and metal dotted the space, and the floor was covered in a thick layer of dust. A chunk of red metallic scrap metal hung from the ceiling a few meters away, suspended by a frayed wire and casting an eerie shadow over the space between them.

"What is this place?" Charles asked.

"It's what's left of a bunker, one of the old military installations from before the Reclamation."

"Makes sense." Charles nodded slowly.

How much sense did that make to him? Did Charles have a full grasp of history, of the conflict that had fueled this place's creation, of why, if Charles *were* made of nanites, how this bunker and the others like it would be the only places with any of hope of containing that threat?

The guards led them away from the van and toward a door frame at the far end of the cavern.

They passed through the door frame and into a hallway made entirely of red metal. The lighting, Sahaan noticed, was newly installed. Portable LED lumens had been stuck to the ceiling at intervals between the facility's original lighting implements, which either sat inoperable, had been smashed or contorted, or were simply missing from their allotted place in the ceiling.

They turned three times, then walked up one short flight of stairs, and finally arrived at a red, metallic door. The guards opened it, and Sahaan followed Charles and the guards inside. They arrived atop a narrow walkway looking down over a large room. Dust spots on the floor showed that it had been recently stripped of much of its furnishings, and a table, chairs, and bed had been newly placed, clean and pristine.

The guards motioned for Charles to descend the stairs

into the room. He complied, and Sahaan followed. Charles, Sahaan noticed, seemed to be getting better at moving his body. Charles held the railing all the way down the stairs but had not seemed to trip or overreach his footing even once.

"Why don't you have a seat?" Sahaan suggested.

Charles pulled out one of the chairs and sat.

Sahaan took another and sat across from him.

"What now?" Charles asked.

"Now we talk."

"What about?"

"You said you knew what would happen to me if I went outside the walls."

Charles nodded.

"And you said you would be okay?"

Another nod.

"What else do you know about what's outside the Reclamation?"

Charles quirked his head.

"Everything inside the walls is a country called the Reclamation."

Charles nodded slowly. "What's outside. It's... cities and people. Lots of people."

"Do you know about the terraforming?"

Charles frowned. "Yes."

"Is something wrong?"

"Yeah. The people outside don't like the terraforming."

Sahaan couldn't stop himself in time from visibly jolting. He noticed that the guards were muttering also.

"Sorry, do you mean the people outside the Reclamation or the people inside the Reclamation don't like the terraforming?"

"Not in the Reclamation. The people outside. They're annoyed with it. It's not working."

"Then, why are they still doing it? Why do we still see hills rise up and deflate when we look out over the walls?"

"It's complicated. It's... It's hard to explain."

"We've got plenty of time." Sahaan shrugged. "Try me."

Charles furrowed his brow and scanned the dismal, empty room covered in dust. He let out a sigh, then looked at Sahaan. "Have you ever had to keep doing a thing, not because you liked doing it, but because it's what you've always done, and there are other people who depend on you doing it, but not because they need it, but because they can't stand the idea of it *not* happening? Because they're more afraid of being without it than of wasting time on continuing to do something useless?"

Sahaan nodded very slowly. Yes, politics was rife with such comprises. He knew that very well. And, once again, he reminded himself, Charles was *not* a child. He only looked like one.

"What else can you tell me about outside the walls?"

A pause. "I'm not sure. There are cities. People go about their lives. They have jobs. There's stuff that needs to get done. All the time. I used to be very busy."

"You were one of the people outside the walls, before you came here?"

Charles looked up at the guards. He frowned, then, hesitantly, he nodded to Sahaan.

One of the guards on the balcony walkway pulled out a handheld and spoke something into it.

"You're very different, physically, from the people in those cities," Sahaan observed.

Charles nodded quickly. "I changed."

"Clearly."

Charles sighed. "I know that I shouldn't have normally been able to get inside the walls, to even get *near* the walls. But I found a way." Charles simply paused his speech. He sat, staring at Sahaan blankly.

"A way?" Sahaan tried.

Charles contorted his facial features. "I'm sorry. There's so much I don't remember. I don't remember how. I remember discussions about whether to do it or not. I remember that I wanted this. Everything else is a jumble. I can't remember specific conversations I had. You know about... No, you couldn't."

"Couldn't what?"

"The people outside, they talk completely differently now. It wasn't like that before. Back during... let's call them the hostilities. Do you know what I mean?"

Sahaan nodded.

"During the hostilities, we still used vocal sounds for interpersonal communication. It's not like that anymore. It's digital now, over radio frequencies." Charles laughed a bit.

"Why are you laughing?"

"Sorry. I just remembered trying to convince some-one that speech would be better, even though it was less efficient. I was arguing. It just struck me as funny because I'm having so much trouble communicating now com-pared to before."

"Are you sorry you came here?"

Charles shook his head slowly. "I know it's important."

"Why?"

"Because things aren't okay the way they are."

"You mean, having the division between the Reclamation and outside."

Charles shook his head. "I mean, sure, that's not great, but what I really mean is, even just outside the Reclamation. With the others. Things aren't okay. A century is a long time to be changing yourself and not seeing any benefit from it. It's made people... I don't know. Anxious. Malcontent. Ready to tear everything down. Ready to do something else."

Another murmur from the same guard into his handheld.

Charles put a hand to his face. "I shouldn't have told you that," he whispered to Sahaan. Then he looked up at the balcony and said, "most people out there *aren't* extremists."

The guards did nothing but stand.

Charles turned back to Sahaan. "I'm sure most of *you* aren't extremists, either."

"We're not," Sahaan said.

"But that's what we couldn't know," Charles said. "Your political organization. What has my presence done here politically? Has my showing up empowered your extremists?"

Gadh.

Ugh.

Sahaan was quick enough to hide that reaction, though. "It's too early to tell, but even if it has in the short term, I think we'll end up better for having met you in the long term."

Charles smiled weakly. "I hope so."

"Sir!" One of the guards called down.

"Excuse me," Sahaan said, then walked up the stairwell.

The guard who'd called down approached him at the top of the stairs. "President Aavee would like to speak with you, sir."

Sahaan glanced at his handheld. No signal.

"I'll show you the way to the surface. Follow me."

"Dr. Ekeer?" Charles called up.

"Yes?"

"Where are you going?"

"I need to make a call. I'll be back soon."

Charles visibly gulped.

"I promise."

Sahaan walked out the door, following the guards. The nanite-bodied had found a way to transmute themselves into our wall slabs and keep most of their memories. The political ramifications would be immense. What was he going to tell the president?

No sooner had Sahaan reached the surface than his handheld erupted in a flurry of notifications, but he decided to ignore them for the moment so he could take stock of the surface. None of the base structure remained above ground. He had emerged from a simple stairwell dug out of the earth. The only other visible terrain feature was the road, some twenty kilometers away that led to its own hole in the ground. That must have been how his vehicle had come in.

He got to work on his phone, but didn't have time to scan more than a couple of emails before he received a call from the president's office.

"Sahaan?"

"Yes, Mr. President. It's me."

"How are you holding up?"

"As well as can be expected, Mr. President."

"What's he like?"

"He's... not a boy, sir. I mean, he's clearly an adult in a boy's body. And, he admitted just now, he's one of them."

"Should I wait for a debrief?"

"Sir, the military is here and they're recording everything. I don't think there's any point in trying to keep my conversations with him a secret. I'm not even sure we should. Mr. President, this is it. It's contact. After over a century."

"Sahaan. They've turned one of our wall slabs into a *person*."

"I realize that, sir."

"Good thinking, by the way, bringing the old military installation back online. That should minimize any threat to Citrine while we figure out a way to transport him safely to Portal City."

"Sir, I'd like to keep Charles here."

"Sorry. Say that again. He has a name?"

"Yes. It's Charles."

"No family name?"

"If he has one, he hasn't shared it."

"Why do you want to keep him in Citrine?"

"Because—" How to explain? Sahaan found himself suddenly irritated that he had to explain such things to his own boss. He shoved the emotion aside and focused on how to best elaborate his stance. "Because the people in Citrine, and the spokes more generally, are starting to tell themselves that Reconciliation and the hub cities don't care about them or their safety. If we bring him into the hub, they won't have their people monitoring him anymore. They'll go on telling themselves that we're not on their side, and I'm convinced that pretty soon, the story will be that we're conspiring with the nanite-bodied against them. The mayor of Citrine practically told me as much earlier today."

"I agree with you, Sahaan, but I think it's all the more reason to bring him in here, where we can better control the messaging to the media, where everyone will behave more predictably."

"Sir, if I could just—"

"You have until we can prepare adequate safeties for his transportation. Is that clear?"

"Yes, Mr. President."

"And I heard you put Bharo on the Adamantine situation."

"Yes, sir. I did."

"Good work there. Learn as much as you can, Sahaan. I want twice-daily updates to the capitol. Keep yourself safe out there."

"Yes, Mr. President. I will."

Sahaan pressed the red button on his handheld to end the call. He looked back down into the pit he had emerged from and noticed, over near the vehicle entrance, two young soldiers unloading crates from a military vehicle that he hadn't heard approach.

"What are they doing?" Sahaan asked his two escorts.

"Those are software engineers," one of them said.

"They're doing something to make the old systems work better," the other added.

Sahaan had a frightening flashback to fourth grade,

when he'd first learned about pre-Reclamation history. Before they'd had the wall slabs, a certain number of young people had to give up their lives to become human computers, each one wired into the bases to give the defensive systems a kind of randomness that the nanite-bodied's computer algorithms couldn't quickly adapt to.

He didn't have to ask that of these young people, and he would do everything in his power to keep it that way.

When Sahaan returned to Charles's cell, he peered down from the balcony to see that Charles had lain down on the bed provided. At the sound of the door, Charles sat up, threw his legs over the bed, stretched his arms, and gazed up at Sahaan... How exactly to describe it? With eyes full of some meager hope, perhaps? At the very least, glad that Sahaan had returned.

Sahaan walked down the metal stairs and sat down at the table in the same chair he'd taken before. Charles remained at the edge of the bed.

"Is everything all right?" Charles asked.

Sahaan nodded.

"The rest of the Reclamation... I bet they're afraid of me. Afraid that I'll explode into a billion nanites, or something like that."

"Not everyone is afraid."

"Just most of them, then?"

"Perhaps. Part of my job is to help explain things to people so that they're only afraid of what they should be afraid of."

"You don't seem afraid of me."

"Should I be?"

Charles shook his head. "I don't think so. I'm pretty

sure I won't explode into a billion nanites, anyway."

"Do you know..." Sahaan searched for the right words. "Do you know how you entered the Reclamation?"

Charles stared at him blankly many more seconds, then shook his head. "I remember talking about it with others before, but like I said, the details are all fuzzy. The first thing I remember here is you talking to me next to that... pavilion."

"Do you remember your goal?"

Charles's eyes brightened. "Contact. It's something I've always wanted. To talk to—" He suddenly gazed off past Sahaan's shoulder and squinted.

"Something wrong?"

Charles shook his head. "A word I can't translate. I guess 'human' will do. Although they—we consider ourselves human, too."

"How many others want contact, too?"

Charles's grimace grew more severe, and he remained silent for many moments. "It's really complicated. And there are a lot of details that are hard to remember. A lot? I think."

Sahaan realized in that moment, that getting Charles to remember the intent of his compatriots was crucial. Charles's arrival had been perfectly ambiguous. The Reconciliation party would interpret it as the thing they had always wanted—contact. The Guardian party would interpret it as their worst nightmare come true—invasion, the breach of the walls. In a sense, both were right. Unless Charles proved harmless, or proved hostile. But how to prove it?

"Dr. Ekeer?"

Sahaan realized he'd allowed himself to become lost

in thought. "Yes?"

"Can you tell me more about what the Reclamation is like?"

"What do you want to know?"

"We know about the roads out to five isolated cities, and the seven others in the center. Is that all of them?"

"Yes."

"What are their names?"

"Portal City is our capitol, and the portal connects it to Alterra, the parallel world that Le Choglamsar and Stok Thiksay came from ninety years ago. There's also Besserine, Dazine, Adamantine, Adrine, Barine, and Eline in the hub. The spokes are Cynine, Bengine, Exenine, Enerine, and we're in Citrine."

"I just remembered something."

"What's that?"

"Some people are worried. That you'll want to expand your hub."

Sahaan nodded slowly. "We've anticipated that fear. Some of us. We'd like to establish contact and negotiate terms of expanding the wall system."

"Others think you can't expand it anymore."

What to say to that?

Sahaan crossed his arms. "We're committed to the integrity of the existing walls and we have adequate means to reinforce them." Not entirely true anymore, but since Charles had said he didn't remember how he'd arrived, it probably couldn't hurt. He'd probably noticed the construction crews replacing the wall panel on their departure and was certainly bright enough to put the details together, but that didn't diminish the political necessity of the lie. Sahaan caught the click and chatter of the guard talking on his handheld behind him.

Charles frowned. "Sorry. I didn't mean that to sound threatening."

Sahaan leaned forward. "Then you'll need to tell me more. Everything you can remember about your society. This is how we get rid of that fear. Understanding. Talking to one another. Tell me this, then. What do you know about us? We know you don't have satellites in orbit, not that we can see, anyway."

"We don't need satellites. Nanites crawl on top of the field projected by the walls and look inside. And we noticed your satellites. There are a lot of stories about what it's like here. There are opinions..." Charles screwed his face up. "I'm sorry, trying to remember this stuff... It's very hard."

"Are you in pain?"

Charles nodded and lay down on the bed.

Sahaan stood up. "I don't want you to hurt yourself on my account."

"I'll be all right," Charles muttered, his face to the wall.

"Should I come back later?"

"Give me a minute."

Sahaan waited for many minutes, then asked, "Charles?"

No response. Sahaan stood and walked over to him. He put a finger on the boy's neck and indeed felt warmth and a pulse. His chest was rising and falling.

Sahaan walked up the stairs as silently as he was able, then said to the guards in a low voice, "He appears to be sleeping. I'm going to arrange for accommodations in the city. I'll be back in about an hour."

The guard saluted his acknowledgment, and two others joined up alongside him to escort him to the surface. Sahaan glanced at sleeping Charles on his way out and sighed. The boy had better become able to share more about the nanite-bodied society. It was the only way Sahaan could imagine that they would be able to avoid the disastrous election outcome of a Gadh presidency.

When Sahaan emerged from the bunker a second time, the sun had fallen low in the sky, turning the magenta sky a deep umber. Long shadows from the walls around the complex shrouded the vehicle entrance, but a lamp set up beneath the canopy of a tent illuminated the software engineers, busily tapping at keyboards atop makeshift desks.

His handheld stole his attention, erupting in another flurry of delayed messages and notifications. In summary: the election polls had swung considerably in Gadh's direction, but most polling agencies expressed doubt as to whether or not it was enough to win him the election; Adamantine had shut down their side of the Adamantine-Citrine wallroad, then opened it up again; Lachel and Jaan had both texted him asking him to call as soon as he could.

He instinctively hit his speed dial for Lachel.

"How are you?" she asked.

"Good. Better."

"How is he?"

"He's... interesting. He says he doesn't remember much."

"You don't believe him."

"His sharing more would help us trust him more. But,

I don't know. If they really have found a way to take a nanite-bodied and put their minds into human bodies, sure, memory loss seems reasonable, if not a mild symptom. How are you?"

"All right. Give or take. Worried about you."

"I'll be fine. The one thing he doesn't seem is dangerous."

"I'm trusting those political sensitivities of yours to remain alert. I want you home when this all over."

"Alert as ever."

"Promise?"

"Promise. How's Jaan?"

"Asking about you a lot. Want to talk to him?"

"Of course."

"I love you."

"Love you, too."

Some shuffling of the handheld, then, "Dad?"

"Hey, Jaan."

"Dad! Are you all right? You're talking the nanite-bodied boy, right?"

"All we know is he used to be nanite-bodied. He looks human, now. And he gets tired like we do, at the very least. We'll know more in the next couple of days."

Jaan's voice took on an uncertain tone. "Are we in danger? I mean, they took out of a piece of our wall. Can they do that again?"

"I honestly don't know, son. But I'm going to do everything I can to find out. And, if there is a danger, I'm going to do everything I can to keep it from hurting you and Mom and the Reclamation. That's a promise. It's probably going to be a while before I can come home, so I need you to be especially good for your mother while I'm gone. Can you do that?"

"Sure, Dad! You got it."

"Love you."

"Love you, too."

Sahaan hung up and immediately dialed Bharo.

"Hey," Bharo's voice intoned. "How you doing?"

"Pretty well. I saw you got Adamantine to open up their wallroad. Thanks for that."

"No prob. You know the Adamantine city government. All you have to do is suggest infrastructure funding at them and they'll be all over any request."

"What'd you have to promise them?"

"A park restoration we would have granted them anyway."

Sahaan chuckled. "Nice work."

"Thanks."

"The polls are showing Gadh has lost his lead."

"Yeah," Bharo's voice intoned despair instead of relief. "I think you might have been right. The media has never liked Gadh, and I think they may be trying to paint a rosier picture than is justified. If you squint really hard at the numbers, maybe you could draw that conclusion. According to my read, Gadh now has seven cities locked down, enough to secure a Guardian victory. I mean, I just don't get it. The nanite-bodied might be able to break through our walls now, but how can they expect *that man* to keep them safe?"

"They don't want us doing what we're doing now."

"What's that?"

"Talking to the 'invader.'"

Bharo began talking, more incredulity in the form of a minor rant, but Sahaan's mind had begun working another angle, one he hadn't considered until this moment.

Sahaan interrupted Bharo mid-sentence, "Hey, when is the soonest you could get out here?"

"I take it I'm packing light?"

"Yeah."

"Tomorrow morning. Maybe tonight if there aren't any logistical issues catching the last Adamantine train."

"Go find out. Keep me apprised. I've got to run."

"Hey, mind telling me what's so urg—"

Sahaan had already hit the button to end the call. He shot back down the stairs into the dilapidated hallways of maroon metal, tracing his way back to Charles's room. He'd realized, speaking with Bharo, that, being in Citrine, the government officials he was giving transparency to were generally hostile to the notion of Sahaan carrying out his investigation. As long as he was around, they wouldn't dare, but Sahaan had been going up to the surface.

Sahaan shot into the room, ran to the balcony railing, where he saw two women and a man in white robes standing over Charles.

"Stop at once!" Sahaan roared as he clambered down the stairs. "I am Dr. Sahaan Ekeer, Senior Consul to the President of the Reclamation, and I demand to know what's been done to Charles, what more you planned to do, and who ordered it."

One of the two women stepped forward. "Dr. Ekeer, please calm down."

Sahaan did his best to tower over her, frowning. "What have you done to him?"

She bit her lip. "We have injected him with a common sedative and a solution of nanites programmed with our best software for combating the de— nanite-bodied."

"What will it do to him?"

"If he has any other nanites in him, it will destroy them."

Sahaan did his best to make his eyes spit fire. "What's your name, doctor?"

She finally seemed perturbed. "Anati Paape."

"And your supervisor?"

She gave the name of a senior medical official in Mayor Samaapt's government.

"You had better hope, Dr. Paape, that Charles suffers no ill effects from these injections."

The male doctor, who'd been snarling, stepped forward.

"Why are you protecting him? Let's just disassemble him and be done with it."

Dr. Paape turned her head and had begun to reprimand him, but Sahaan cut her off. "We are not animals! We do not kill people trying to communicate with us just because we are scared of them! How dare we be so proud of our humanity, of how different we are from the nanite-bodied of a century ago, when we would stoop so low as to murder someone because they are different from us. And you call yourself a doctor? If I were the Reclamation Medical Consul I would have you thrown out on the street. Get out of here! The both of you. Paape, you stay."

Paape turned and glared at her two subordinates. With a swift tilt of her head toward the door, they were up the stairs and gone.

"Dr. Ekeer—"

"I don't want to hear it, Paape! All I want to know is, presuming his biology is human, is there anything you can do for him right now that will stabilize his condition?"

Dr. Paape took a long breath in and a long breath out. "If he is biologically human, then the second injection will be innocuous. The nanites only destroy other nanites. I would not want to try to wake him from sedation. It would be best for that to run its course. If he does not wake up naturally in four hours, then he will need medical attention. He needs to be monitored by an anesthesiologist during that time. You've just excused one."

"It's going to stay that way. Thank you, doctor. You can go."

When she was gone, Sahaan called down one of the soldiers, and, with as much calm as he could manage, gave him instructions to request that the Citrine Central Hospital's most morally upright and politically neutral anesthesiologist be sent to the bunker immediately, to be paid double for their time.

He then sat down, looking at Charles's unconscious form, splayed out on the bed, little swabs of cotton pinned to his arm with medical tape. "You hang in there," Sahaan said, hoping it would help.

Within thirty minutes, the anesthesiologist arrived, a young man named Upayo Gee, who could not have been more than five years out of medical school. He seemed more nervous than Sahaan would care for in a doctor, but who, once Sahaan explained the situation, seemed to calm considerably and got to work on his patient.

After a battery of tests, the doctor announced that Charles's condition, presuming he was indeed biologically human, was completely normal, and that all that remained at this juncture was to wait for him to wake up.

"You saw it, didn't you?" Dr. Gee asked. "They said on the news you were there when he formed out of the wall."

Sahaan nodded. "One of the most incredible things I've seen in my entire life. Also one of the most frightening."

"Doesn't seem like you frighten easily, though. The whole Aavee administration is like that. It's too bad we can't just have another term of his leadership."

Sahaan smiled. "Thanks. I appreciate that. I really do. But those are the rules. How do you feel about Una?"

"I'll vote for her, of course."

"But?"

"Well, she feels kind of... entrenched. A bit too old guard. People are looking for something new, something different. An end to this weird limbo we're stuck in. We've got walls all around us, and we can't expand them any further, but we can't pull them back either. It'd be nice, for once, to just not have walls. To not have to *worry* about the nanite-bodied. But the world isn't that simple."

Sahaan realized they were both staring at Charles now, watching his chest rise and fall, watching the medical display that Dr. Gee had hooked up to him and listening to its faint, repetitive blips.

"It might not ever be simple," Sahaan said. "But we need government to be competent enough to navigate its complexity. So that we don't end up with murdered emissaries. I was so stupid to leave him alone here."

"It's not your fault our mayor is a reactionary." Dr. Gee tapped his foot.

"It's my job to think of these things in time."

"What will you do about the rest of tonight?"

"I've got a friend coming in from Portal City. Another member of the cabinet. ... Doctor, there's one more thing I need to ask you. Before Charles wakes up."

"Yes?"

"So far we've been assuming that Charles is biologically human. Have you seen anything so far that would suggest otherwise?"

Dr. Gee shook his head silently.

"Thank you."

They continued talking on an off for about three hours, Dr. Gee sharing stories from his time in medical school, which, Sahaan had guessed more-or-less correctly, he'd completed three years prior. Sahaan also told stories about Lachel and Jaan.

Finally, Charles began to stir, and Dr. Gee once again got to work, watching all of his vitals. Charles's eyes fluttered open, and he shot up in his bed, breathing heavily.

"Easy now," Dr. Gee put a hand on Charles's shoulder.

Charles jerked away from the touch.

"Dr. Ekeer?!" Charles called out.

"I'm here, Charles."

"The doctors..." Charles's eyes darted around.

"This is Dr. Gee. The other doctors are gone."

At that, Charles calmed significantly. Dr. Gee reached out again for Charles's shoulder and guided his torso back down toward the bed.

"I'm sorry about that, Charles," Sahaan said. "I won't leave you alone again."

Dr. Gee gave Charles water and some crackers, then took his blood pressure. He later had him take off his shirt and checked his lungs with a stethoscope. The medical instrument blipped throughout, and when Dr. Gee was done, he turned it off, and told Charles he could remove the patches from his arms, legs, and chest where it was connected.

"You're fine," Dr. Gee announced, much to Sahaan's relief.

Charles smiled as well. "Thank you, Dr. Gee."

"Just doing my job." Dr. Gee proceeded to pack up his equipment, letting Sahaan know that he could be called back at any time if Charles's condition were to change.

Sahaan thanked the doctor, and returned to his seat at the table. Charles stretched, got out of the bed, and joined him.

"You hungry?" Sahaan asked.

Charles nodded.

Sahaan looked up at the guards, who acknowledged the request and took to their handhelds.

"How long has it been?" Charles asked.

"About three and a half hours."

"I definitely didn't mean to sleep that long."

"It wasn't your fault."

"They sedated me?"

Sahaan nodded.

"Anything... else?"

"Yes."

"What was it?"

"Nanites. Programmed to destroy all other kinds of nanites."

Charles frowned, but nodded.

"Yeah," Charles said. "That won't do anything."

"You're sure?"

Charles nodded again, more vigorously. "Oh, yes. Physically I'm just like everyone else here."

"You seem pretty certain of that."

"I remember that that was the idea. We were pretty sure it was the only way to make communication possible. And it's also why I have trouble remembering things."

"Why's that?"

"Like I said, we don't *talk* like this. I mean, we do talk, but not with sound. It's data transmission over RF. Digital radio signals. It's faster, but, in my opinion, inelegant. And... well... damn, how can I explain? Oh, okay. So, you're Dr. Ekeer, right? Doctor is your title?"

"Yes."

"The word for 'doctor' in the kind of speech I'm describing isn't a word at all. What I would do, if I had the title of doctor, is attach a provisioning file to all of my speech acts, and the file would contain my credentials. Others would return a digitally signed copy of that provisioning file to me in their responses. If someone wanted to be really rude, they could refuse to digitally sign the provision or even omit it from their communication. This would be the equivalent of me refusing to call you 'doctor' and just using your first name. Or saying, 'hey, you.'"

"I'm astounded you can speak our language at all."

"I... solved that somehow. What's frustrating is remembering the general shape of my life, the events, the contours of emotion, but specific conversations, pieces of data, is all a blur. Just thinking about it—" Charles stretched out his arms and released a wide yawn. "— makes me sleepy."

The door atop the balcony clanged open, and new soldiers entered, one carrying a tray. The soldier with the tray descended and sat it down across from Charles. Atop it lay a steak, a salad, a small jar of sauce, and a glass of sparkling water.

"Set that here," Sahaan ordered the guard, who looked up at the balcony.

"I said, put it in front of me," Sahaan said.

The soldier complied.

Sahaan noticed multiple guards on the balcony pull up their handhelds and begin muttering furiously into them.

"I'm going to sample everything," Sahaan said, taking up the silverware. He cut himself a piece of the steak and held it up. "I mean it," he called up to the balcony. "If there's any reason I should not put this steak in my mouth, it would be best to tell me *now*."

"Sir," one of the guards called down. "Please hold a moment."

He walked down the stairs, approached the table, then whispered in Sahaan's ear. "We are mostly certain about these cooks. Mostly. But if you want us to be absolutely sure, we will need to call someone else in."

"Please do that," Sahaan whispered back.

The soldier took the tray back with him.

Charles stared across the table at Sahaan, his expression difficult to read. Not upset. Perhaps disappointed. But only somewhat.

"Do the nanite-bodied handle fear any better than us?" Sahaan asked as casually as he could.

"From what I have seen," Charles said, "No. They— we haven't figured out how to evolve out of that one yet."

Sahaan tried a weak smile. "Something we still have in common, then."

A new dinner was delivered about an hour later. Sahaan

taste-tested everything, but this time the guards didn't stop him. He handed the meal over to Charles, who at first eyed it warily, then picked up a fork, holding it around the base with his fist. He stabbed into the steak, pulled at it at a bit, then took up the knife in a similar grip and began stabbing at the meat. He kept at that for about a minute, then gave up on the silverware entirely and proceeded to stuff the steak into his mouth with his hands.

Sahaan wondered out loud about meal etiquette amongst the nanite-bodied, to which Charles replied that none of them had needed to eat in over a hundred years. They had multiple ways of recharging instead. One could do so wirelessly, which was something akin to fast food. A "real meal" consisted of injecting oneself with packets that provided energy of varying frequency and modulation patterns.

Charles grinned over his new steak.

"What is it?" Sahaan asked.

"Well," Charles wiped his mouth with his sleeve. "I remember thinking about this beforehand—you know, having to eat. To be perfectly honest, I found the concept a bit... revolting."

"I take it the experience of it has proved somewhat better than that."

"Taste is amazing! I love it."

"There are a lot of different foods you can try."

Charles furrowed his brow.

"Yes?"

Charles finished tearing through the steak with his teeth, chewed, and swallowed. "Just something... I'm not sure. My main reason for coming here was to make contact, of course. But there's something else..." He shook his head and tore into the steak again. His expressive remained pensive while he chewed and swallowed. "I can't remember. Maybe something to do with my job?"

"What was your job?"

A long silence while Charles tore into the steak and chewed again, looking off over Sahaan's shoulder. After he swallowed, he sat for a long time. "A scientist, maybe. Something like that. In a sense, we're all programmers. But I worked on the code that organized the information in a database. I think it had something to do with atoms."

Charles finished up the last of the steak, then paused, his eyes wide with surprise, then all at once he released a loud belch. He put a hand to his chest and looked at Sahaan with a concerned expression. "Was that normal?"

Sahaan almost laughed. "Yes. But... well, people usually hold it in."

Charles frowned, and Sahaan worried that he'd insulted him. But then, Charles interjected, "we gave up too much."

"Do you mean the nanite-bodied quest for perfection?"

Charles nodded. "I have to admit, there are perks. If only I could give you the experience of our internet. I'm not sure it's even describable with your words." Charles shook his head. "What's your job, Dr. Ekeer?"

"I'm on the president's staff."

Charles's eyes went wide. "The president? Of the whole Reclamation?"

Sahaan nodded.

"And the government is in Portal City?"

"Yes."

"What do you do for the president?"

"I write most of his speeches. Whenever we have guests from other cities, I make sure that all the accommodations are taken care of. I advise him on policy. That kind of thing."

"Sounds like a hard job. I've never been able to imagine myself in politics."

"What are your politics like? Do you have a president?"

Charles bunched up his brow. "That's— No? I think? I'm not sure. Politics is hard for me to think about." Charles yawned widely, not covering his mouth.

"Do you have political parties?"

Charles frowned, staring into space for many moments, then shook his head. "I'm not sure. Sort of. Probably. How about the Reclamation? I take it you continued a Veda-style government?"

Sahaan nodded. "There are some differences, but basically, yes. We have two major political parties, Reconciliation and Guardian."

"Which are you?"

"I'm part of the Reconciliation party."

Charles's expression turned apprehensive. "Reconciliation because... you want to contact... us?"

Sahaan nodded. "And Guardian wants...?"

"More walls," Sahaan said softly.

Charles frowned.

"Can you blame them?" Sahaan asked.

"No, I suppose not. If I were... if I had been *homo sapiens sapiens* from birth, I would probably want more walls, too."

Sahaan silently remarked to himself Charles using the

term *homo sapiens sapiens* instead of the old term *homo sapiens inferus*, which the nanite-bodied had lobbed around with wild abandon a hundred years ago during the hostilities, while Sahaan's own ancestors had used 'deranged' to describe the nanite-bodied.

"Not all of us do," Sahaan remarked. "In fact, a sizable chunk of us don't."

Charles nodded. He eyed the salad on his plate, looked at Sahaan, then at the salad again. Finally, he said, "Can you show me how to use that utensil? The only other thing I can think to do with these leaves is put my face in them."

Sahaan let out a small laugh and proceeded to instruct Charles on how to use a fork.

Sahaan and Charles talked for some time after Charles finished his meal. Charles detailed more differences between nanite-bodied and *homo sapiens sapiens*, such as not needing to sleep and extended lifespan. The nanite-bodied who Sahaan's great-great-grandfather had spoken to were only just now starting to die of old age. Rather than becoming androids, they'd sought instead to perfect the biological. Immortality, it seemed, remained out of reach.

In return, Sahaan gave Charles a rundown of his daily duties for the president. The topic of the election came up, and Sahaan told Charles about the Guardian candidate Abhiman Gadh, but left out the part about Charles's appearance swinging the election in his favor.

Another topic Sahaan avoided was that of his ancestry. Sahaan's last name wouldn't be noticeable to Charles, but his paternal grandmother's maiden name would be.

She had been the daughter of Mox Thiksay, son of Stok Thiksay, the one who'd been responsible for bringing the wall technology from Alterra to Asura, the one who'd made the Reclamation possible. Without the help of the Alterran government, it was widely believed that the nanite-bodied would have been able to break through the defenses of all the remaining military installations and convert their inhabitants into nanite-bodied. Even if Charles had chosen to give up his prior form and take a *homo sapiens sapiens* body, Sahaan wasn't willing to take the risk of telling Charles about that particular piece of his biography just yet.

The more they talked, the more Charles yawned and complained of feeling light-headed. Eventually, he insisted on lying down, upon which he promptly fell asleep and began snoring.

Sahaan sat at the table, leaned back in his chair, and went over the evening in his mind. Charles was such a conundrum. The idea of meeting the nanite-bodied face-to-face had been part of the Reclamation's cultural imagination for decades. Novels and television shows had explored fictional scenarios that had made it possible. Never had such stories imagined the nanite-bodied taking the form of human children with poor motor control and lacking table manners.

Had he established that Charles was not hostile? Almost certainly. What remained to be seen was whether or not he were some kind of sleeper agent. And, begrudgingly, Sahaan had to admit that the only place with the resources to make that determination properly was Portal City. With that, his mind turned back to his country's political problems and the election.

What a mess.

The door above clanged, and Sahaan looked up to see a familiar face peek through.

"There you are!" Bharo called down.

Sahaan drew a finger up to his mouth and nodded toward Charles.

Bharo seemed to catch his meaning and began carefully down the stairs. Sahaan noticed then that he was carrying a brown paper bag with the Hedgerow logo printed on the side. Bharo sat the bag on the table in front of Sahaan, then, still looking at Charles, said, "so, that's him, huh?"

Sahaan nodded.

"Think he'll sleep all night?" Bharo asked.

"Hard to tell. He was sedated earlier."

"Sedated?" Bharo looked worried. "Why did you do that?"

"I didn't. Mayor Samaapt sent in a group of medical thugs. I got here just in time. And it's why I asked you to come so quickly. We can't leave him alone. Not until we get him back to Portal City. Maybe not even then. Thanks again."

Bharo took a seat where Charles had been sitting. "I got you covered. So, what has he told you so far?"

"It's a bit jumbled. Apparently, the nanite-bodied have stopped using vocal speech. They communicate in digital transmissions now. They somehow made it so that, on taking this body, he can speak our language, but he has trouble remembering the details of his life before. He's told me about his job and about his family. Interesting societal differences, too, like no food. But nothing on their politics or government. About all I got was that it's different."

"Did you say no food?"

"The nanites recharge over RF, too, and then fuel cell ATP. They don't need sleep, either."

"Huh." Bharo turned to look at Charles on the bed. "Guess he's making up for lost time."

Sahaan chuckled. "Perhaps. How's everything going up there?"

"Not too bad," Bharo said. "The President's telling everyone that you're on it, which is making everyone feel better. I heard some stories about the police having to establish curfew in Bengine and Enerine, but no major social unrest. Hopefully it stays that way."

Bharo gazed over at Charles apprehensively, then he nodded at the door.

Sahaan, taking his lead, stood and led Bharo up the stairs, where they exited the room, but remained just outside. Sahaan closed the door behind them.

"The guards okay?" Bharo asked.

Sahaan nodded.

Bharo crossed his eyes and his expression grew stern. "The question though, that keeps getting asked in the media, is, 'Can they do it again?' And it's a question we need to answer fast. We can replace this wall slab, and, currently, thirteen others, but if they do this fourteen times or fifteen times, then we will be in major trouble."

Because there would be irreplaceable gaps in the wall—the Reclamation's worst nightmare, the plotline of various horror movies and thriller novels. Asking Charles directly was out of the question. Sahaan didn't trust him enough yet. For all he knew, conversations with him could be going to back to the nanite-bodied. If they were hostile, and if they learned that all it would take to breach the Reclamation was fourteen more targeted wall conversions...

Sahaan bit his lip. "I'll see if I can get him to tell me what their plans for that are. But he might not know."

Bharo's eyes widened. "He's the only shot we've got at knowing."

"What's the President's strategy?"

"The first is you. Find out from Charles whether or not they can do it again. The second is Alterra. If they can start an emergency mining effort, we might be able to cobble together two or three more walls. But that's only a stopgap."

Sahaan took a deep breath in and out. His mind shot back to the study group he'd led in high school, the one he'd botched. That, at least, had only been a study group.

"I'm glad you're here, Bharo."

"Anytime. Now, how about you eat your food then get some sleep yourself?"

"What time is it, anyway?"

Bharo chuckled. "Eleven-thirty."

Sahaan scoffed as he pulled the bag open, only then realizing how hungry he was. "Thanks for bringing food."

"No problem."

"Have you eaten?"

"I had mine on the train."

Bharo filled him in on the innocuous details of the cabinet activities while Sahaan ate through his dinner. After finishing the last of the potatoes, he said, "I want to be here when he wakes up."

"You sure?"

"Last time I wasn't here, it didn't go so well."

Bharo called down one of the soldiers and muttered something to him. The soldier retreated up the stairs and disappeared out the door.

"What was that?"

"He's getting us a pair of cots," then he whispered. "You've got to keep your mind sharp."

Sahaan nodded. Perhaps with friends like Bharo and a President like Aavee he might be able to pull through this one.

Sahaan fell asleep the very moment he lay down on the cot. His sleep was dark and dreamless, an empty void that absorbed all passing time. He awoke to the shake of his shoulder, and Bharo's voice.

"Sahaan. He's awake."

Sahaan rolled over and pulled himself out of bed, still groggy. Charles was sitting at the table, looking bright-eyed and swinging his legs back and forth in the air.

Sahaan stifled a yawn as he approached. "Charles. Good morning. I want you to meet my friend, Mr. Bharo Meharab."

"Nice to meet you, Mr. Meharab."

"Nice to meet you, too, Charles."

"How did you sleep?" Sahaan asked.

The question seemed to perplex Charles momentarily. "All right, I think. I can tell I feel better, recharged, but I had *dreams*. Strange sensation. I'd read about them, but I can't imagine anything that would have prepared me for it. I dreamed I was back at home and the Reclamation was expanding the walls. But then everything was changed and I was back here and I was in a human body again. And none of that struck me at the time as being

78

that odd. I accepted the inherent strangeness of those hallucinations. It was unsettling. I'm not sure we were all that wrong in giving those up."

Bharo gave Sahaan a wide-eyed look, which Sahaan read immediately as a kind of unspoken, '*this* is who we've been trying to contact for fifty years?' Sahaan winked in response. Yes, Bharo. This is it.

"Are you hungry?" Sahaan asked.

Charles nodded vigorously, and this time Sahaan didn't even have to look up at the soldiers. One began chattering on his handheld at the mention of food.

Charles turned his head, craning his neck to look at the empty bag that had contained Sahaan's dinner the night before. "What is 'The Hedgerow?'"

"Dr. Ekeer's and my favorite restaurant in Adamantine."

"You were in Adamantine, Mr. Meharab?"

"Yup. Took the train from there last night."

"Do you work with Dr. Ekeer?"

Bharo nodded. "I do. I'm Communications Liaison to the Chiefs of Staff of the President of the Reclamation. It's my job to know what's going on in the media politically."

Charles perked up at that. "Has your internet changed in the last hundred years?"

Sahaan looked at Bharo. "We've made the transfer protocols more efficient. Video, in particular, can be streamed much faster. But that's about it."

"Our internet is completely different," Charles said. "We experience it. And it's... fused with how we talk. It's all the same thing. The internet *is* communication."

Sahaan and Bharo shared a look.

"Does that mean that..." Sahaan struggled for a polite way to word the question. "Are there individuals, or are the nanite-bodied one big consciousness?"

"Oh, no." Charles shook his head. "I know where I end and others begin. There's a boundary. But if I'm authorized to have an experience, I can communicate to someone else and share their experience, wherever they are. I'm still me, and they are still them, but we're together, even though we might be physically separated by hundreds or thousands of miles. Sorry if that's confusing."

Bharo shrugged. "It makes a kind of sense."

Sahaan churned that one over in his mind. No wonder it was hard for Charles to talk about politics. The political dynamics of such a people had the potential to be remarkably complex... or perhaps also remarkably simple.

"Dr. Ekeer?"

"Yes, Charles?"

"What will happen to me now?"

Bharo looked at Sahaan, who nodded his assent.

"We're preparing to move you to Portal City," Bharo said.

"What for?" Charles asked.

"Citrine," Sahaan jumped in, "is, in some ways, not suitable for us. We had that unfortunate incident earlier with those doctors, for which I'm very sorry. In Portal City it will be much easier to prevent such incidents from happening."

"I see." Charles stared at the floor for some time.

"You'll like Portal City much better, I think," Sahaan added with a note of optimism. "We had to throw this place together without notice, but they're going to make sure your environment in Portal City is comfortable, accommodating, and safe. Right, Bharo?"

Bharo nodded.

"I... appreciate that." Charles's voice had taken on a slight tone of skepticism.

Sahaan noted it and decided to charge forward. "It would help our preparations to know... Charles, do you expect anyone other nanite-bodied to enter the Reclamation in the same way you did?" Political capital with Charles thoroughly spent, he noted.

Charles frowned and shook his head. "I don't know. Maybe. Maybe they can't. Or maybe some don't want to. I'm not sure."

"Will anyone be upset if you don't come back?" Bharo tried.

Charles shook his head vigorously. "No. I'm supposed to stay here."

"To what end?" Sahaan didn't realize that the tiniest hint of frustration had slipped into his question until it was out of his mouth.

Charles bunched up his forehead, shook his head wildly and slammed his fists on the table. "I don't know! I can't remember. I used to know and it's so frustrating to not remember and have you not believe me. I knew that you'd all decide I was a monster!"

Bharo stood, walked to Sahaan and pulled him up out of his chair by the arm. Sahaan acquiesced to his friend's grip. Bharo nodded up toward the door. Charles had wrapped his arms around his head and put his head in his lap.

Sahaan walked up the stairs and out the door in a fugue. What an idiot he'd been. Stupid. Politically inept.

The door shut behind them.

"Sahaan!" Bharo was holding him by the shoulders

"Yes?"

"Remember that girl you dated your freshman year? You came home livid because you'd had a fight, and you were convinced it was the end of the world?"

"Yeah."

"It's not the end of the world. It wasn't then, and isn't now. You're right. He's not dangerous. I'm convinced of that after only ten minutes of seeing him awake. He's too... weird. He's like their version of a computer geek."

"He did say he was a scientist. Some kind of programmer."

"No surprise there. Now pull yourself together. Why don't you go up to the surface and call your family, call the president, link in with home now that I'm here? You and he both need to calm down and process what just happened."

"Sure." Sahaan shook his head. "You're right, as usual."

"I'll send a soldier if anyone else tries to barge in."

And with that, Bharo was back inside Charles's cell, and Sahaan found himself walking through the hallways of C8 in the poor, shuddering lighting, wondering just how he'd let that conversation go so wrong so fast.

The first call Sahaan made on the surface was to Lachel, who was still doing well. All of her classes had been canceled, as had school for Jaan. A curfew was now in effect across the Reclamation, and people were getting restless. Lachel, typically resourceful, had organized a grocery shopping expedition with other parents in their community, and they had acquired ample supplies. If the situation continued to deteriorate, they would not starve, but so far the police were able to keep things under control and the military had not gotten involved... yet. Jaan was well and asked about him often. Sahaan talked to him, too, reminding him to stay alert and be extra helpful to his mom.

"What's the boy like?" Jaan still wanted to know.

"He only looks like a boy. He's actually a lot older. And he's very scared. He doesn't have all his memories from before he came here, and what he does have is a jumble." Perhaps, Sahaan thought, it would be best to get some proper medical attention on him. He had, after all, meta-morphosed out of a wall. And, come to think of it...

"Are you coming home soon?"

"The day after tomorrow."

"Are you sure?"

"Mostly sure. You'll be the first to know if that changes."

"It'll be better when you're back."

"Then I'll do my best to get back."

After he'd ended the call, Sahaan dialed into the President's office.

One of the office's many secretary staff answered. "Office of the President."

"Hi, yes, this is Dr. Sahaan Ekeer calling for Dr. Khoj Anaveshan."

"One moment."

The familiar deep, older voice answered the phone. "Dr. Ekeer?"

"Hello, Dr. Anaveshan. How are you doing?"

"Could be better, though I can only imagine how you must be doing. They say you were there? You saw it happen?"

"I did, yes."

"And you're talking to him now? He's really one of them, but made into a human boy somehow?"

"Yes, that's about the gist of it."

"Amazing."

"Dr. Anaveshan, I need to know, has anyone been doing any analyses of the area where the wall turned into Charles— the boy, where the wall turned into the boy?"

"I sent a team out there this morning. They should be reporting in by noon, I would expect. It's the question the whole scientific community is asking. How did a piece of metal turn into a boy without nanites able to come anywhere near it?"

"Right. Have you ever heard of that kind of material transmutation happening under circumstances that don't involve nanites?"

"None."

"Can you keep me updated on what your team finds out?"

"Of course! I'm glad someone else is taking an interest in the scientific aspect of things. You remember the reason we have the walls at all, right?"

"I think the Alterrans noticed that the area around their portal kept nanites out and they dug up the metal. Am I remembering that right?"

"You are. And the human toll here was enormous because we didn't apply our scientific minds in the right way. We just kept throwing energy and people at the problem. I'm trying to keep us from repeating those old mistakes."

"Thanks, Dr. Anaveshan. Do let me know if there's anything I can do to support your efforts."

"Of course. I'll be in touch."

Even if Charles couldn't remember what they needed to know, if they could figure out *how* his transformation had occurred, they could potentially stop it from happening again. And the party that figured out how to do that would be the savior of the Reclamation. Just the kind of thing that could turn an election back around.

The last call Sahaan made was to the president, who was busy preparing for his day trip to Alterra, but was quite happy to hear that Charles now had adequate protection and that Sahaan had thrown his support in with Dr. Anaveshan's efforts.

"One more thing," the President said. "Last night, we got an update from the team here. The Portal City facility for Charles will be operational by end of day today. We're preparing secure transport tonight."

"Already, Mr. President?"

"That's right. They've been working around the clock. The cabinet and a lot of others think that expediting his transport will help minimize the growing civil disorder. If it gets much worse, they'll be asking me to get the military involved, and the last thing Una needs right now is a Reconciliation president declaring martial law."

"Understood, Mr. President. I'll make sure Charles is ready to go."

"Thank you, Sahaan."

"Good luck on Alterra, Mr. President."

Sahaan ended the call, then typed out a text message to Lachel about his updated schedule.

He took a deep breath. His confidence restored, he trod back down the stairs into the bunker. Damage wasn't permanent, he reminded himself. Broken bridges could always be rebuilt. With relationships, honesty and openness could mend a lot of hurt. It was time to see just how skillfully he could apply that principle.

When Sahaan walked into Charles's cell, both Bharo and Charles looked up at him from their respective seats at the table below. With a calm smile, Sahaan proceeded down the stairs and took his place at the table.

"I was just telling Charles about the cabinet and our different consuls."

"And about the differences between the Veda government and yours," Charles added helpfully.

"Right. That too."

"Great," Sahaan said. "I'm glad to hear that you've been doing well. Charles, I need to apologize for raising my voice earlier. I'm very sorry to have upset you. I'd like to explain, and also to ask for your help." This was it. Either tactical genius or a major blunder. "I've decided I want to trust you with this information. Perhaps it will help you understand my position. Your body formed out of a wall panel, Charles." A flurry of handheld activity from above him, including chatter audibly loud. He didn't care. Sahaan continued. "I wanted to find out if we should prepare for others coming here, or if it would be just you. It would also be helpful to know where they might appear if they are coming, mostly for those individuals' safety as they enter. A lot of people in the Reclamation are very frightened right now."

Charles nodded very slowly. "Thank you, Dr. Ekeer."

"Call me Sahaan," he added, before Charles had a chance to continue.

"Sahaan. Thank you. It means a lot to me that you're

willing to share that. I... had guessed about how this body was formed from where I woke up. I also think I kind of knew from some half-formed memories of conversations from before I came here. If I'm completely honest, I think you should prepare for more nanite-bodied to come here the way I did."

The soldiers on the balcony began practically shouting into their handhelds.

"But!" Charles turned toward the balcony and shouted over them. "Listen! It's important. I don't remember if there was any interest from others in coming. More of them *can* come, but most of us don't want to. I had a particular interest in coming here, one that I, frustratingly, can't remember. It was unique. No one else has *my* interest. But maybe some will choose to come. If they do, they will try soon, and I suggest you have somewhere safe for us to live. And, I'm sorry, but I have no way of knowing if the people running the conversion process will choose Citrine again or some other slab of your walls."

"How many new visitors should we expect?" Sahaan asked.

"Likely one or two. Maybe three or four at the very most," Charles said. "Four would be extraordinary."

"What makes you sure about those numbers?"

Charles bit his lip. "I don't wish to offend you. There's no delicate way to say this. Remember what I told you yesterday about eating?"

Sahaan nodded.

"What was that exactly?" Bharo asked.

"The process of eating, from the perspective of a nanite-bodied (again, forgive me, but there's no delicate way to say this), invokes a sense of disgust. In fact, that also goes for the vast majority of your biological processes. Most of them will not want... this. If you are worried about an invasion, I am not aware of one. What I can recall is that once I did what I did, everyone else would understand how I'd done it. Everyone else now knows how to enter the Reclamation the way I did. But most won't do it. I remember that it's hard. Since the means of entry removes our physical and mental upgrades, our military wouldn't be interested. Intellectuals? They are more interested in perfecting our home. They do not view any potential for perfection here. Politicians? The journey would be a political setback. Businessmen? The journey would be dangerous and not useful for trade. I cannot see anyone being interested. Except for me. But I do not know all seventeen million others. It seems likely that there exist a handful of other unique individuals who will possess some personality quirk that makes this journey compelling. I cannot tell you how many of those there are."

Bharo was giving Sahaan that look throughout Charles's speech. It was the look he gave whenever there would be an impending media disaster. Charles's confession would also make the civil disorder worse.

"Thank you, Charles. That makes sense. I want you to know, if there's anything I can do to help you remember why you came here, please let me know what that is. It sounds like the Reclamation had some kind of personal meaning for you. Is that right?"

Charles sat and stared with the most painfully perplexed expression on his face. "I think so. Ugh. It's the most terrible feeling. I can see the conversations in my memory, but the details are all a jumble. Do you still have physical libraries?"

Sahaan and Bharo shared a look.

"Yes," Bharo said. "Why? Something to do with why you came here?"

"Maybe..." Charles let his voice trail off, then he added. "If it's ever possible, I would like to visit one. The nanite-bodied don't have them anymore. Everything is digital. The guiding principle of our city structures is that they most efficiently house and protect the biological components of our physiognomy. There is no room for a building dedicated to books."

For the first time, Sahaan saw an expression on Charles's face that he would interpret as anger. "I think that revision was a move away from perfection rather than toward it."

"You didn't like your old home much?" Sahaan tried.

Charles's face lightened. "There were things I liked. Visiting the central spire of Redwing. Walks down the streets of—" A single tear slide down Charles's face, and all at once he screamed and slapped at his face.

The soldiers reached for their weapons, and Bharo immediately called up to them to hold their fire. Sahaan jolted out of his chair and crouched next to Charles, who was now shaking to the point of spasms, taking Charles's hands in his own. "Charles! Charles! It's all right. They're just tears. It's perfectly fine."

Charles closed his eyes, which then sprouted more tears. "What *is* this? Why am I—? Sadness makes water erupt out my *face*?"

"Yes," Sahaan said. "Sadness makes us cry."

"Why did I do this to myself?" Charles said. "Why?

Why did I do this?"

"I don't know, Charles. But we'll figure it out together."

Sahaan calmed down Charles, and Bharo calmed down the guards. Food arrived for all three of them, and they ate a solid breakfast, Charles barraging them with questions around the intricacies of table manners throughout.

After they'd finished, Sahaan announced the updated timeline for their departure.

Bharo studied Sahaan at the announcement, and then, half an hour later, excused himself to the surface to make some phone calls. There, certainly, he would discover the deteriorating state of civil order throughout the Reclamation. Sahaan could only hope that getting Charles to the capitol would quell the unease. On the other hand, it would only be a matter of time before Charles's revelation would leak into the media, and that would certainly make things worse.

Thinking it would be best to keep further revelations until they reached Portal City, Sahaan intentionally kept their conversation light. Charles asked about what other surprises he could expect from his body, some of which he understood were socially fraught, others of which he didn't. Sahaan did his best to explain.

Bharo returned after about an hour, by which time the conversation had turned to the Reclamation's two political parties and how they'd come about. Sahaan had explained the history of Mox Thiksay's children, his daughter Vibha and his son Param. Both had inherited Mox's fiery spirit, love of history, and determination to protect the Reclamation, but they'd drawn two different conclusions about how to go about it.

Vibha thought that the best defense was to establish formal diplomatic and economic treaties with the nanite-bodied. She was the one who had come up with the term "nanite-bodied," as opposed to the old term, "deranged," which everyone had used until that time. In her estimation, the Reclamation could only ensure its continued safety through contact.

Param, on the other hand, thought that defense was only possible through an expansion of the wall network and the advancement of the quantum field science they were based on. Param believed that communicating with the nanite-bodied was a waste of time and ultimately dangerous since it was likely to lead to further hostilities.

Their arguments started young. Mox had already steeped them in Reclamation and Alterran history throughout their youths, and both children were engaged and attentive learners. By the time they were in their teens, their political values had emerged, and they entered in ideological warfare with one another. Rather than come down on one side or the other, or even just calm their debates, Mox encouraged them to argue even more, figuring that the child with the best idea for the future would prevail.

But Mox died very suddenly of a heart attack when Param was only twenty-one and Vibha eighteen. Their mother tried to settle their ideological dispute, but by that point, winning the debate had now become intrinsically tied to winning the approval of the parent who could no longer give it. Their debate took on a personal dimension, and their relationship deteriorated even further. They both entered politics, then Parliament, where they recruited so many others to their views that they re-organized the five existing political parties into two new ones. Reconciliation formed around Vibha; Guardian around Param.

MPs who represented the hub cities found themselves falling in with Vibha. Their constituencies were largely more affluent, had better access to education, and that meant generally a tendency to view solutions in terms of manipulating the dials of complex systems, systems like social and economic dynamics between populations.

MPs who represented the spoke cities represented a much different population. Less affluent and less well ed-ucated, not to mention surrounded on all sides by enemy territory, they tended to see defense in simpler and more obvious terms: walls keep out the enemy; military spend-ing makes us safer. Complex discussions about the defen-sive properties of treaties and economic agreements were completely ineffective on this group. Such MPs fell in with Param.

Param had also died young, nearly two decades before Vibha. Her brother's death affected her profoundly. Dur-ing the last two decades of her life, Vibha had started to see things differently, but her change of heart had proved ineffective against the two-party system, against the po-litical foment that she herself had created, and the bitter contention between Guardian and Reconciliation had continued right up through the present day.

Sahaan was able to tell the whole story, neatly avoid-ing the fact that Vibha was his grandmother by using her maiden name, Thiksay, instead of her married name, Ekeer, the one he'd inherited.

Charles listened attentively throughout Sahaan's telling. When he was done, Charles sat quietly for many moments.

"How do you feel about the Thiksays?" Sahaan tried.

"Me?" Charles shrugged. "I don't know. Stok was a man who wanted to protect his home and save his spouse's life. I can't say I blame him too much. I think, if I was more into the idea of perfecting the material world, I might not like him very much, because of what he did, but that's never really been my thing. There's something else about how we think about him, but I can't quite place it." Charles closed his eyes, shook his head, and yawned. "Sorry. Is it okay if I lie down?"

Sahaan nodded. He glanced at his handheld noticing that it wasn't even noon yet. He took the opportunity to have a private conversation with Bharo outside of the cell.

"We have to get a good doctor to take a look at him when we get him to Portal City," Sahaan said. "This is the third time he's fallen asleep because thinking through his memories overtaxed him."

"I'll set that up," Bharo said.

"How bad is it up there?" Sahaan asked.

"Still getting worse. Enerine, Bengine, and Cynine have requested that Portal City military forces supplement their police force. If this keeps up, the president will be forced to declare martial law, probably tomorrow at the earliest. The more fringe elements of the media are blaring louder than ever. The radical Guardians are encouraging people to overthrow their local governments, saying a nanite doomsday is imminent, and the radical Reconciliationists are demanding we take down the walls ourselves to let in more nanite-bodied envoys."

"One more favor, then. Find out how Dr. Anaveshan's group is getting along."

"Oh? What's going on with the science division?"

"A team of his is analyzing the area around the pavilion where Charles appeared. They're trying to figure out how they converted a wall slab into a boy without nanites."

"Got it. Will do."

And Bharo was away.

Sahaan returned to watch a sleeping Charles, alone with his old thoughts and feelings about his family. How could he get the two sides to realize that they were both actually on the same side? The rhetoric coming out of both of their extreme elements was ridiculous. Open up the walls? Take up arms against your forced mutation? Insane.

And all because two siblings couldn't agree on how to solve a problem. It was as though, no matter how hard he tried, the two factions just pushed further and further away from the mutual understanding he was trying to create.

Bharo returned some time later, bringing lunch with him. They managed to rouse Charles, who found himself famished. They spent the afternoon describing more details of Reclamation government. Sahaan tried a few stabs at getting information from Charles about how nanite-bodied government worked, but each time he did, Charles bunched up his face or shook his head or simply stared off into space.

Later on, Sahaan asked for some paper and a pencil,

and drew out a map of the Reclamation and the local geography to the best of his ability. "We know there are nanite-bodied cities in these four locations, the closest cities to us."

Charles nodded. "Oh. Yeah! This one is Archway, this is Eveling, that's Nightbridge, and on the coast is Northstar."

Sahaan and Bharo shared a pleased expression. They were the first people in the Reclamation to learn the names of nanite-bodied cities. For eight decades, ever since the launch of the first satellites, Reclamation maps of the world had merely labeled the nanite-bodied cities with question marks, though some fringe Guardian groups were now distributing maps marking them with hazard symbols instead.

Before long, the soldiers on the balcony became more active, moving in and out of the room, talking on their handhelds. More of them appeared, too.

"Everything all right?" Bharo called up.

"Just preparing for the move," one soldier called down.

A half an hour later, a soldier called down that they would be underway within five minutes.

"Are you ready?" Sahaan asked Charles.

"I think so. How long will it take to get to Portal City?"

"Normally, about three and half hours," Sahaan said. "But our train won't be stopping in Adamantine and Adrine like a normal train would."

"Three hours," Bharo added. "Give or take."

"I think I'll be glad to be in Portal City instead. Even if my... living quarters are much the same."

"You aren't a prisoner, Charles," Sahaan insisted. "You

haven't done anything wrong."

"I also haven't proven out my intentions. I'm aware of my position here."

Sahaan was reminded just then just how un-childlike Charles was, and just how much they'd been through together in their short time here. Now it was time for the next step.

Soldiers called down for Charles, Sahaan, and Bharo to climb the stairs and exit. Sahaan looked back on that drab room with fondness as they left. He caught a glimpse of his empty bag from The Hedgerow on the table as a soldier shut off the lights.

It was time for the next stage in their investigation. It was time to help Charles fully remember his past so that they could determine the true intent of the nanite-bodied. Sahaan wanted an answer to the age-old question. If the nanite-bodied were still basically hostile and Charles were a personality anomaly, then Reconciliation would be forced to adopt a militarily and scientifically defensive posture. If the people who sent Charles here did intend him as an envoy and couldn't anticipate or prevent his memory loss, then Guardian would be forced to accept that negotiation of territory rights was the new political reality.

Sahaan said a silent goodbye to Citrine. He'd come here intending to teach people about himself and Reconciliation. Instead, the city had taught him quite a bit.

He shut the door to the room and hurried to catch up with the military entourage leading Charles away.

They returned to the same van they had used to enter the facility, still parked in the large, vacant, concrete space where they had left it. Soldiers climbed in alongside Bharo and Sahaan, the doors were shut, and the window-less space closed in around them.

Sahaan heard doors opening and closing. The sound of the motor erupted from the front, and then the feeling of motion, turns, inclines, turns again.

They remained silent.

Sahaan found it odd. There had been just as much surveillance in the bunker, and yet here, with the soldiers sitting so close beside them, conversation was stifled somehow.

Charles stared at the wall behind Sahaan, and Sahaan watched his expression throughout. He seemed lost in thought, then pensive, then frustrated, then pensive again. All at once, his whole face lit up.

"Sahaan!" Charles sat up straighter. "I've remembered something. About our politics—"

The engine stopped and the soldiers stood, interrupting Charles's sentence.

"What is it?" Sahaan asked.

The doors to the van were being opened, soldiers were all around. They were at a part of the Citrine train station that Sahaan had never seen. A train lay in view, and some ways off was the platform for standard commuter trains, which he recognized. The crates and machinery in this part of the station indicated that they'd be taking a line normally used for freight.

"Should I tell you... here?"

Sahaan glanced around. Beyond a cordon, he could see media representatives ready with handhelds poised to take pictures. "Perhaps not. Let's wait until the train."

They walked a short distance to the train. Bharo eyed

the media, giving them his flat, cheery-but-distant expression, while Charles, Sahaan noticed, seemed lost in thought. Perhaps trying to remember more.

When they reached the train, the soldiers motioned for Charles to head toward a car in the rear, while Sahaan and Charles were being guided toward the front.

"Wait," Sahaan said. "We ride with Charles."

"Orders from the president," the soldier said.

"Let me see those," Bharo stepped forward.

"Me too," Sahaan added.

The soldier, clearly the group's leader by the rank pinned to his uniform, pulled up his handheld and transferred the document to both Bharo's and Sahaan's devices.

"Does it authenticate?" Sahaan asked.

"Yes," Bharo said.

"Mine too."

Bharo bit his lip and gave Sahaan his 'this smells' expression. But what could they do? Violate a signed mandate from their boss? They would have to dig into it when they arrived in Portal City.

"Are there any soldiers assigned to the train who weren't part of our contingent at the facility?" Sahaan asked the soldier. "Anyone new or recently reassigned?"

"No, sir," the soldier said. He transferred two more documents to Sahaan showing the soldiers assigned to the train and those assigned to Charles's cell in the bunker respectively. The former was an abbreviated version of the latter.

"And you trust all of these soldiers?"

"Yes, sir. With my life."

Sahaan glanced at Bharo. Bharo shrugged.

Sahaan took a deep breath and walked to where Charles stood. He knelt, so as to meet Charles at eye level.

"We're going to be in separate cars. All the soldiers are the same. You'll be fine."

"What I have to tell you, though—"

"You'll tell me in Portal City."

"We'll wait then. Like you taught me about Guardian and Reconciliation. Waiting to realize that they both actually want the same thing. Different, but actually the same."

Sahaan thought he caught just the slightest hint of a wink. But did Charles know what a wink meant? Perhaps. And why was he bringing up the parties again? Sahaan watched as Charles walked away, led by the soldiers toward the rear car.

Sahaan turned and walked with Bharo toward the front car.

"What did he say there just now? Something about the parties?"

"'Different, but actually the same.'"

Bharo bit his lip, mulling that one over himself, too, apparently.

Sahaan climbed into the train, soldiers all around him, but his mind kept replaying his interaction with Charles. What could it have meant? Clearly it was something to do with what he'd remembered, but he had only reiterated what he'd learned about the Reclamation's politics. Something about that phrase, "different, but actually the same." Nanite-bodied and *homo sapiens sapiens*, perhaps? They shared the same genetic heritage. The nanite-bodied had been making modifications for more than a century. They'd changed much, but at the heart of every

Reconciliation hope was the idea that they still could be communicated and negotiated with. Charles's existence itself had proved that out, so that information was nothing new.

What then?

Bharo yawned and stretched in his seat.

"Have you gotten any sleep yourself?"

Bharo shook his head. "I was just thinking it would be a good time to doze off."

"Go for it. Unless you have any idea what Charles might have meant just now."

"Nope. It's an odd thing to remark on. I'm not sure how it could be related to their politics or their stance on anything."

"Me either."

Bharo adjusted himself so that his head was positioned between the seat and the wall of the train car and closed his eyes.

Sahaan retrieved his handheld and sent a text to Lachel that he was on his way home and would be able to see them as soon as Charles was safely in the facility prepared for him in Portal City.

The train climbed up the mountain range, and outside, through the south window, the peaks of the Asym mountain range cast long shadows over one another, only just barely visible over the walls protecting the road. The train twisted and turned through the mountain valley, then began its descent.

Sahaan noticed something out the window. He squinted, wondering if his eyes were playing tricks on him. Some trick of the light of the setting sun against the—

All at once, a sharp jolt forward. The train accelerated, and the air became hot, so very very hot. Brightness filled his vision and a roar screamed into his ears. There was not the chance for even one more thought before he lost consciousness.

"We interrupt regularly scheduled programming to bring you a breaking news announcement.

"At 4:32 pm today, the train carrying the nanite-bodied visitor was derailed in the wallroad region connecting Adamantine and Citrine while descending from the Asym Mountains.

"The derailment happened simultaneously with an explosion that destroyed six wall slabs and has created—"

The anchor took a moment to collect herself.

"The gap of six wall slabs has created the first ever full breach of the Reclamation's defensive wall. Automated systems have confirmed that nanites have penetrated the Adamantine-Citrine wallroad area.

"Our own defensive nanites have become active throughout the Adamantine-Citrine wallroad. So far, the invading nanites occupy an area of approximately half a kilometer of the wallroad, and our automated defenses are holding them back. Again, all our diagnostic systems indicate that the containment zone is stable and that our automated defenses have prevented further incursion.

"The emergency reactors in both Adamantine and Citrine have been brought online, and the power supply to the wallroad's automated systems is stable.

"As for the passengers of the train, it is unclear at this time how many survivors there are. The explosion appears to have obliterated the middle two cars, tearing the train in half. The back two cars were propelled back toward Citrine and the front three cars forward toward Adamantine. Emergency rescue workers have been dispatched to both halves of the train wreck.

"President Aavee has released a statement that his government has begun exploring options for restoring the Adamantine-Citrine wallroad.

"An additional presidential decree has declared martial law throughout the Reclamation. All citizens and residents are to fully comply with the orders of all military personnel, who have been mobilized throughout the country. Citizens are urged to stay indoors and to travel only as necessary for food and supplies.

"I repeat, our walls have been breached, and the Reclamation is now under martial law. We will provide you with additional information as it becomes available."

PART II

Boundaries

"Charles."

"Yes?"

"You want us to believe that the Senior Consul to the president, the leading authoritarian overlord of the Seditious Party, simply sat and talked with you for nearly two days. That he taught you table manners, and about human tears. That you discussed the surface details of Reclamation political organization. That you tried and struggled to remember details from your time as a deranged. Is that all? Are you sure you are not leaving anything out?"

"Yes. I'm sure."

"We think there's more you're not telling us, Charles."

"I'm sorry you feel that way. There's no more I can tell you."

"There is at least one thing. The political element about the deranged you remembered before getting on the train."

"It doesn't matter. And you won't believe me, anyway."

"You will tell us."

"Fine. But, you won't like it."

"Tell us."

—

Sahaan awoke to two sensations: bone-splitting pain and the sound of voices all around him. At first they didn't make much sense. Words, certainly, but nothing his brain could put together. Throughout his body coursed the most horrific pain he had ever endured.

"Can you hear me?"

A light in his eyes. Finally, words that made sense.

"Yes." His voice came out as a kind of gurgle, but he was mostly certain he'd articulated the word.

"Prepare a stretcher." A man's face formed in his field of vision. All at once, he turned and called out over his shoulder. Red and blue lights strobed over his face, red then blue, red then blue. He seemed to be doing something else, something with some instruments near Sahaan's torso, but Sahaan couldn't feel anything besides the pain, which had begun hitting him in waves. The swell of a wave was almost worse than the omnipresent background pain he'd woken to.

"What's happened?" Sahaan asked.

"Please stay calm, sir," the medic asked.

"I have to know about Charles," Sahaan said.

The medic ignored the request and continued working.

"The nanite-bodied visitor who was in the back car. What happened to him?"

The medic stopped only momentarily. He waved over to someone beyond Sahaan's limited field of vision, then continued to work.

"He's agitated," the medic said while working.

Sahaan couldn't see whoever it was the medic was talking to. But within moments he found consciousness slipping away. They'd sedated him. Damn medics.

Ah, well. They *were* trying to save his life after all. But what about Charles?

When Sahaan woke again, he found himself in a hospital room. Machines beeped and hummed around him. He lay upright on a bed, and a doctor stood by his side tapping into a handheld. She glanced over at him and smiled.

"I'm Dr. Aarogy. How are you feeling?"

"Terrible."

She gave him a knowing nod. "Any place where the pain is particularly bad?"

"My left side?" He realized, then, that that was the epicenter from which the waves of pain throbbed. "My left side," he repeated with more certainty.

"You sustained an impact from a component of the carriage."

"What happened?"

"An explosion. The two middle cars of the train were obliterated. Your car and the two other front cars were propelled forward, then derailed."

"And the two back cars?"

"Pushed back toward Citrine."

"This is... Adamantine Central Hospital?"

Dr. Aarogy nodded.

"Doctor, this is of the utmost urgency. Please contact the Citrine authorities on my behalf and ask them to confirm whether or not Charles survived."

Dr. Aarogy frowned. "The situation regarding Charles is complicated. President Aavee has requested to debrief you himself. However, before that can happen, I need to make sure you're well enough."

"How long will that be?"

"Long enough that I can be certain that minor exertion won't worsen your condition."

Sahaan released a deep breath. "My friend, Minister Bharo Meharab. What happened to him?"

"Minister Meharab is in critical condition. He is in surgery now. I'll keep you up-to-date on his progress."

"And my condition?"

"I believe you will make a full recovery."

Even now, the throbs of pain in his side were getting somewhat better. That was probably just the drugs, though.

"Thank you, doctor. For everything. If there is anything you can tell me about Charles before my debrief, I would very much appreciate it."

"It *is* all over the news." Dr. Aarogy motioned her head toward the holographic television panel in the wall, the controls for which were built into the bedside near Sahaan's hands. She crossed her arms and let out a capitulatory sigh. "Charles was not found in the wreckage of the two cars that were pushed back toward Citrine, only his guards were. No one knows where he is."

Sahaan squinted. "How...? I don't understand."

"I'm sure President Aavee will be able to tell you more. Try to relax."

"Has my family been contacted?"

"Yes. Arrangements are being made for your wife and son to come here. It's been difficult—" She suddenly seemed to think better of this line of explanation, but then seemed to decide to proceed forward anyway. "The normal commuter trains have been shut down as President Aavee has declared martial law."

"I see."

"Please let me know if you experience any sudden changes. You can watch the holocaster if you like, but I advise you to avoid news segments about the incident with the train for the time being."

"Thank you, doctor."

Dr. Aarogy left him with a smile. Adamantine hospitals were good. When Bharo pulled through, it would be thanks to their surgeons' skill. And he insisted to himself that Bharo would indeed pull through.

He reached for the holocaster controls, then decided against it. He didn't want to see aerial views of the train wreckage. Not just yet, anyway. He lay back and closed his eyes, trying not to think about that pain in his left side.

As he lay, Charles's last words to him came back to him, repeating themselves over and over in his mind: "Guardian and Reconciliation, waiting to realize that they both want the same thing. Different, but actually the same." Some kind of code... or indicator, a signpost, but indicating what? Pointing to what?

He worked that riddle over in his mind until he found himself drowsy and drifting off into sleep.

Sahaan's alarm clock rang, jolting him out of slumber. He pulled himself out of his bed, the pads of his pajamas smooshing between his feet and the carpet. In his grogginess, he instantly thought of school, but then realized that it was the weekend. He had no school today, and the reason his parents had had him set his alarm was that today was their big trip to Portal City. And then he remembered—today he was going to see his grandmother again.

Dad got along with grandma alright, but Mom always got so quiet when grandma was around. Sahaan had noticed that Mom never said much of anything around her and, if Sahaan asked her for something, she always gave him short answers, usually just "no." He'd learned not to ask her for things when they were around his grandparents.

His first thought was of what to read on the train. It took an hour to get from Eline to Portal City, which would allow him to get at least one good book in. But which one? He moved instinctively to the two tall bookshelves near the door to his bedroom and gazed over the spines. How to choose?

He eventually decided on two books, figuring he could make up his mind between them on the way to the train station. He pulled them off the shelf and stuffed them into the backpack at the base of his desk. Atop it lay his history and science homework—done—and his math homework—not done. He always saved math for last, and he always regretted that. He couldn't help that he liked the other subjects so much better, though.

He pulled off his pajamas and threw on some pants and a T-shirt. He then thought better of the T-shirt and opted instead for one of his nicer shirts. He was going to meet grandma after all.

"Everyone in the Reclamation and Alterra knows who your grandmother is," his father had told him five years before, "but not everyone has to know about you. Your grandmother thinks that our whole family is responsible for leading the country into a better future, but I want you to know that I don't agree. I love your grandmother, but she's wrong in this. You're not to take responsibility for things that happened before you were born."

"Will someone still lead the country into a better future if we don't?" Sahaan had asked.

His father had sighed. He hadn't seemed to like the question.

"That's... Well. It's like this. Your grandmother chose to go into politics. And that was her choice. But I didn't have to go into government, and so I didn't, and neither do you. Right now your whole life is ahead of you, but the older you get the more your choices narrow. You'll realize more and more that it's important how you spend your time. You get a choice about how you can best help the people around you. Being a good citizen in your local neighborhood is a fine choice. Just because your grandmother thinks that government is the best choice doesn't mean that it is. You shouldn't even be worrying about that now. So, if Grandma talks to you about the government, you let me know, okay?"

"I will." Sahaan said the words out loud as he checked his collar in the mirror. Not too shabby. Now, what else would Grandma be looking for? She always honed in the most minute details. It was simultaneously irritating and invigorating. The game of making himself the most presentable he could was, in a way, kind of fun.

A knock on his door.

"Sahaan?" his mother called.

"I'm getting dressed," Sahaan called back.

"We're starting breakfast soon."

"I'll be down in a bit."

"Don't take too long."

Pants not scuffed. Shirt not wrinkled. Well, not too wrinkled. Books in backpack. Anything else? No, that would do.

A day in Portal City. He could hardly wait.

"Dad!"

Sahaan woke with a jolt and found Jaan clutching at the metal railing of his bed.

"Hey, son!" Sahaan tried to sound energetic but still felt groggy, likely from the drugs. "Great to see you."

Lachel hovered into view behind him. Her hand reached his and he clasped it tightly. "I'm so glad you're all right," she said through a wan smile. She held back the tears admirably.

"You can't imagine how good it is to see you two," Sahaan said.

"There are police and soldiers *everywhere*," Jaan said. "It's unreal. And school's been canceled, but Rahan and I have been texting the whole time about what's going on and when we heard about the train everyone freaked out. But then we heard you'd been taken the hospital and you were fine. You're fine, right Dad?"

Sahaan laughed. "That's what they tell me."

He put on as serious of a face as he could muster. "You've been behaving and helping your mom, right?"

"You bet!"

Lachel nodded, albeit with a bit of a furrowed brow... but just a bit. "He's been helpful. Most of the time."

"So, Dad, it's all over the news that Gadh and the other Guardian politicians are saying that the government can't keep the nanite defenses up for very long. They're wrong, aren't they?"

Sahaan quirked his head. "Nanite defenses?"

"Then they haven't told you," Lachel said. "The explo-

114

sion that struck your train also destroyed six of the wall slabs in the Citrine-Adamantine wallroad. The nanites from outside have breached, but the government insists that our automated defenses are stable."

Sahaan took a moment to process the severity of that. No wonder Aavee had declared martial law. Sahaan looked at Jaan and summoned all the authority he could muster. "Guardian is wrong. We know our defenses work, and there's no reason to believe they'll fail." What he wouldn't tell his son, is that Guardian was technically right in that the nanite-bodied could at any time roll out improved programming capable of penetrating the Reclamation. They had no way of knowing... unless Charles was alive and could be found.

"How long will martial law last?" Jaan asked with a small frown.

Sahaan shook his head. "I don't know."

"Your father's had a rough time of it, Jaan."

"Sorry."

Lachel continued. "President Aavee is here, too."

Sahaan nodded slowly.

"I am *so* glad that you're all right."

"It's good to see the both of you."

Jaan burst into another question. "What's President Aavee going to do next, Dad?"

"Well, first we've got to clear the nanites out of our territory, then restore the walls, then we'll have to find Charles."

"On the news they said he'd forgotten everything," said Lachel.

"He remembered one thing."

"What was it?" Jaan insisted.

Sahaan shook his head. "He didn't have a chance to tell us. There were reporters all around us at the station, and then we got on the train. That's why we have to find him."

Lachel nodded. "We should let you talk to the President."

Sahaan returned a nod. He looked at Jaan and thought of the time they'd introduced him to the President, Aavee being all smiles and charm and Jaan being scared stiff with nerves.

"Love you both," Sahaan said. Lachel gave his hand one more squeeze, then released and guided Jaan out the door.

Not moments after they had exited, President Aavee and his entourage of three dark-suited agents entered the room. Aavee strode up to Sahaan's bedside while the agents fanned out around the room. Sahaan had experienced this enough times not to be fazed by it.

"Sahaan," President Aavee said, "so glad to see you're safe and on your way to a full recovery."

There was something about the President's demeanor that Sahaan couldn't quite place. He had always, in Sahaan's memory, held himself perfectly at ease despite the severity of any situation. He was doing the same now, but minor details felt... off. The breach of the walls had slipped through even the President's practiced serenity.

"Any news on Bharo?" Sahaan asked. "Last they told me, he was in surgery."

"He's out now, but they don't know any more. It was successful, but they're waiting to see how he responds."

Sahaan nodded. "The doctor told me about martial law and I learned about the nanite breach from my fam-

116

ily."

"Sounds like you've been debriefed already." The president grinned. "I should have just sent your family and saved myself the trip."

Sahaan laughed.

"But, seriously, this is one hell of a situation we're in. I've shut down all transit between the cities except for military trains. I've asked all the mayors and regional councils for a daily report, but after two days I'm still waiting for a response from the local governments of Cynine, Exenine, and Enerine, so who knows what's going on there. And then there's Citrine—"

"They're completely cut off."

"Yes, but the mayor has been in constant contact with us."

"Making sure we're still here?"

The president nodded. "Nothing like a disaster to bring people together. Mayor Samaapt, at the moment, seems more afraid of permanently becoming an island than displeasing his party's leadership. For the moment, he's not toeing their line."

"What's the plan to restore the road?"

"We're going to pull all of Adamantine and Adrine's backup walls out of storage and haul them up to the exclusion zone. Then we'll push the slabs into the zone with military-grade tractors and force the nanites back out the breach. Then we can simply replace the slabs. The Service wanted me to hold off so that they could thoroughly analyze the explosion, but I told the military to proceed with the wall replacement."

"You don't want them programmatically adapting."

"How easily we forget pre-Reclamation history. People crowded into tiny, dirty bunkers. Half of them giving up their higher cognitive skills to supplement the systems that kept the nanites out. If your bunker lost a handful of computer sub-systems or more than a few human computers for any amount of time—" Aavee snapped his fingers. "—the nanites broke in and morphed everyone in your bunker into one of them. They call themselves 'Guardian.' Which party insisted on maintaining the emergency subsystems? Which party focuses our spending on the maintenance of our existing infrastructure? Of our emergency power stations?" The President seemed to look beyond Sahaan for a moment, then his attention snapped back, but he remained silent.

"What about the polls?" Sahaan asked.

The last traces of amiability dropped out of the President's expression. "It would be the height of imprudence to check *polls* during a national emergency of this magnitude."

Sahaan smiled gently. "Of course. But, if you *had* happened to catch the polls on the way here, say in an off moment, when you needed a mental break anyway, what would they—?"

"There is now an eighty-nine percent chance that Gadh will win." President Aavee paused, both exasperation and despair seeping in at the edges of his expression and demeanor. "I swore an oath," he continued, "to protect the Constitution of the Reclamation and all of her citizens. I will continue to do that to the best of my ability for another six days, even if a majority of those citizens prefer the illusion of security to the genuine article."

Sahaan took a deep breath. "My last question, Mr. President. What happened to Charles? The doctor said that he wasn't found in the wreckage."

President Aavee motioned to one of the agents. A female agent near the door stepped forward toward the bed and tapped at a computer tablet, then handed it to Sahaan. He found himself presented with a video playback interface.

"Hit the play button," the president said, and Sahaan did so.

At first, Sahaan wasn't sure what kind of video he was watching. It was filmed without color and extremely grainy. He realized momentarily that the light in the background was the coruscating trainwreck, and that a black-ish bulk nearer to the camera was a derailed car that hadn't caught fire.

"Watch near the right edge," the president added.

Sahaan's eye had indeed caught a vehicle, hard to make out, but visible, careening into view. It stopped at the edge of the wreck, and two individuals emerged from it, entered the wreck, hauled a person out, put him into the car, then re-entered the car and drove off.

"How soon after—?" Sahaan started.

"They arrived one minute and thirty-seven seconds afterward."

"Then they knew." Sahaan bit his lip. "Reclamation citizens caused the explosion."

"The proper classification is terrorist."

Sahaan reeled. He felt sick and almost dizzy. If it had somehow been the nanite-bodied... then... but terrorism? People inside the walls intentionally detonating an explosion that would take out a wall... All so they could get at *Charles*.

The president took the computer tablet from Sahaan,

drawing him out of his thoughts.

"What's our plan?" Sahaan asked.

"They must still be in Citrine somewhere." The president grinned. "And, as I said, Mayor Samaapt has been very receptive to working with us. The only price I have asked of him is the local government's full cooperation in tracking these individuals down."

"And is he complying?"

"So he says. For the time being, we have no way of corroborating his actions." President Aavee let out a short laugh.

A thought struck Sahaan all at once. "And Dr. Anaveshan's team?"

The President's eyes lit up with the same realization. "Yes, they must be stuck there. I'll make sure we find out how they're holding up. Now, get some rest. I need you back to one hundred percent. Thanks for taking care of Charles so well in Citrine. When you're feeling up to it, I'll need a full write up of your time with him. Is there anything I should know now that will help us locate him?"

Sahaan thought that over a moment. "No, I don't think so."

"I'll let you rest, then."

"Thank you, Mr. President," Sahaan said.

The president and his entourage retreated out the door, and Sahaan let himself sink back into his pillow. He'd only been awake for perhaps ten or fifteen minutes, but already he felt exhausted. He decided to close his eyes, just for a nap, but he found himself drifting back to sleep all the same.

Sahaan had read his book dutifully on the train but had

put it down when they'd entered the Portal City limits. The land between Eline and Portal City was covered in fields of grasses and wildflowers and dotted with young trees, all imported from Alterra and transplanted sixty years prior. It was a serene but monotonous landscape and his book easily won out over it. Once inside the city limits, however, all of that changed. Large buildings dotted the landscape and grew ever larger as the train hurtled onward. Sahaan caught a glimpse of skyscrapers before the train dipped underground, and the only view from the window was the emergency lights within the tunnel.

Sahaan turned to his mother. She was staring at the front of the train car, already in cocoon mode. She couldn't wait for this to be over, Sahaan guessed. His father sat next to her, reading something on his tablet computer.

He nudged Sahaan's mother with his elbow and drew the tablet closer to her. "I've gotten us a five-thirty train back, so we can leave at five. We'll tell them Sahaan has school tomorrow."

Sahaan wouldn't mind spending more time in Portal City, but he dared not say so. Besides, he rather liked his grandmother. He wasn't quite sure why his mother didn't like his grandmother. It had something to do with politics, which didn't interest him in the least. He was far more interested in stories. So far, good stories had made him laugh, they'd made him cry, they'd made him want to learn anything and everything about history, they'd inspired him to do better in school, and on and on. Books had given him so much, and his parents supplied him with new ones readily.

And grandma always let him talk about stories to her. She'd even told him one. It was about her own grandfather, a man named Stok Thiksay, who had come to Asura from Alterra when there hadn't been Portal City or Eline or any of the other cities. Only the nanite-bodied and their nanites everywhere. In fact, when Stok had first arrived on Asura, the nanites had nearly transformed him into a nanite-bodied, but he'd been rescued by soldiers from a bunker called A5, and that bunker had stood where the city of Adrine was today. Stok had eventually opened the portal back to Alterra and brought the wall slabs—they were, in fact, an Alterran technology. And slowly, over the course of thirty years, they'd created more walls, at first just defending the remaining bunkers, then connecting them with wallroads, and later pushing the nanites out of the hub completely.

Everyone knew the story of Stok Thiksay, but not many people were direct descendants of him. Grandma had taken the family name of Ekeer when she'd married, but it was her Thiksay lineage that she remained loyal to. "It makes our family special," she'd told him. "We're people, just like everyone else," his father had told him later.

Unlike his mother, his father seemed to get along with his grandmother. He disagreed with her, but they got along just fine.

It was too bad they didn't visit his other grandparents more often, the ones who lived in Cynine. He'd visited them only once. It was a much longer train ride, and more expensive, too, his parents said. His other grandparents lived in a small house at the very edge of the city. At first he thought he'd never seen such a large lawn in front, but then his grandparents had shown him the huge field in back.

"Wow," Sahaan said. "It's beautiful! So much open space!"

"There'd be even more if we could get more walls," his grandfather had said. Indeed. At the edge of his grandfather's property, Sahaan could see the towering gray edifices stretching off into the distance. "There's another thirty kilometers of land between here and ocean, but it's all Deranged territory."

His mother had given her grandfather a look.

He'd responded in kind.

"What kind of tree is this?" Sahaan had asked, and the conversation had turned to the different flora that they'd received from Alterra.

The trains began to brake, and the tunnel opened up into the expanse of railway platforms that composed Portal City Station. Four major lines, each with enormous signs above them indicating which cities they ran to— Dazine, Adrine, Enerine, and above him, then over his head, the enormous letters spelling out Eline.

One day in Portal City, and he had to spend the whole time at his grandmother's retirement party. Sahaan wished, for just a moment, that they could see more, that his mother could get over whatever bugged her so much about her mother-in-law, that they'd all get along and decide to take a trip to the Museum of Natural History or the Portal City Central Library. But no. Train in, retirement party, train out.

He released a small sigh as the train came to a halt, and his father stood up and began pulling their day bags from the overhead luggage rack. His mother remained seated for many moments before standing and silently taking up her things.

Sahaan did the same.

"Dr. Ekeer."

Sahaan awoke to discover a nurse at his bedside.

The nurse continued. "The doctor says you're ready for some food." He rolled a tray into position so that it was suspended over Sahaan's abdomen. Looking over it, Lachel sat in the corner, smiling. Jaan sat next to her, his face glued to his handheld.

"Thank you," Sahaan said to the nurse, who proceeded to read some of the monitors at Sahaan's bedside, then left the room.

The meal that lay before him was a simple plate of crackers, cheese, and a cup of purple liquid, probably juice. He wasn't hungry in the least, but he forced himself to have some of the crackers and cheese. His side still hurt and a headache pulsed behind his forehead.

"How are you feeling?" Lachel asked.

"Good," Sahaan lied. For all his political acumen, he was terrible at lying to Lachel.

"Not worse, I hope." She stood and walked to his side.

"No." At least he could answer that one honestly.

"How long was I asleep?"

"About six hours. It's after eight in the evening."

The curtains were drawn over the room's window, but no light leaked in at the edges now.

"Mom," Jaan called out. "It's starting!"

"What's starting?" Sahaan asked.

"The president is giving a speech," she said.

Sahaan grimaced. With both himself and Bharo out of commission, it would have been up to a junior aide to draft it. Sahaan's headache intensified. For the president to need to give a speech without his Senior Consul...

"What happened?" Sahaan asked.

"Gadh gave a speech a few hours ago." Lachel pursed her lips.

"And?"

Lachel released a sigh. "He said that the explosion constitutes an act of war, and he announced his intention, upon becoming president, to expand all the walls by a kilometer every year for all four years of his term. He said he's changing the mandate of the Guardian Party. Their goal is now to push the walls out until the Reclamation covers the entire planet."

Sahaan's jaw hung slack. He blinked a few times. "You're joking."

Lachel shook her head. The expression on her face broke his heart.

"That's insane."

"Adults are weird," Jaan announced. "Do you want to see President Aavee's speech, Dad? I can put it on the TV."

"Yes, Jaan. Please do that."

Jaan took up the remote and activated the holocaster on the far wall. The president, now apparently back in Portal City, sat in his office in the Hilltop Suite. They entered the speech mid-sentence. "—have now cleared nanites out of one-third of the area of their incursion. We believe we can have the rest cleared out by midday tomorrow. After that, it is only a matter of time before we can lift the exclusion zone and restore train service to Citrine.

"So far, we have held back details about the explosion that derailed the train carrying the nanite-bodied visitor,

Charles. Many assumed that the nanite-bodied created the explosion either to gain entrance to the Reclamation or to recover their citizen, or even both. According to an alternative theory, it was Charles himself who caused the explosion. However, now that we have had time to thoroughly investigate all of the evidence, it is confirmed that none of those scenarios are true, and it is my unfortunate duty to report to you the truth.

"The explosion was an act of terrorism, committed by citizens of the Reclamation. Their goal appears to have been to capture the nanite-bodied visitor. Creating the first-ever sustained, permeable breach of our walls was, to their minds, a price worth paying in order to achieve their objective. We will find them, we will bring them before the law, and we will teach them that it certainly was not.

"This government, a Reconciliation government, for as long as it remains, will track down the individuals who have killed Reclamation citizens, destroyed our defensive fortifications, and kidnapped a guest to our country. And yes, until proven differently, we must assume that Charles is a guest, and we will treat him with humanitarian dignity.

"One hundred and twenty-one years ago, Stok Thiksay delivered us wall technology from Alterra, and that has allowed us to rebuild our cities and re-establish our way of life. However, this technology has natural limits. If we push beyond those limits, it will eventually fail. Who or what will guard us then?

"The terrorists who committed this act of sabotage—"

President Aavee's voice diminished to mute, and at the same time, his holographic image faded away to empty space.

"What happened?" Lachel asked.

Jaan pulled up his handheld. "It's stopped streaming, too..."

The holocaster jolted to life again, now showing a news anchor.

Sahaan and his family exchanged confused looks. They were interrupting the president for a newscast?

"We interrupt... We're interrupting to bring you this late-breaking news. Eight minutes ago, alarms were triggered along the wall system bordering the Eline-Besserine train line just two kilometers outside of Eline. Camera systems have confirmed that another wallslab has been converted into a person. The process appears identical to the one that affected the wall slab in Citrine during Senior Consul Sahaan Ekeer's political rally. Authorities are en route to the site— One moment."

The news anchor put her hand over her ear.

"This visitor is female," the news anchor said. "She says her name is Samantha."

Sahaan's grandmother didn't have any time to talk to him or his family before the event. They arrived at the venue just before eleven, which Sahaan thought was pretty early (and it seemed his parents had thought so, too), but even as they arrived, his grandmother had already been cornered by a crowd of news reporters, and Sahaan recognized other people from holocasts surrounding her as well. He wasn't sure what all their functions were, but he knew they were part of the government.

At school, he'd noticed that some kids told him they thought his grandmother was awesome (even though they'd never met her), while others called her names. None of the other schoolkids seemed to have a neutral opinion on her. It was the same with the news, which his parents encouraged him to ignore. He was supposed to ignore his classmates, too, especially the ones that seemed to hate her.

So far, he'd managed to never get into a fight over this, mostly owing to the fact that he found it easy to calm other kids down. He just kept asking them questions, trying to understand how they felt. It came naturally to him.

His family took their designated seats at one of the many round tables dotting an enormous ballroom, and they proceeded to wait in silence. Sahaan looked around the room, but couldn't find any other kids his age in attendance. All the adults were busy hurrying around.

Eventually, his grandmother came running over to them. She wore a long, blue dress, and had her hair rolled up into a bun, a style he'd seen her wear before only on the holocasts.

"Bahaar, Saana, and Sahaan! How you've grown! So wonderful to see you!" She gave Sahaan's father a hug, then a strained hug to his mother, and finally she knelt down to meet Sahaan eye to eye. "You still reading stories?"

Sahaan nodded. "I can't wait to visit the Central Library again."

"You come up to Portal City again soon and we'll make a day of it. If your parents approve, of course."

Sahaan's father smiled and nodded. His mother remained stoic, although normally, she also approved of his passion for reading.

Sahaan's grandmother stood. "Sorry about earlier. I

saw you, but I just couldn't get away from them."

"We know the drill," Sahaan's father said.

"Well, I am glad you're here. All of you." His grandmother seemed to be directing that last statement at Sahaan's mother directly.

"Thank you for having us." His mother spoke lightly, just loud enough to be heard over the crowd.

"MP Ekeer?" A man appeared at their side. "The MPs from Besserine have just arrived and are asking to meet you."

Sahaan's grandmother smiled and nodded, then looked at Sahaan and his family. "Duty calls. We'll catch up after the reception, I hope."

"We have a five-thirty train," Sahaan's father said. "Sahaan has school tomorrow. We were hoping maybe after the main event we could chat for a bit?"

Sahaan's grandmother nodded. "Of course! I'll make sure to tell Sahayaak. He'll make sure to arrange it. At four-thirty, then, after the main event?"

"Sounds good." She looked at Sahaan. "I'm looking forward to hearing about all the books you've been reading." Then she turned to his mother. "And Saana, I'm so very glad you were able to make it. It's wonderful to see you here. Thank you."

"Don't mention it." His mother seemed to be in shock, her words barely audible.

And with that his grandmother disappeared into the crowd, following the man who had appeared, apparently toward the Besserine MPs. Sahaan sat down and smiled, thinking of the trip he would get to take in the near future to the Portal City Central Library.

—

Sahaan and his family sat, watching the holocast in rapt silence. Samantha was given clothes, escorted into a heavily armored van, similar to the one Sahaan had ridden in with Charles, and from there, the journalists were cordoned off and Samantha was spirited away.

Her route would probably be circuitous and very few would know about it, Sahaan guessed. It's what he would do. Her destination would, of course, be the secure area they had set up in Portal City for Charles.

Ah well, Sahaan thought. It was someone else's turn now. For the time being, he was merely to lie here and recover. He also imagined, momentarily, the mood in the Hilltop Suite when they'd had to tell the president that the broadcasting agencies had cut him off. He was glad he'd avoided that one.

Once Samantha had departed on her undisclosed journey, the news reverted to Guardian's reaction to the president's speech. They oscillated between insistence that the walls be expanded regardless of the cause of the explosion and insinuations that the president's terrorism analysis was mistaken or an outright lie.

Somewhere during a Guardian commentator's rant, Sahaan glanced at his family and noticed that Jaan had fallen asleep against Lachel's side.

"The president arranged for secure lodgings for you, I hope," Sahaan said quietly.

"Yes, the hotel is right next to the hospital. It will have military guards."

Sahaan nodded toward Jaan. "You should take him to get some proper sleep. I'm not in any danger." The pain in his side had, in fact, diminished, and the headache had turned out to be transitory.

Lachel roused Jaan and walked him over to Sahaan.

"Night, Dad," Jaan said in slurred speech.

"Night, Son."

Lachel kissed Sahaan on the forehead, smiled, and took Jaan toward the door.

"You're the best, you know that?"

Lachel smiled back. "Love you."

"Love you, too."

Sahaan took a deep breath and returned to watching holocasts, absorbing all the political opinions and watching the progress of the crews pushing the nanites out of the Adamantine-Citrine wallroad. They were now over halfway complete, and scans of the wallroad area were reporting the newly reclaimed area to be nanite-free. It was about the only good news available. Reconciliation and Guardian voices were louder and more extreme than ever. Sahaan couldn't help but think back to his grandmother's last and most famous speech, the one he himself had witnessed as a child, the one that had put a chink in the armor of both sides of the political divide, a moment that had made it seem that the Reclamation might be politically capable of reclaiming itself.

So much for that.

And here he was, a lone voice in the wilderness, and stuck in a hospital bed no less.

He watched the news until his eyelids drooped, at which point he turned off the holocaster and let himself drift off to sleep.

He awoke later not to a nurse, but to someone new, a young man he had perhaps seen around the Capitol Offices but whose name he had never learned.

"Sorry to wake you, Dr. Ekeer."

"It's alright, Mr...."

"Vitar, sir."

"Mr. Vitar. I've seen you around the Capitol Offices, correct?"

"I'm an associate secretary for Dr. Anaveshan, sir."

Sahaan smiled. "How is Dr. Anaveshan?"

"As well as can be expected. He managed to avoid the worst of the rioting in Citrine, but one of the scientists in his unit is in the Citrine Hospital."

"I'm sorry to hear that. I didn't realize he'd gone out to Citrine himself."

"He was on the last train that made it through, sir. In fact, he's on the phone right now, and he can tell you more about it."

"Please." Sahaan motioned for Mr. Vitar's handheld, which he promptly handed over.

"Dr. Ekeer?" Dr. Anaveshan's voice sounded strained and the audio quality was somewhat grainy.

"Yes, this is him."

"Phenomenal discovery, Dr. Ekeer. Truly phenomenal. This is an encrypted line, by the way. I knew last night, but I had to make sure we could talk privately, you see. There's no telling how much worse it could make things if this gets out the wrong way."

"Have you figured out how they do it, then? How they turn the wall slabs into people?"

"I think so. We'll need to get back to Portal City and run more experiments to be sure, but we're more or less certain now. As you know, because a matter transmutation has clearly taken place, the mind jumps to nanotechnology, as that is the obvious way that we transmute matter at the molecular level. But it makes no sense for that to be the mechanism in this case because the walls repel nanites. Always have, always will.

"So, we went looking for a way to transmute matter that didn't involve nanite manipulation. At least not direct manipulation. Have you perhaps read about a set of experiments performed one hundred years ago on Alterra, just before the Reclamation was founded? About the walls and high-energy radiation?"

"I'm afraid that's not my field, doctor."

"They were testing to see if the walls could be attacked through means other than nanites. They discovered that gamma and other high-energy radiations interacted with the walls' quantum field, ultimately changing the elemental composition of the atoms they struck. The iron in the walls shifted to manganese or cobalt. They could also 'push' the elements into compounds and new configurations by varying the angle of the radiation emitter. Despite all this, as long as a wall slab remained metallic, it kept the metaxic field property that keeps nanites and other microscopic paraphernalia out. It was calculated that the amount of energy required either to reduce a single wall slab's iron down to argon or to compact it enough to form a gap would require the energy output of a medium-sized fusion reactor. In other words, breaking down every single wall slab in the Reclamation would require energy beyond even the nanite-bodied's generation capabilities."

"But they've done something different with the same principle, right?"

"Yes. We think they've bombarded our wall slabs with enough high energy radiation to reduce its atoms down into a configuration of carbon, oxygen, and various other elements—into that of a person. And there's something else. I recall you telling me that Charles believes he's a nanite-bodied person, correct?"

"That's correct. Should he not?"

"It's almost certain that the process that created his mind is a copy process, not a transfer process. The nanite-bodied *are* made of nanites, but unless they've discovered something about consciousness that we don't know yet, then the person that served as the template for Charles's mind is still living his own life somewhere beyond our walls.

"What I am willing to admit is the possibility that the idea is for Charles and Samantha to go back out into nanite-bodied territory at some point and be transformed into nanite-bodied organisms. They would then, theoretically, be able to share the experiences of their time in the Reclamation in a way that is much deeper than any form of communication we understand. We know that they've supplemented verbal speech with digital transfer as far back as the war."

"Did they really expend a medium-sized fusion reactor's worth of power for each of these events?"

"If we're right, then Charles and Samantha each took about ninety quadrillion kilowatt-hours."

"Yikes. Should I be getting myself tested for radiation exposure?"

"In the experiments, the radiation had to be very focused, and the metaxic field acted as a sink. The wall slabs absorbed all of it. A test couldn't hurt, but I suspect you're fine."

"Good to hear. Thank you for contacting me directly, doctor. You're right that we need to be careful about how we roll this information out, especially now."

"No problem. Is there anything else I should look into while I'm in Citrine?"

"Not that I can think of. I hope the scientist on your team is on the mend."

"That has yet to be seen. He took a club to the back of his neck. They tell me there's a chance he'll be paralyzed."

"I'm very sorry to hear that."

"We've entered dangerous times. Take care of yourself."

"Will do. Thank you, doctor."

Dr. Anaveshan hung up. Sahaan passed the handheld back to Mr. Vitar, who had stood waiting patiently throughout the entire conversation. He took his leave and left Sahaan alone in bed to think.

The nanite-bodied could have destroyed a wallslab or turned it into anything, really. And yet they had chosen to make it into a human being. And Charles was a copy. Presumably this Samantha, too. Sahaan was looking forward to meeting her.

However, the matter of gaining the information to calm everyone down couldn't wait the days it would take Samantha to remember anything useful to them. What he needed now was news of the search for Charles. His memories of nanite-bodied society were the one thing that had the potential to diffuse this entire situation. If they could just get him back.

But how?

Once his grandmother had departed, Sahaan returned to sitting together with his family in silence. Eventually, more adults joined the table, and his father struck up a conversation with the man sitting next to him. An older woman eventually arrived next to his mother, and even she began speaking as well, leaving Sahaan between the two of them to sit and wait.

His parents had warned him that it might be like this.

"It's going to be a big event. There might even be media there. Your grandmother is famous, you know. If there's not a lot to do, please just sit quietly. We'll make it up to you next weekend. We promise."

Next weekend had better be that trip to the Central Library.

Sahaan sat and let his mind wander off to the book he'd been reading. He'd had to stop at one of the most annoying places to leave a book—three chapters from the end. If he'd had his backpack, he might have even tried to get his book out, but it had been stashed somewhere by the concierge under his father's name.

He sighed, thought of his book, and continued to wait.

Perhaps an hour or so later, a glass was rung a few tables away. The woman holding the glass introduced herself as the Parliament Majority Leader and asked for silence. She made her way up to a stage at the back of the room, where she took up a microphone, thanked everyone for coming, then began talking about Sahaan's grandmother and all the wonderful things she'd done as a Member of Parliament. It was largely all stuff Sahaan had heard before from other adults—founded the Reconciliation party, then after a disastrous election twenty years ago, which resulted in eight years of a Guardian government, his grandmother had taken over leadership of Reconciliation in parliament, which had been the majority party ever since.

'Reconciliation' and 'Guardian' were just words to Sahaan. He didn't know what they meant and wasn't sure he cared all that much what their difference was. The fact was, they didn't seem all that different to him. Everyone wanted to keep themselves safe from the nanite-bodied, right? What was all the fuss about?

With a sigh, he joined in the applause when the speaker finished. A man took her spot on the stage and began another speech. This one was about specific things she'd done in parliament to bolster support for the Reconciliation party.

Bored as he was, Sahaan managed to catch the applause for this one just in time, too. He yawned and rubbed his eyes, wondering if he'd even recognize the third speaker or not. When he looked up at the stage, he discovered his grandmother had arrived there.

"Thank you, all of you, for coming," she said. "It is a great honor to see all of you here today. My career has been... let's call it eventful." A small laugh went up from the crowd. "At times, I'll admit that, in my heart of hearts, I was not entirely sure we would pull through. But here we are. Twelve years of Reconciliation government and the next election appears as promising as the last.

"This election cycle, I will not be joining you in campaigning. I leave Zenith House in your hands. I leave the party in your hands, to carry us into the future.

"Now, at the end of my career, I finally have a moment to look back, to reflect, to take stock of all that I have seen. Even some things that I have not seen. Recently, I had the opportunity to go much further back. My grandson, as it turns out, is enamored of stories." She winked at him, and Sahaan jolted, eyes wide and back braced against his chair.

"Taking a lesson from the wisdom of the young, I myself have gone back to the oldest stories about politics. One of our ancient philosophers remarked that, humans being social creatures, that there were many forms of human association—family, friends, business associates—but, he added, no association was more important nor even more noble than the associations created for the purpose of maintaining safety and prosperity within the city, the form of a social organization which was, at his time, the most complex one in existence. His word for city, *polis*, could be made into an adjective, *politike*, which he used to describe the social behavior most befitting a citizen.

"Humbling words. I wonder how many citizens today would agree with the great philosopher that politics is the noblest human association." Another small round of laughter. "No human being is perfect. This imperfection, ironically, is what we struggled so hard to preserve during the Long War. Our ancestors chose, in the face of relentless military opposition, to preserve the shreds of humanity they held onto.

"Looking at my own life, I see all the things MPs Agrim and Karana have mentioned, but I see the missteps, too. The things which, given a rewind and a playback, I would perhaps do differently.

"As I am sure many of you know, my brother Param passed away a little more than a year ago. He spent a year being treated for the cancer which he ultimately succumbed to. During that time, and in the months prior, our relationship changed. I realize that, though I couldn't pinpoint exactly when or how it happened, I had let my thinking about his and my relationship change. In one stage of my life, he had been my beloved brother, with whom I maintained an ideological disagreement. Somehow, by the time I entered parliament, he had become the enemy, the one who would bring ruin down upon us if his ideology triumphed over mine.

"His illness did not allow me to maintain that illusion, and I had done far too much damage to our relationship in the intervening years to fully heal those wounds. Were I given a 'do-over,' so to speak, I would worry much less about proving myself right and much more about how *politike* I was behaving toward my own flesh and blood.

"Reconciliation, in the sense of contacting the nanite-bodied and establishing their intentions, is, I maintain, the best way to achieve security for the Reclamation. In this position, I have not the slightest doubt. However, a number of citizens, including my late brother, do not agree with us on this. We must strive to do what we believe is right and best, but we must not forget that *politike* demands cooperation, integration of good ideas, compassion, and mutual trust.

"The Guardian party is not our enemy, at least not today. But I fear the direction in which current political rhetoric is taking us. If we let ourselves forget, on both sides, that our grandparents fought tooth and nail to secure our freedom and our prosperity, that we essentially want the same thing, if we eventually forget that we all, deep down, desire a secure and prosperous nation, then we may end up fighting a war with one another, and nothing I can imagine would weaken national security more than that.

"I leave parliament to you, the up-and-coming leaders of the Reconciliation Party. Going forward, do remember that you will be defined just as much by the bridges you burn as the ones you build. Thank you."

Sahaan still sat stunned. He clapped, but his mind reeled. And, momentarily coming out of his catatonia, he realized that the applause had been somewhat half-hearted. He looked around the room. Some severe expressions, some frowns. Not everyone though. Had that speech... not gone over well?

Sahaan had liked it very much.

After Mr. Vitar left, Sahaan checked the time and discovered it to be seven in the morning the next day. He didn't feel the slightest bit tired, and, thankfully, his side seemed to be even better. He tested himself by shifting his weight a bit in bed, and a sharp pain shot up his spine. He instantly relaxed back into the mattress. He wouldn't be going anywhere anytime soon.

He decided to catch up on the news until his family returned.

In summary, securing the Adamantine-Citrine wall-road area was proceeding as planned. A full two-thirds of the exclusion zone had been reclaimed. Details of the plans to restore train service to Citrine were being finalized by President Aavee's government. Gadh was painting the whole affair as a massive political failing of Reconciliation government. He had begun claiming that during a Guardian government, no wall slabs would have been blown up or transmuted. He had additionally begun referring to Charles and Samantha as "invaders," a term which other Guardian pundits had immediately picked up.

Martial law and the curfew remained in effect. Rioting had been quelled in the spoke cities where it had initially flared up in the wake of the train explosion, but it seemed a tense and fraught lull. Everyone seemed to have a sense that another incident could spark further civil disturbances. For the time being, at least, the military seemed to be keeping order.

A nurse arrived with breakfast, and his family appeared shortly after he'd finished eating. Lachel and Jaan both asked how he was feeling, to which he responded that he seemed to be improving. All three of them proceeded to watch the news together.

At about noon, the news erupted into a flurry of announcements that Samantha had arrived safely at the secure facility in Portal City, which had been set up for Charles. Discussion with her had thus far yielded nothing that Sahaan had not already learned from Charles. She seemed to suffer the same affliction as he did—while not reticent to be questioned, any minor recollection of nanite-bodied society induced extreme fatigue and at times frustration.

Sahaan resisted the urge to get on his handheld and see if he could find out more about how the investigation was going. It was possible they'd uncovered something from her that Charles had been unable to remember, but which they weren't willing to share on the news.

The nurse who brought Sahaan's lunch also had a bit of news. "I thought you'd be interested to know that Dr. Meharab is awake now. I think the doctor might be asking you to get out of bed and walk around tomorrow or the day after. If that's the case, you'll be able to go see him, if you'd like."

"I'd like that very much," Sahaan replied, glad for more good news.

And the good news just kept coming. He and his family cheered when the news showed the final wall slab of the Adamantine-Citrine wall being moved into place. Within an hour, it was reported that additional sweeps of the wallroad for nanite activity had turned up negative, and repair crews were en route to restore the damaged train tracks.

Still no news on *who* had caused the explosion.

Just as Sahaan was mulling that over, Mr. Vitar appeared at the door.

"Vice President Dokha to see you, sir."

Jaan's eyes lit up. "You think I can ask him about the Quantums?" The vice president had a reputation as a sports aficionado. At the last summer family luncheon, Jaan, the vice president, and his two sons had spent perhaps an hour talking about professional voidball.

"Maybe next time," Sahaan said.

Lachel gave her usual smile. "Come on, Jaan. Let's take a walk to the hotel."

Jaan begrudgingly followed his mother out the door past Mr. Vitar. Vitar himself promptly disappeared, and the vice president entered the room.

"Good to see you, Sahaan." He approached the bed and sat. His movements were tense, betraying that despite the good vibes projecting out of the news stations, all was not well. The vice president was a tall man with dark hair and handsome features. He dressed well on most occasions, but today he wore only a plain white collared shirt and slacks that had seen better days. He'd come here in a rush.

"Good to see you, too, Mr. Vice President. How is everything?"

"As you've probably seen from the news, we've restored the wallroad to Citrine, and Samantha is safely in the containment facility in Portal City, but we've got two major problems. The mayor of Citrine spoke a big game in working with us to apprehend the terrorists, but he has done little or nothing to actually help. Short of ordering the military already there to start ransacking private property, we're at a loss as to next steps. Additionally, our undercover agents in other spoke cities have identified at least three other potential terrorists groups, ones which simply haven't had the opportunity to strike yet. This problem has morphed from a single missing visitor to a full-on threat to national security."

Sahaan shook his head. "As I told the president, I can't think of anything about Charles that would help us find him now. As far as we could tell, he was human. He fell asleep a lot. That will be a liability for whoever has him now." He shuddered to think about that. He hoped that Charles was not being physically mistreated.

"I need your help with another matter."

"Yes?"

"Tomorrow I'll be going in to talk to Samantha."

"Have we learned anything from her that's not on the news?"

"I'm afraid not. Anytime her interrogators take the conversation in that direction, she'll reply with something vague, or just stare at them blankly, then yawn, then ask to lie down. They've lost hours of potential discussion time that way."

"That sounds like Charles. No. It sounds worse than

Charles. Charles seemed to be trying to remember things. And details would surface on occasion."

"Do you believe the sleepiness is genuine?"

"With Charles, yes."

"Any advice on how I should proceed?"

"Get her talking about the generalities that she can remember. With Charles, the more he talked about generalities the more he strayed into details. At the end, he seemed to remember an important detail, even."

"Oh? The president didn't mention that."

"It was right before we got on the train. There were media people there, so I asked him to wait until we got to Portal City. I still don't know what it was. But he did say, right before we got on the train, that Guardian and Reconciliation were waiting to realize that we both wanted the same thing. 'Different, but actually the same,' he said."

"What do you suppose he meant by that?"

"I'm not sure." Sahaan shrugged. "I've been rolling it over in my mind these last two days, and I still don't know. We got that far because I shared our high-level political organization with him. He found the whole history of the two parties interesting. You might take Samantha down a similar line and see if you can get her to the same realization."

"Sounds like a good place to start."

"You could see if she likes voidball." Sahaan winked.

The vice president smiled. "Somehow I doubt it, though I suppose it's worth a shot at this point." The vice president stood. "Thank you, Sahaan."

"Mr. Vice President."

With that, the vice president turned and left.

His gait was too tense. The feelings of normalcy coming out of the media seemed now a ruse, a false signal. At least three other terrorist groups, who might at any time decide to blow up a chunk of wall, and an election in less than three days which appeared would go to Gadh.

Unhappy thoughts, these.

His family appeared in the doorway, however, and at least in that moment, Sahaan was again able to smile.

The speaker who followed his grandmother wore the oddest expression on his face as he approached the podium, and when he began speaking he made these strange little interruptions. It was as though he now had reservations about the kind words he was saying about Sahaan's grandmother. There was so much about adults that Sahaan still didn't understand, but he did guess that his grandmother's speech had made a number of her friends angry with her.

Sahaan found himself perplexed. He thought on all the things he'd observed, all the incongruous details, and then, without notice, the pieces flashed together in his mind. His mother's family, he now realized, espoused Guardian ideas, and his father's family, clearly, was Reconciliation. But neither of his parents were much interested in politics. In fact, they seemed to go out of their way to not talk about politics. They'd removed themselves from it, escaped it as best they could.

The last speaker ended his speech, and an army of waiters and waitresses began delivering plates of food. Everyone ate, and the mood returned to more or less amenable. His father talked to the man next to him, and his mother to the woman next to her, but there was still something in the atmosphere. Sahaan sensed it. Something was wrong.

More remembered details came together in his mind, coalescing with his recent epiphany. A time on the playground when he'd prevented two other boys from getting into a fight, a time when he'd noticed something another student had said had made his teacher angry, and he'd talked to his classmate later and told her she should avoid saying things like that. Sahaan had assumed this was all perfectly normal, but none of the other students did this.

It was as though he was sensitive to... something.

Before Sahaan knew it, the clock at the far side of the auditorium showed four twenty-five, and Sahaan's parents were excusing themselves. He followed them dutifully. They weaved around the circular tables, toward the stage, but then turned out a door beside it rather than ascending onto it.

They entered a backstage hallway, which led them around to a room behind. A man's voice became audible as they approached, very loud and irate.

"Vibha, this is insanity! Do you realize what you've done to the party?"

Then his grandmother's voice. "Not you, too, Niraash."

A woman's voice. "He's right. This is a complete disaster. And it will take us at least two election cycles to clean up the damage. If not more."

"What does that mean?" his grandmother insisted.

His grandmother and her two interlocutors came into view now. They stood in a backstage conference room with a large table and numerous pieces of paper taped to the wall, most of them filled with text.

"It means," the man named Niraash took a step forward, "that we will now have a lot of work to do to convince our base that the party's founding member isn't in fact a Guardian in disguise."

"That is *not* what I said."

"That is what everyone in the audience heard," the woman said. "They heard Vibha Ekeer tell the entire party that we are to reach out and embrace the backward, idiotic ravings of redneck yokels."

Sahaan noticed his mother stiffen her back and purse her lips. His father clenched his fists and his eyes widened.

His grandmother met Sahaan's eyes, and her entire countenance dropped. She tensed, then her eye twitched, and annoyance became anger. A lifetime of political training could not possibly have taught her how she could contain the situation presented to her now, an older Sahaan would come to realize.

She did, however, the best she could under the circumstance. Looking directly at the woman, she said. "You are a disgrace to the Reconciliation party. That is my family at the door."

His mother took a step forward. "And I suppose that makes me the backward, redneck yokel." At the time, Sahaan had been frightened at the escalating rhetoric, but he would look back on this moment as one of the bravest things he had ever seen his mother do, and he would never be more proud of her than in that moment.

The woman deflated, and the man called Niraash frowned.

"Let's go," Niraash said.

The woman followed him silently away. His mother and father glared at them the entire way as they left.

His grandmother came over to them, hugged Sahaan's

father, and said, "I'm so sorry, son. You shouldn't have seen that. I didn't realize how badly I'd misled the party. I didn't think it would be like this."

"You did the right thing tonight, mom," his father said. "I'm proud of you."

She smiled, and Sahaan thought he caught a tear. "My darling boy."

Her grandmother released him and turned to Sahaan's mother. "Saana, how can I ever—?"

"Thank you," his mother said. And, much to Sahaan's amazement, she embraced his grandmother in a hug. Even Sahaan's father seemed shocked.

"What happens now?" Sahaan's father asked.

His grandmother took a deep breath in and out. She shrugged. "The party goes on. Wherever it will."

"I really liked your speech," Sahaan said. "Especially the part about the philosopher. Did you really read him because of me?"

"Absolutely."

"Can you show me the book?"

"Sure," she said tentatively. "It's a hard one, though."

"I want to try."

Both his parents were now wearing smiles.

They sat and talked for a bit. His mother and grandmother seemed to be having a frank and honest chat for the first time in Sahaan's life. It seemed like a small miracle to watch them interacting. He realized, then, that there had been a tension between the two of them that had only been at the very edge of his perceptions. Not caring about grandma's party, he'd noted her behavior as a curiosity. But now...

At five, they hugged, said goodbye, and left. They

picked up their things from the concierge, hailed a cab, went to the train station, and waited to board. It had begun to rain, and Sahaan could make out the droplets splattering the domed glass roof of the train station far above his head.

He thought about his books, about the books his grandmother had read, about Guardian and Reconciliation, and then he turned to his father.

"Dad?"

"Yes, son?"

"Can telling people stories help them see things in different ways?"

"I don't see why not."

"So, if I come up with a story, and if I tell it just right, I can help people understand each other better, and maybe yell at one another less?"

"Seems... possible. Difficult, probably. But possible."

Sahaan had decided, just then, at the age of twelve, exactly what he wanted to do with his life.

Evening rolled around, and Sahaan found himself drifting off to sleep against his will, despite the fact that the upcoming election had taken over the news cycle. With nothing noteworthy (or at any rate reportable) about the progress in finding Charles, and with Samantha safely ensconced in one of the securest facilities in the Reclamation, policy debate between Una and Gadh had come to the fore.

The polls now showed Una catching back up to Gadh, since Reconciliation's handling of the aftermath of the explosion was largely considered impeccable. Additional political points had been scored for getting Samantha safely to the capital.

He awoke at seven the next morning, now only two days away from the election. He found Lachel at his side, Jaan slouched into her. He smiled, seeing the two of them here.

He decided not to wake them and instead used his handheld until the nurse arrived with breakfast. He tried shifting his weight again, too, which today didn't result in nearly as much pain.

Doctor Aarogy returned just before noon and indeed wanted for him to try taking a walk. After dressing in an additional layer of gown, a walker was pulled up to the bedside, and Sahaan slowly sat up, pulled himself out of bed, and managed to move across the room at a decent pace.

"Great job." Dr. Aarogy smiled. "This is excellent progress."

"I haven't made it to Bharo's room, yet." Sahaan laughed. "Is he expecting me?"

"He is."

Lachel, Jaan, and the doctor followed at his side all the way out the door and down the hall. Dr. Aarogy indicated a right as the hallway ended splitting into two perpendicular corridors. Feeling winded and exhausted, Sahaan wanted to ask how much further, but decided not to, for Lachel and Jaan's sake.

"Here." The doctor indicated an open door not much further after the turn.

Sahaan hobbled in.

"Sahaan?" Bharo's voice rasped a bit, but sounded firm.

"It's me, Bharo." He fell into a seat at his friend's bedside, while his family took up positions on the other side of the bed.

"Hey, kiddo." Bharo smiled at Jaan. "Hi, Lachel."

"Hello, Dr. Meharab," Jaan replied.

"Hi, Bharo." Lachel smiled.

"How are you feeling?" Sahaan asked.

"Like I was hit by a train."

Sahaan chortled. "And you wonder why they give me the speech writing jobs."

"You all caught up on the news?"

"Yep. I take it they told you about Charles, and about this new one, Samantha."

Bharo nodded. "The vice president was here. He filled me in." He turned momentarily to Jaan. "You've been following the Quantums?"

"Well, their last game was canceled. But when they start up the season again..."

Bharo nodded.

"Lachel," Bharo said. "Is it all right if Sahaan and I talk privately for a bit?"

Lachel nodded and guided Jaan out of the room.

"Feel better, Dr. Meharab!" Jaan said.

Bharo turned to Dr. Aarogy. "Doctor?"

She nodded toward Bharo's bedside console. "Hit the button if you need me."

"Thank you."

Once the doctor had shut the door, Bharo shook his head. "I don't like this, Sahaan."

"The election? The reports of the terrorists?"

"I don't like those either. I was talking about Samantha."

"I had the same thought when talking to the vice

president. We got much more out of Charles in much less time."

"Exactly. After twenty-four hours with Charles, we'd established a few things, found some directions to take the conversation further. It sounds like Samantha is different. They're not learning *anything*. That's why the vice president is taking over himself."

"She might just need more time."

"Maybe. But also, why send two?"

"Charles did guess that there could be others."

"Sure. But I imagine someone over there is signing off on these procedures now, even if Charles managed to slip through because he was the first one. You got the same call I did from Dr. Anaveshan, right? About how these have to be sinking an enormous amount of energy into these events?"

Sahaan nodded.

"Why do this twice? Why another visitor while Charles is still here?"

"Maybe they can tell he got kidnapped?"

Bharo's eyes went wide. "Let's only hope they can't tell *that*."

Sahaan took a deep breath. "Are you suggesting we do something differently?"

Bharo shook his head. "No. It just... it just doesn't feel right!"

Sahaan had learned to trust Bharo's intuition.

"You're worried about Charles," Bharo said.

"Yeah," Sahaan admitted. "It's odd. I feel like I should be worried about the election, or even about Samantha, but I can't stop thinking of how I could possibly help find Charles. It seems now like the only thing I ever really did for him was tear that damned doctor off him—" Within a matter of moments, Sahaan's mind had moved from the incident with Dr. Paape to the nanite injection she had given him to the fact of a specific Reclamation legal mandate.

"My god... Bharo, remember Dr. Paape? She gave him a nanite injection."

Bharo's eyes lit up. "Those nanites are almost certainly traceable!"

Sahaan tried to stand, took it too quickly, and felt a jolt of pain shoot up his spine. He howled and fell back into his seat, which caused another, duller version of the pain.

Bharo slammed the button on his console, and a nurse came immediately in.

"Yes?" he said.

"Please get Mr. Vitar. It's urgent."

The nurse nodded and ran off.

Sahaan sat with his eyes closed, willing the pain to diminish, but it wasn't cooperating with him. So instead he stayed as still as possible. He heard the sounds of Mr. Vitar arriving and Bharo asking for a secure handheld connection to the Hilltop Suite. Vitar responded that he was on it, and it was then that Sahaan heard a throat clearing from beside him.

Sahaan opened his eyes and found Dr. Aarogy standing over him with crossed arms. "Dr. Ekeer?"

"Yes?"

"Did you try to stand up the way you normally do?"

"Yes."

"Please don't do that again. Not for a while, anyway."

"Yes, doctor."

"Thank you."

"I got this," Bharo said, just as Vitar returned with a phone.

"Thank you," Sahaan grunted as he pulled himself carefully up into his walker. The long way back to his room didn't seem so intimidating. As he walked out the door, he heard Bharo giving the orders to organize everything: find Paape, get the signature of the nanites she used, get the satellites scanning for them.

"You're in a good mood," Lachel said as she and Jaan joined at his side.

Sahaan nodded. "Bharo helped me remember how to find Charles."

Jaan held up his handheld. "Check it out, dad! Una just took the lead."

Sahaan smiled. At last, it finally seemed that everything was going to turn out all right. There was just one thing niggling at the back of his mind: Bharo had some kind of intuition about Samantha. And the thing about Bharo's intuitions was that there was usually something to them.

When Sahaan had finally managed to get himself back into his hospital bed, he wanted nothing more than to close his eyes and rest.

"Any dizziness?" Dr. Aarogy asked.

Sahaan kept his eyes closed. "No. Just tired."

"That's fine. How about pain?"

"Some. But dull."

"Also good. Sounds like your body needs a break. Try to relax."

"Thank you, doctor," he said. But how could he relax? His mind was going a million miles a minute. He wished he could be tied into the Hilltop Suite, directing the search for Charles, rallying the leaders of the military teams who would go in and pull him out, telling them everything he knew about Charles.

His body ached, and drowsiness kept his eyelids held fast.

He forced his eyes open. "Lachel?"

"Yes?"

"Can you wake me up if there's anything on the news about Charles?"

She smiled and nodded, kissed him, then returned to Jaan, who had found some new tidbit about the election on his handheld. Sahaan let himself drift off to sleep.

It was a deep sleep, and before long he began to dream.

He dreamed of the ocean. Not the ocean near Besserine, but a wide, open, wild ocean. He stood on a beach, and there were no walls in sight anywhere on land, nor aloft buoys on the water. Somehow, he wasn't afraid of nanites.

Gulls circled about a large rock protruding from the water, some ways out into the ocean. He had only seen gulls once before, on Alterra. He'd gone through the portal, taken a train to Delta Province, and seen the great floodplain where the river spilled out into the ocean.

There were no gulls on Asura anymore, and the biologists told them they would need to reclaim much more coastland if they were ever going to be reintroduced.

Sahaan also spotted a crab scuttling across the sand—another creature from his visit to Alterra. And plants—so many plants—many of which he had never seen in such abundance and others he didn't even recognize. There were grasses up further beyond the dunes, seaweed woven into the sand of the beach, driftwood logs.

The sea left foam wherever it receded.

Sahaan walked up to the edge of the water and watched the ocean, listening to the crash of waves and the screeches of the gulls. He heard another screech and turned.

Figures had appeared upon the grassy dunes. There were two of them. They towered over him, five or six meters tall each. Their bodies shimmered gray, and their eyes were fiery orange orbs. Their legs were haunched back like a quadruped's, but they stood upright. Their feet and hands were enormous, shimmering, metallic claws. Orange holograms danced across the surface of their bodies, always changing shape and form, too quickly to see if they were comprised of lettering, shapes, or some other form of symbology.

One of the creatures opened its mouth and shrieked, but it did not move or change its stance. Sahaan decided that it was not a threatening act, although the noise had indeed sounded shrill to his ears.

The creature shrieked again, twice, in the same pattern as the first time.

All at once, the creature beside the one who had shrieked seemed to morph, its body parts bulging and elongating. The second creature exploded, sending blobs of gray goo hurtling in all directions. Where they landed, the blobs spread out across the ground, consuming the beach, turning it all into a monotony of metallic gray.

The gray hurtled toward Sahaan, but there was nowhere to go. The ocean behind him, the expanding gray mass before him.

The first creature shrieked again, the same pattern,

but somehow sadder this time, as though begging him to understand what it was trying to communicate, as though that would save him.

Sahaan turned, jumped into an incoming wave, and swam, fighting against the ocean. But where was he swimming to?

"Dad?"

With a jolt, Sahaan awoke. Jaan was shaking his shoulder. "They got him, Dad. You and Dr. Bharo. You saved Charles."

On the holocast, Sahaan struggled to see through blurry vision as he fully opened his eyes, how a contingent of both police and military were leading Charles out of a house at the edge of Citrine, while simultaneously leading four men in handcuffs toward a circle of police cars.

Sahaan registered the announcer's voice. "The visitor is back in the custody of government officials and is currently being transferred to the secure facility in Citrine until arrangements can be made to transfer him to Portal City. Naturally, the hope is that, once united with Samantha, the two visitors will be able to work together to tell us more about their purpose here.

"In recent polling news, Pragati Una of the Reconciliation Party has gained a ten-point lead over Guardian candidate Abhiman Gadh. The quick and efficient response to the terrorist attack on our walls, as well as the response to our most recent visitor has increased confidence in the leadership skill of the Reconciliation Party."

Lachel and Jaan both clapped.

"Awesome job, Dad!" Jaan was beaming.

Lachel was smiling at him, too.

Sahaan smiled back. "It was nothing. I should have re-membered that detail much earlier."

"You remembered it in time," Lachel said. "That's what counts."

Perhaps. But what was he missing? He couldn't get Bharo's observation out of his head. Why two? What was the point? And what had Charles been trying to tell him? He would at least be able to find out the answer to the lat-ter question very soon.

"Mr. Vice President?"

"Sahaan?"

"How are things going with Samantha?"

"This line is secure?"

"So Mr. Vitar tells me."

A pause. "Not well."

"Nothing at all?"

"She brings the conversation always back around to being hungry, thirsty, or tired. She avoids answering any questions. This is not how you described Charles to the president."

"No. Charles was very talkative. Personable. He did get tired a lot, but he also seemed to be trying to answer our questions. Has Samantha complained about her memory at all?"

"No. I'm skeptical that she's even trying to remember anything."

"Any ideas on next steps?"

"One of the researchers here had an idea for a line of questioning. We'll try tomorrow." The Vice President sti-fled a yawn admirably, but Sahaan caught the telltale muffling of it over the phone line.

"Thank you, Mr. Vice President."

"I'll let you know as soon as we learn anything."

Sahaan ended the call. He looked up at the clock on the wall. Nine in the evening, only three full days before the election, Samantha was being unhelpful, and Bharo's intuition was telling him something was wrong. No matter which way he took his mind through the problem, Sahaan came back to the same conclusion: he had to go see Charles himself.

Sahaan summoned Mr. Vitar. When he'd arrived, Sahaan returned the handheld and asked him to send for Lachel. With a curt nod, Vitar vanished, and not a few minutes later, Lachel appeared in the door. She stood tall and proud. She walked toward him resolute. Despite having worn the same clothes the whole time she'd been here, she'd done up her hair as best she was able. She stood over him and she held his hand.

She looked into his eyes. "You know something."

"I have suspicions of something."

"Tell me." She had always been able to do this. He was an open book to her.

"Bharo is worried about the situation with the visitors, and Samantha is not turning out to be anything like Charles. Now that Charles is safe again, we can ask him about what he remembers, but the only people who can effectively do that, after what he's been through, are Bharo and me."

"You're going to Citrine, then." Not angry. Not needy. Not even disappointed. Just plain matter of fact. A statement of the necessity of the situation.

"That was my thought."

Lachel sighed, smiled, and nodded. "Do you think it's dangerous?"

Sahaan shook his head. "I just don't know. I want to believe Charles. I still have some suspicions, but all his behavior so far has been exemplary."

"Jaan and I should go back to Portal City, then."

Sahaan shook his head. "I was thinking you two should stay with your sister for a few days."

Lachel looked at him, must have seen the worry etched into his face. He'd given her all the pieces, and she'd put them all together herself. She squeezed his hand harder, kissed him, then said, "I'll figure it out."

She inhaled and exhaled deeply, then set his hand down, and straightened her back. "Do you know if we're making progress?"

"How do you mean?"

"Not the two of us. I mean the Reclamation. I used to think, before, that Reconciliation was constantly making things better for everyone. But everywhere I look now, there are limits. We can only know so much about the nanite-bodied. Our walls can protect us only so much. Half our country wants to vote for a presidential candidate who is clearly incompetent. Some of our own people have even turned on the walls. Has the last hundred years been just an illusion? Were the dissidents right after all? Should we have simply evacuated to Alterra and closed the portal?"

"I think our way of life is worth something," Sahaan said. "Even for all that."

Lachel nodded. "Come back." Spoken in a whisper, but with eyes firm and full of energy. Ready to tear the world apart for him, if need be. But all he needed, for the time being, was for her and Jaan to stay away from both visitors for the next three days.

"I will."

With that, Lachel turned and left.

Sahaan sat and thought for many moments. He thought about the next time he'd get to take Jaan to a voidball game. He thought about that dinner with Lachel he was supposed to have had a week ago. He thought about the two of them holed up in Barine at Nishkap's bachelorette-pad.

Finally, he was able to wrench his mind away from those worries to his new goal: to get himself discharged from the hospital and on the morning train to Citrine.

Sahaan rang for a nurse, who appeared promptly and was shocked to discover that Sahaan wished to discharge himself. He deflected Sahaan's insistence admirably, but when Sahaan started to get himself up out of the hospital bed, the nurse was forced to make a nighttime call to Dr. Aarogy.

The nurse pushed the handheld into Sahaan's ear, and Sahaan grabbed it up.

"Dr. Ekeer?"

"Speaking."

"The nurse tells me you intend to discharge yourself?" The exasperation in her voice was evident.

"That's correct."

"Doctor, there is a wide array of medical reasons why that is a bad idea at this time. Besides, where do you intend to go?"

"Citrine."

"Doctor." Her voice now bordered on condescending. "Have you considered that perhaps you might not be

161

psychologically ready for train travel?"

"National security, doctor. I'll endure what I must."

"Even so, the logistics of transport at this time—"

"I'm sure the expenses can be covered one way or the other."

"You might sustain further injury. In fact, I would say that would be quite likely."

"And your prognosis on my eventual recovery if I sustain further injury?"

"When it comes to your spine... anything could happen doctor. Most injuries can be recovered from. Some can't. What I can tell you is that this plan is extraordinarily risky."

"I find the risk justified, doctor."

"Can I at least convince you to wait for a morning train? That will give me time to write up notes for my staff about what to prepare for you. We should send someone with you as well, at least for the train journey."

"I appreciate that very much, doctor. Thank you."

"Just remember me when they give your lifetime recognition award."

Sahaan smirked. "Will do."

The call ended on the doctor's side, and to the nurse's obvious great relief, Sahaan lay back down on his bed. The moment Sahaan was settled, the nurse ran out of the room, as though Sahaan might imminently change his mind and decide to try to get up again.

Sahaan picked up his handheld and dialed Bharo.

"Hey," his friend intoned.

"Hi, Bharo. I've gotten the doctors to agree to discharge me tomorrow morning."

"You're going to see Charles."

"Yeah."

"He's the key to all of this."

"Have you thought any more about what he said, about the two parties being different but actually the same?"

"Yeah. It's just, we already *know* that. We've known that for as long as they've existed. Your grandmother said as much thirty years ago."

"Well, it looks like I'll be able to ask him about it myself before too long."

"You going to be all right? I mean, are you sure you're up for the trip?"

"I have to be."

"I wish I was going with you."

"You should stay here. Anything could happen. I just only hope his kidnappers didn't mess him up. For his sake and ours. You focus on getting better. Stay tied into the Hilltop Suite. If this situation goes sideways again, I'm going to need you again soon."

"If I'm perfectly honest, I'm worried about what 'going sideways' would mean at this point."

"Tomorrow's problem. We should both get some rest."

"You're right. Just one more thing."

"Yes?"

"Remember in undergrad, there was a Guardian punk who threatened Lachel after a rally, and you ran in and got pummeled?"

"Yeah."

"Lachel and I were there to pick you up last time. Are you sure you don't want to wait just a little while longer?"

Bharo's reasoning was impeccable, as always. "The election is only three days away, and you said yourself that the situation with both Charles and Samantha doesn't feel right. We have to act now. And if Charles is going to talk to anyone after what he's been through... It's got to be one of us."

A long pause. "Okay. Take care of yourself, Sahaan."

"You too, Bharo."

Dr. Aarogy arrived promptly at eight-thirty the next morning. She carried with her a computer pad, and in her wake followed a small army of medical staff. They first closed the curtains so that Sahaan could get himself dressed properly, then opened the curtains and helped Sahaan get out of bed and into a wheelchair.

One of the staff, another doctor, appeared next to Dr. Aarogy.

"This is Dr. Darshak."

Sahaan introduced himself.

"Dr. Darshak will be accompanying you as far as Citrine Station."

"Thank you for making yourself available for this," Sahaan said.

Dr. Darshak nodded curtly, his expression flat.

The two doctors receded into the hall while other staff busied themselves packing up Sahaan's things. Before too much longer, the doctors returned.

"This is where we part ways," Dr. Aarogy said. "Good luck, Dr. Ekeer."

"Thank you," Sahaan said, hoping his smile fully conveyed how appreciative he was for her help. For all their help. He could only hope that his trip to Citrine would prove worth the effort, expense, and risk.

Dr. Darshak took Sahaan's wheelchair and rolled them

down the hall, into an elevator, through reception, and out to a van waiting in front of the hospital. The morning air felt wonderful on his skin. He'd been cooped up indoors for far too long. Even the rush of a passing gust of wind lifted his spirits.

The doctor came around in front of Sahaan and extended a cane toward him. Sahaan took it in his left hand and slowly pulled himself up to a stance, Dr. Darshak bracing him by his right arm. Together, they were able to move forward into the van, where Sahaan strapped himself in and set his cane upon the floor beside himself. Dr. Darshak entered through the opposite door of the van and instructed the driver to take them to Adamantine station.

The van took off away from the hospital, across a country road, its periphery dotted with Alterran flora. Before long, they merged onto a highway, the tall, gray walls visible not more than twenty meters beyond it.

"How many other patients have I diverted you from, Dr. Darshak?"

Dr. Darshak remained impassive. "They all have other doctors now."

"I apologize for the inconvenience."

"You talked to the first visitor, correct?"

"Yes. For three days."

"What do they want now, after all these years?"

"He didn't know. He had memory problems."

"So he says."

"I believe Charles's confusion was genuine. But there was something he remembered. I think it was something crucial. He wanted to tell me about it before we got on the train in Citrine." Sahaan examined the doctor's face.

His brow was knit and he gazed impassively forward. Seemingly impassive. There was something more. "You don't believe the visitors have anything of value to share?"

Dr. Darshak released a sigh. "I tend to vote Reconciliation. Most especially when I see a candidate like Gadh. I recognize him as a pompous, arrogant fool. But I understand the appeal. You see, doctor, I don't really want 'reconciliation,' in the sense of the process rather than the party. We used to ask ourselves how we were going to make the Reclamation better. We talked of adding new cities. We talked of new infrastructure, new parks, new beaches. What happened to all that? I don't care what the nanite-bodied do so long as they don't bother us anymore. I understand the practical limits and political dangers of expanding the walls. But I don't particularly want us contacting the nanite-bodied, either. I want them to just leave us alone."

"I'm not sure we'll ever be certain that they'll leave us alone if we don't talk to them. Do you know why they're not talking to us this way?"

"On the news, they said it's because they changed their language."

"Charles told us that the way they communicate has changed so much that this is actually one of the more efficient means of communication."

Dr. Darshak shook his head. "It's all so complicated."

Sahaan took a moment to ponder the irony of Dr. Darshak possessing an advanced degree in medicine. He suppressed a smirk. "Politics has always been complicated."

The van exited the highway, and Adamantine Station's blue facade came into view on Sahaan's left. Beyond it, he could see the highway turn into the enormous suspension bridge spanning the Asym River. Soon, they would be entering the service road connected to the station's departure terminal.

"How are you feeling?" Dr. Darshak asked. "Any dizziness or fatigue?"

"I feel fine," Sahaan replied, quite honestly. The thought of boarding the train did induce a bit of trepidation, but he then thought of coming home to Lachel, of Jaan growing up in a world safe from the threat of having one's body forcibly altered, of all the people counting on him to figure out what the nanite-bodied wanted.

The van came to a halt in front of the departure terminal, and Sahaan began the arduous task of getting himself out of the van, stabilizing himself, and then moving through the terminal with Dr. Darshak at his side. An eerie vacancy permeated the terminal. There were people, certainly, but they were mostly station staff and military. Martial law, Sahaan recalled, though he supposed the president might be close to lifting that decree. If Samantha were to finally start talking, that might just do it.

Sahaan found himself able to walk with the use of the cane, albeit slowly, through the terminal. Where there would have normally been queues, there was only empty space. The ambient music from hidden speakers seemed too loud, though its volume was in fact quite low.

He and Dr. Darshak bought tickets from the single open kiosk. Sahaan's government ID sufficed to clear both of them without further inquiry. They then proceeded through the terminal and down a long flight of stairs onto the platform for Adamantine-Citrine line.

When they reached the bottom of the stairs, the train became visible, a sleek, white row of passenger cars, very different from the military train he'd taken out of Citrine five days prior.

"How are you doing?" Dr. Darshak asked.

"Fine." Sahaan wondered how often he'd have to validate his condition for Dr. Darshak.

They boarded at once, found their seats, and Sahaan let out a long breath as he sank into the soft cushions. He closed his eyes and took more breaths in and out. If he was honest, his back and his side were on fire.

"Here." Dr. Darshak's voice.

Sahaan opened his eyes and found the doctor standing before him holding a pair of pills.

"What are these?"

"A painkiller. It was in your IV before, but you've been off that for a few hours now."

Sahaan grabbed them up. Probably a sedative, too, but he wasn't about to argue. As long he was lucid when they arrived in Citrine.

"Water?" the doctor asked.

"That would be nice."

The doctor rummaged around in his bag, which he'd stored over their seats, and produced a water bottle. Sahaan took it, gulped down the pills, and then the rest of the water as well.

"Thank you," he said.

The doctor sat down across from him. He did his best to avoid eye contact with Sahaan, giving Sahaan the distinct impression that the doctor was holding back a question.

"Something on your mind?" Sahaan asked.

The doctor shook his head. Then, all at once, said, "You must get questions about your family all the time."

Actually, most adults, like the doctor, avoided the topic for the same reason he likely was. "What do you want to know?" Sahaan asked.

"We were so keen to show the Alterrans the error of their ways in splitting their University and Monastery the way they did, and here we are doing the same thing all over again with political parties just four generations later. What was Mox *thinking*?"

"Mox wasn't trying to create political parties. He just wanted his kids to think critically about solutions to our problems and come up with plans. He just assumed that they would eventually come around to the same conclusion. It didn't work out that way. I don't think even my grandmother wanted to create a new party. It just kind of formed around her."

The train car had seen a steady stream of military personnel entering and taking seats, but only about a third of the seats had been taken. A chime sounded, and an automated message announced that the train would be departing soon.

"They couldn't see that that would happen?" Dr. Darshak asked.

Sahaan shook his head. "Not even nearly. In politics, we make the best decisions we can based on our experience, but the effects, especially the very long term effects, are rarely discernible in the present. Take our present situation. Charles and Samantha are both an extraordinary opportunity to learn more about the others we share this world with. It's also a very dangerous situation that has to be carefully navigated. I can steer us through the current storm, even make sure we're set up for the next ten or twenty years, but I can't know what effects my decision will have fifty or a hundred years out. I have to count on the fact that the system will provide a steady stream of recruits into my field, who will steer through all of my unintended consequences down the road."

"Because people are complex."

Sahaan nodded.

The train's engine kicked in, and an automated message announced that the doors had been locked and the train was now underway.

Sahaan noticed his eyes had started to droop. "Was there a sedative in that medication?"

Dr. Darshak nodded. "It's primarily a painkiller. But, yes. It's a mild sedative."

"Will I be awake when we arrive?"

"You should be. It's a very small dose."

"I'll just rest my eyes then."

The doctor nodded, and Sahaan closed his eyes and let his mind rest. He felt awake enough at first, but all at once, no time seeming to have passed, he awoke to the sound of voices. Loud voices. His eyes flitted open to the visage of Dr. Darshak standing over him looking out the window of their train car. Across the passageway down the middle of the train car, a pair of military officers was staring out their window as well. The lighting in the cabin had dimmed and a red light strobed through the cabin. The light, Sahaan realized, was coming from outside—shock jolted him fully awake. Those were the emergency lights built into the walls lining the railway on both sides.

He caught one of the voices around him, a female officer trying to turn on the holocaster built into the ceiling of the train car. She succeeded, and a journalist appeared, hovering above them all. The officer yelled for everyone on the train to quiet down while simultaneously raising the volume of the broadcast.

"—containment fields are again holding off further incursion from this latest incident.

"For viewers just joining us, an incident has occurred at the nanite quarantine center where the visitor named Samantha was being held. The center has been overrun with evolver nanites. According to the final data transmitted from the center before its primary systems went offline, Samantha herself was the source of these nanites. Full quarantine procedures were initiated the moment the release of these nanites was detected. An estimated ninety-six government researchers and military personnel were trapped inside. It is believed that all of these individuals have been forcibly transformed into nanite-bodied, but we will not know more until reconnaissance nanites can be programmed to enter the center. Vice President Aasaan Dokha was also inside the center and is presumed to have been transformed as well. Emergency generators throughout Portal City have been activated, and the center's containment fields have so far prevented incursion beyond the quarantine center itself. President Aavee is preparing to address the nation, which will be broadcast shortly..."

Sahaan felt his pockets, pulled out his handheld, and dialed the Citrine regional government. After focusing the distracted and frantic receptionist, Sahaan managed to get a line into Citrine's quarantine center.

"Sergeant Major Semaag. Make this quick."

"Senior Consul to the President, Sahaan Ekeer. I need to know Charles's status."

"As far as we can tell, sir, he's the same as always. We're watching him on the cameras now. I'm having everyone evacuated to the very perimeter of the complex. I'm not risking anyone in there at this point."

"You said no change, right?"

"Yessir. No change. What do you think they did to set off the other one?"

"I'm not sure they did anything at all, Sergeant."

"Would you like me to call you back on this line if Charles's situation changes?"

"Yes, please."

"Good luck, sir."

"I will be seeing you soon." Sahaan glanced out the window. They had passed the crest in the mountain pass. "From the looks of it, I'll be in Citrine within the hour."

"See you soon then, sir."

Sahaan ended the call and sat down.

Dr. Darshak sat down across from him, staring over Sahaan's shoulder, mouth agape, stunned. He seemed to collect himself and looked at Sahaan, taking a deep breath.

"I suppose you'll be heading back right away then. I mean, not much to do in Citrine besides figure out how to get the Charles one safely out of the Reclamation, right?"

Sahaan shook his head. "Not at all."

"How do you mean? Isn't he a ticking time bomb?"

"I don't think so."

"Oh?"

"I think he's genuine." Sahaan revealed a smirk. "And I think I've finally understood what he was trying to tell me three days ago. 'Different, but actually the same,' he said."

Dr. Darshak raised an eyebrow. "I'm not following."

"He and Samantha aren't alike at all. From the same place, but actually different."

"I'm not sure I follow."

"I could still be wrong. I'll have to talk to Charles in person to find out." Sahaan leaned back in his seat. Out the window, the walls still flared red. Inside his train car, people were still talking in raised voices. Sahaan sat calmly, the train tipping forward as they began their descent from the mountains.

He was about to bet his life that he was right. Was he that certain? Certain enough to risk it for Lachel and Jaan and the Reconciliation Party and perhaps even the entire Reclamation?

Yes. He most certainly was.

The subsequent hours passed through Sahaan ephemerally—a fraught conversation with Lachel, a protracted conversation with Dr. Darshak about Sahaan's theory, exiting the train, hailing a cab to the facility, Dr. Darshak insisting on coming along, at least as far as the facility perimeter to see how Sahaan's hypothesis would be proven out. Even Sahaan's physical pain seemed a distant and insubstantial thing, barely registering as his mind ran through the scenarios. If he was right, how to convince people, how to make contact, how to keep Charles safe? So many problems, and very few individuals he could really trust.

The cab driver let them out at the gates to the facility, the driver obviously impatient at Sahaan taking so long to get himself out of the car. As soon as he'd received his fare, his car hurtled off away from the place.

A man with a Sergeant Major's uniform approached Sahaan and Dr. Darshak. Three other officers stood at his sides.

"Sergeant Major Semaag?"

"Dr. Ekeer. Welcome."

The sergeant held forth a computer tablet, and Sahaan took it in his right hand. Its display showed Charles, sitting alone in the same room where Sahaan had talked to him three days prior. Charles had his head on the table, his arms wrapped over it.

"He's been like that since we evacuated to the perimeter," Semaag said.

"Thank you," Sahaan said. "I'll be going in now. Please show me the way."

The sergeant and his subordinates bristled.

"Is that wise?" Semaag asked.

"Perhaps not," Sahaan admitted. "Or perhaps I'm right. Either way, I can only find out by going inside."

A female officer at Semaag's side spoke. "Permission to accompany Dr. Ekeer, sir."

"Me too, sir." One of the male officers.

Semaag paused glancing between the three of them. "Permission granted."

The two soldiers saluted.

"Good luck, Dr. Ekeer," Semaag said. "Sergeants Niska and Aant will show you the way."

Dr. Darshak stayed behind, asking the Sergeant if he might be allowed to watch Sahaan's progress.

"Thank you," Sahaan said to Niska and Aant, once they were out of earshot of Darshak and the Sergeant Major.

The two officers nodded and proceeded to guide him to the familiar stairs in the ground, through the dark, crimson, metallic corridors, passageways that held an eerie nostalgia for him now. He'd come so far, and yet, here he was, back at the beginning.

The soldiers opened the door into Charles's room, and Sahaan saw Charles's head rise, then his eyes light up in recognition.

"Sahaan!"

The sergeants took up positions by the door, while Sahaan made his way slowly down the stairs. "Hi, Charles."

Charles's smile was bittersweet. "It is good to see you."

"It's good to see you, too."

"I have to ask you... The reason that everyone left a few hours ago... There was another visitor, wasn't there?"

Sahaan pursed his lips. "Yes, there was." He took a seat across the table from Charles.

"And they attacked the Reclamation, didn't they?"

Sahaan nodded.

Charles's head dropped. "I'm sorry. I suppose I'll have to leave now."

Sahaan shook his head. "Not if I can help it."

Charles looked up with wide eyes. "Really? Even after—?"

Sahaan smiled. "You told me already, 'different, but actually the same.' You weren't talking about Reconciliation and Guardian, were you?"

Charles smiled and let out a small laugh. "No. I wasn't."

"You were trying to tell us about the Reclamation and the nanite-bodied nation. You're as politically fractured as we are, aren't you? All these years, we've just gone on assuming that you're a single people with a single ideology. But even if you evolved, you evolved out of *us*, and some elements of human nature don't change. Like politics."

Charles nodded. "Not *as* politically fractured, but rather *more*. I can't even begin to explain our politics to you. It's vastly complicated. But it's the reason I'm here. I wanted to understand what it's like to be human, and this was the only way to do it. I wanted to read books. We don't read books anymore. Inefficient, someone decided. But all of these decisions about efficiency have added up to an experience that's *stifling*. At least, I feel it is. Not everyone does. I think most people don't. But I needed to get out."

"I'm glad you've been able to remember."

"I just wish I could remember more of the details. There are reasons that the others aren't talking, and it's related to politics, but that stuff is still hazy."

One of the sergeants on the balcony began taking a call on her handheld, and Sahaan and Charles both turned their attention to her. She wrapped her free hand over her mouth as she spoke. A few moments later she waved for Sahaan.

"Just a moment," Sahaan said to Charles, then pulled himself up out of his chair and headed toward the stairs.

The soldier, seeming to remember his condition, rushed down the stairs, meeting him at the base.

"Sir," she said in a whisper, "something is happening outside. They're saying it's a hologram from the nanite-bodied, being projected into all twelve cities. Our handhelds won't work in here, but I can get a computer, if you would—"

Sahaan nodded his head vigorously, and the sergeant ran back up the stairs. Sahaan returned and sat across from Charles.

"I'm glad to see you weren't too badly injured from the crash."

Charles winced. "One of those men was a doctor. They did help me recover. All in all, they could have been a lot worse. I think they left me alone because they were scared of even touching me. They were so frightened."

"A lot of people are very frightened now. But I hope that this newest development will help calm everyone down."

"Oh?"

"A holographic message from the nanite-bodied. They're bringing us a computer so that we can watch together."

Charles raised an eyebrow.

"That's surprising?"

"Somewhat."

"You don't recall any political group that would want to do that?"

Charles seemed to ponder that a moment. He yawned, shook his head, and said. "I think there's one. But something about them achieving it is surprising. I think they're not very powerful. Perhaps the least powerful. I have this image in my head of a dispersing cloud, and I'm not sure why."

The door to the cell opened, and the sergeant returned, hurrying down the stairs.

"Well, let's hope this answers both of our questions," Sahaan said.

He took the tablet computer up from the soldier.

"Thank you, Sergeant."

She saluted. "Yessir. I've made sure it's set to start from the beginning, so you'll be at a couple minutes' behind real time."

Sahaan almost offered for her and her companion to join them, but didn't. They were likely duty-bound to hold their stations. Too bad. This was history in the making.

He propped the computer up on the table so that both he and Charles could see then hit the play button on its interface.

The steps in front of the Hilltop Suite in Portal City appeared. Atop the steps stood the hologram of a girl, her holographic nature evident from the blurriness of the projection, her partial transparency, and the presence of intermittent scanning lines. Besides that, she appeared a perfectly normal girl with brown hair and eyes and wearing a dress that was common for twelve-year-old girls throughout the Reclamation.

"Citizens of the Reclamation," the projection said. "My name is Catherine, and the country I represent, which lies outside your borders is called the Pinnacle. I am here to break the long silence between our peoples. Charles will not have been able to tell you very much, and we fear what Samantha may have already done. We send this message in the hope that all is not lost, in the hope that we can begin a dialogue.

"The reason for our silence is complicated. It is related to our political configuration, which will take some explaining. I hope you will indulge me as I attempt to relate the context that will make our reasons for silence apparent.

"Political systems of past human configurations have typically existed along a single axis, its extremities often labeled 'left' and 'right.' The 'left' typically counts itself amongst the elite and desires changes that will further cement its power within the existing political order. The 'right' typically reacts against that order, hoping to prevent additional changes and to ground society in principles it perceives to be eternal. Human societies have fallen into this familiar pattern for thousands of years. We find now, after our extensive modifications, our situation analogous, yet also much more complex.

"Our political system exists along three axes. Imagine a three-dimensional coordinate system filled with various interlocking shapes. Those shapes are our political parties. When we communicate the names for them amongst ourselves, we are in fact sharing with one another an asset file containing a three-dimensional model for that party's corresponding shape in the Cartesian coordinates of the political model-space.

"The first axis of our political system is our relationship to ourselves. We call this the i-axis. Groups left on this axis believe that we have not advanced nearly far enough, and that, for all of our modifications, a myriad of evolutionary-biological flaws remain, which must be corrected. Groups right on this axis believe that humanity's best configuration so far has been either past versions of ourselves, or, in extreme cases, you. Peripheral groups on this axis would be willing to evolve themselves back into your form of humanity and join your society, if they could.

"The second axis of our political system is our relationship to our biosphere. We call this the e-axis. Some context here is required. The same as you have had satellites to look at us, our nanites have crawled over the top of your walls' field of repulsion and watched you as well. We have seen the many beautiful plants you have imported from the world beyond the portal. This contrasts sharply with our own endeavors to create a viable, self-sustaining ecosystem of nanite-organic flora, all of which have failed miserably. No serious attempts have been made in this field in the last thirty years. Groups left on this axis believe it is enough for us to continue to reshape our landscape to meet our needs. Groups right on this axis believe either that we need to acquire your flora and evolve it, or simply to let it spread across Asura as it is, unaltered.

"The third and final axis of our political system is our relationship to you. We call this the h-axis. For an explanation here to make sense, it is necessary to go back in time one hundred and twenty-one years. From the perspective of our ancestors, you unlocked a portal and gave our great-great-grandparents access to a parallel world, which they promptly tried to assimilate into nanite form, as they had done to everything on Asura. To their shock and amazement, the people of that world were able not only to repel and evict our evolvers, but also brought to Asura the wall technology which has enabled your country to flourish. This event was traumatic, instigating a deep and lasting fear within our society. Our technology, which we thought to be the greatest achievement of human civilization, which had allowed us to utterly dominate Asura for nearly a century, had become completely and utterly thwarted in a span of hours. Those to the right on the h-axis have maintained silence because they fear what you might do to us if provoked. They imagine an arsenal of anti-nanogenic weaponry just waiting to be deployed from the parallel world. Those to the left on this axis have maintained silence because communication does not fit in with any of their goals, which is simply to find a way past your walls. They have already partially done so, in the form of Samantha.

"The man who was the template for Charles is a member of a political group I will call 'decelerationist.' They are hard right-i, hard right-e, and center-h, a political orientation which should now be clear from my description. Samantha's homunculus received a minimal personality template from an individual of left-i, center-e, hard left-h party. She should be neutralized if she has not already self-deconstructed.

"And now myself. I represent a small and shrinking party whose political center is at zero-i, zero-e, and zero-h. The future we imagine for Asura is unique amongst all the parties. We imagine an Asura of connected cities, where each city is populated by humans, some like us, some like you, and many other kinds of humans in between, perhaps even other kinds yet to be imagined. In such a world, no one would worry about anyone forcing anyone else to evolve into another configuration. Such choices would be made freely by individuals, and minds would be changed with words rather than through the physical manipulation of that individual's component molecules. Most importantly, this world would have no walls, because there would be no need for them.

"Most of our society believes such an Asura to be impossible. A daydream. An impossible utopia. We continue to dream regardless.

"Rightwards of our political party, there are those who want to become more like you but are too afraid of you to act on that desire. Leftwards of our political party, there are those who want to destroy you. Our society at large now possesses the ability to send you both envoys of goodwill and envoys of destruction. We cannot tell you which they will be. It will depend on which party they originate from. Our party has neither the political clout nor the resources to do any more than project this meager hologram, but we will continue to work to establish a dialogue. We hope, faintly, that a dialogue is still possible."

The hologram of Catherine flickered, then faded out to empty space.

PART III

Trust

"Charles?"

"..."

"Charles!"

"Yes?"

"What did you think of that just now?"

"... I'm a copy."

"You're a human being with free will and agency."

"I knew that this body had formed from the wall, you know. But I had no idea that there was a real Charles still out there."

"But, do you see what this means? There's a group out there that wants contact."

"They're small. Much too small. Like Catherine said. All the parties rightward of hers are like me. I'm not here to communicate with you. I'm here to *be* you. And the ones leftward are like the ones you remember from before the walls, but worse. They're angry, bitter, and even more convinced that they're right in spite of everything that's happened."

"But it's something. Catherine reached out. She broke a century of silence."

"I'm tired, Saahan. I want to lie down."

"Okay."

"Just one thing before I do."

"What's that?"

"About Samantha. What did she do?"

"She released evolvers into her environment. They've been contained."

"Did she evolve anyone?"

"Yes."

"I'm sorry that happened. Make sure the evolved have access to both water and electricity. They will need a lot of electricity."

"This wasn't your fault, Charles."

"In a way, indirectly, it was."

"Oh?"

"I'm remembering more now. A lot more. He, the real Charles, was the one who figured out how to transform the walls."

The surface of the Citrine base had changed much from Sahaan's first visit here. Before it had been largely empty, save for the few military personnel then assigned to it. Now, an enormous ring of military had encircled the spot where Sahaan stood, the base of the stairwell leading down to where Charles lay sleeping. The two sergeants who had been following in Sahaan's wake saluted him, then strode off toward the bustling encampment.

Sahaan pulled out his handheld and dialed Bharo. The line rang for perhaps over a minute, and Sahaan had just begun to wonder if his friend were all right, when Bharo's voice suddenly burst through the speaker.

"Sahaan! Sorry about that. I was on the phone with the president."

"The president will need a speech, I'm sure."

"He said to have you come back to Portal City right away."

Sahaan grimaced. He'd anticipated this. He'd called Bharo hoping he could get an update without getting that order relayed. "And how will we keep Charles safe?"

"I'm sure the president thinks this is a whole lot bigger than Charles now."

"Charles is key to this. He's *remembering* things. Someone's got to keep an eye on him."

A long silence. "Tell you what. The doctor had me walking last night, so I'll pull your little stunt on them tonight, meaning I can be in Citrine by tomorrow. I can probably fend off the president for another day. Just tell me what you think Charles has left to tell us."

"He's the one who figured out how to turn the walls into people."

A pause. "Well, I'll be... Sure. Yup. I'll be there as soon as I can."

"Thanks. How's everything else?"

"Well, about half of Portal City has applied for a visa to Alterra. The president shut down travel through the portal but decided to lift the train travel restrictions so that those who want to evacuate Portal City can. Most of the capital's citizens have taken him up on that offer. We've got a full mass exodus in progress. Seems most are staying with friends and family in other cities. But it's somewhat backfired. Even the types that normally keep their posts—police, emergency workers, and government officials are operating at something like two-thirds capacity. No one wants to be anywhere near Portal City right now. Gadh and Guardian are having a heyday with this, of course. They're calling Aavee incompetent for the travel decision, and the only part of Catherine's broadcast they seem to have heard is the part about their extreme left still wanting to evolve us all. Una's stance, naturally, is that this is our opportunity to finally make contact."

"And what about the vice president and the others trapped in the containment center?"

"The news just talks about how the containment fields are holding."

"In other words, we're already treating them like casualties."

"Yes."

"No, Bharo. That's not how we play this. My recommendation to the president is that this is our leverage to the nanite-bodied. Their center party wants relations and their right wants access to the human experience. What we want is for our people to be *un*-evolved. It's been two centuries now that we've been at the mercy of their damn evolvers. We need to change that. The initial treaty will be that they return the vice president and all the others to their human forms, and in exchange we will agree not to expand our walls for some number of years, let's say a decade. That gives us plenty of time to expand diplomatic relations."

"Ambitious."

"You're damn right it is."

"Most people can't operate the way you do, you know."

"How's that?"

"See a problem, rush in, solve it."

"At least I make a plan now, before rushing in."

"Granted. I'll talk to the president and see what I can

do. Then I'll work on getting out of here. You going to be near your handheld?"

"I'm going to be underground in the bunker with Charles."

"Probably for the best."

"Thanks. Oh, and have someone in Portal City make sure that there's still electricity available inside the containment area. Charles says they need electricity and water to survive."

"Will do."

The call ended and Sahaan immediately turned off his handheld. The sun was getting higher in the sky and had already managed to burn off the morning mist. Sahaan had begun to sweat. He gazed briefly around the circular military encampment, then descended back into the underground containment center.

It was one of those mornings.

A cool breeze was blowing in off the ocean, and wisps of clouds dotted the crimson sky. Charles couldn't yet bear the thought of going into the office and finding out which sub-atomic particles had folded kataward rather than anaward, or vice versa, the bevy of communiques that would be waiting in his inbox, the myriad tasks he needed to ask and learn about, to make sure that the research was proceeding toward its goal and that no one on the business side would be concerned about delivery dates or costs. Not just yet.

He turned right at Hill Street instead of left, striding uphill instead of down. The streets of Redwing were busy at this time of the morning, people commuting from home to work, buses and trams shooting down the streets on either side, the skyscrapers towering over him. Lining the roads lay the pots of soil, where, just a few decades prior, modified organisms had been planted and nourished, only to all die early and sickening deaths. They'd mulched and burned the plants, but kept the pots of soil, as though holding on to the idea that they would one day become useful again.

Charles climbed further, two blocks more, across busy intersections, car horns screeching and trams passing with a hum, suspended over antigrav rails.

At last, Redwing Spire came into view, an enormous structure towering a full ninety stories. Two circuitous paths interlocked to form its outer frame, one running in a spiral upward, the other downward. At the top lay a large balcony with tables and a café, the perfect spot for looking out over the ocean.

Charles strode up the spire, moving faster now, as though arriving at the lookout sooner would stave off the encroaching needs of his workplace. It was not that he was bad at his job, far from it. It was that he knew the effort to be futile. So they had gone deeper than the sub-atomic and found the quantum folding properties in sub-atomic particles. So what? They'd spent the last two centuries documenting the myriad ways in which those particles folded across six-dimensions of spacetime, and still no end was in sight. Despite all that, the work continued. Society demanded that they know, that the catalogue be complete.

Charles reached the very top of the spire, strode over to the railing at the edge of the balcony, and gazed out at the ocean. He loved watching the water, the way its surface shimmered, especially in the morning sunlight. It seemed to him a more elegant form of what the evolvers were doing to the land, raising hills, flattening them, digging ditches, changing the course of rivers.

It had occurred to the leftists to attack the vestigs indirectly—cut off the flow of the Asym or Enim rivers, whose sources lay in Pinnacle territory; or, compromise the foundations of their walls, especially at weak points like the Asym mountain pass or the marshier parts of the Bekel plains. But there was always that pervasive fear. What would the vestigs from the parallel universe do in retaliation?

So much fear. So much useless, stupid fear. It would take so little effort to just reach out and say something, a simple message. But no. Too politically inconvenient for either side to actually do something, to take a risk of any meager magnitude. And so they did nothing. Charles supposed he might be less annoyed if they were indeed busy with so many important internal issues, but observing his own behemoth of a workplace didn't inspire much confidence. The six-dimensional folding processes of sub-atomic particles had grown so complex that no single human, even with centuries of technological enhancements to their brain, could comprehend the concept in its entirety. The previous generation had been so convinced they'd discovered the deep and glorious truth, the 'end of physical science.' Lying bare before Charles was the honest truth of the endless monotony of sub-sub-atomic particles and their folding properties. What was the point of it all?

Charles took a deep breath and reminded himself that the Tromm Ocean was beautiful, its elegance simple. Waves cresting, flattening, over and over, across an enormous space. Constantly changing itself, yet seemingly perpetual, self-sustaining.

A ping in Charles's mind broke his reverie. He opened the message with a tinge of annoyance. A question from work, already arriving in his inbox, even though it wasn't yet even nine.

Fine. Fine. He'd go in to work, then. At least, since he was here, he could get a voltage. That would take the edge off the morning at least. And the queue at the café was short. Charles strode over and got in line, looking over all the delectables on display—semiconductor biscuits, direct-alternate-twists, even one of his favorites, acid pies. Not for him, though. He'd been carefree with his diet in his twenties, but the ones who let themselves gorge usually ended up overcharging their brains and burning out their silicon-based organs. Repair was costly and Charles was far from spendthrift. He had decided that life path was not for him.

"One voltage?" The cashier asked. "Alternating current, light on the acid, right?"

Charles smirked. "You got it." He'd been coming here for a morning break perhaps too much. He could change careers, he thought just then, but that would only prolong his servitude to this system. He ordered himself to stop thinking about work, at least for now.

"That'll be 3.278 kilobytes," the cashier said, transmitting a payment authorization form.

Charles signed the form and transmitted it back.

"Thanks," the cashier said with a smile.

"Thank you," Charles said, and walked around the side of the counter where a barista worked a large, humming, hissing and occasionally shuddering machine dotted with sockets.

"Order up," the barista announced. "One double-ohm, open circuit."

"How's it going?" Charles asked the barista. He realized, as he said it, it was a selfish act. Anything to distract himself from work. A deeper resolve lay beneath it, though. He didn't want to be like some of the people he worked with, the ones who tended to treat anyone not employed in physics, chemistry, or math as a lesser species.

"Good, man. How about yourself?"

"Well. Looking forward to the weekend, I suppose."

The barista pulled out a plug above what Charles presumed to be his voltage, and the machine sputtered to life, hissing. "Just a few more days, huh? What have you got planned?"

One impulse within Charles wanted to give one of the canned answers: nothing much, just taking it easy, or something equally innocuous. But not today. This was another person in front of him.

"I was thinking of scanning some old books. Perhaps *The Politics.*"

Charles watched for signs of being taken aback, of perhaps the barista feeling intimidated by the idea of scanning rather than simply downloading books, or the idea of being interested in a three-thousand-year-old work like *The Politics*, written when humanity was 'less evolved.' Instead, the barista grinned. "Nice. That'll make a good scan. Have you scanned Rema and Xelas, too?"

"Most of Rema and a bit of Xelas."

"My favorite Xelas is *Banquet.* And there are also Porfini's interpretations of Xelas. His *Debates* are particularly good."

"I've scanned most of Porfini, but not *Debates*. I'll check those out. Have you seen his treatise on justice? He tore a dialogue of Xelas's apart."

"No, I haven't gotten to that one. I'll check it out. What was it called?"

"I'll have to look it up. I think it might just be *Treatise on Justice*."

"Here you go." The barista handed Charles his voltage over the charging apparatus.

"Thanks."

"No prob. Have fun scanning."

"I will."

Charles plugged the voltage into his arm and felt the rush of electricity into his system. He descended Redwing Spire with a smile, a spring in his step, perhaps because of the voltage, or perhaps because he'd had an interesting conversation for the first time in he couldn't remember how long, brief though it had been.

Now, finally, he felt ready to start his busy day.

Sahaan opened the door to Charles's chamber to find that he had returned to the table, sitting with his feet propped up and arms crossed.

"Couldn't sleep?" Sahaan called down as he made his way carefully down the stairs.

Charles shook his head. "Memories are coming faster now. Lots of stuff about Charles's... the other Charles's life."

"Oh?"

Charles smirked. "Mostly innocuous stuff. He's a physicist in Redwing. That's the Pinnacle's capital. It's on

196

a continent west of here, across the Tromm Ocean. There's this café I like— he likes at the top of Redwing Spire. It's connected somehow to me coming here."

"A café?" Sahaan sat down.

"I know. It's weird." Charles pulled his feet down. "I'll bet it's rude to put your feet on the table, huh?"

"Don't worry," Sahaan chuckled. "I'm not offended."

"It's rude for us— them, too." Charles scowled. "This is confusing, Sahaan. I liked it better when I thought I was the only Charles."

"You're the only you."

He was still scowling. "He knew I would feel this way, you know."

"How do you feel?"

"Like a puppet. Created for someone else's benefit."

"I consider you a human being. And I will make sure you are treated accordingly."

"I appreciate that."

A long silence. Sahaan knew what he had to do next. He had walked through the conversation in his mind all the way down the stairs and through the long dark corridors of this ancient military bunker, remnant of an ancient and ridiculous rivalry about what humanity should be. That more than anything else had convinced him to pursue the course he had chosen.

Charles now stared over Sahaan's shoulder, apparently lost in thought.

"Charles?"

"Yes?"

"I have something I want your help with."

"What is it?"

"A proposal that I'm going to make to the president.

It's about a treaty I'd like us to extend to the Pinnacle. The terms are that we would promise not to expand the wall system for a decade, and in return, they will provide us a way to turn the ninety-seven people inside the Portal City quarantine zone back to their original forms. I also want it to outline a framework for the eventual establishment of a full diplomatic relationship, from regular communication channels all the way to embassies, if we can take it that far."

Charles smiled widely and chuckled.

"What is it?"

"Just a memory. Charles wasn't entirely certain what I would find here. He hoped for something just like what you described, though. I'll do what I can to help."

"Thank you, Charles." And now the hard part. Dread was already tormenting Sahaan, deep in his gut, making him queasy, but he tamped it down. It had to be done. "Now, before I ask for any more of your help on this matter, there's something I have to tell you."

"Oh?"

"I haven't lied to you. Not this whole time we talked here, or even before the train. But I have left something out. Treaties are built on trust, Charles. I couldn't go on doing my job if I'd felt I'd misrepresented my side at the very beginning of a treaty's creation. And so, what I have to tell you is this. My full name is Sahaan Ekeer. But my grandfather married a woman named Vibha, whose maiden name was Thiksay. I am Stok Thiksay's great-great-grandson."

Charles blinked, his smile had faded, but he had not taken on a frown either. His eyes remained locked with Sahaan's, impassive.

"Charles?"

Charles spoke quietly. "This is... quite some news."

"I can imagine that the opinion of Stok Thiksay in the Pinnacle is quite poor."

"It is the one thing that all political groups have in common."

"Do you want some time alone?"

Charles paused, looking at the corner of the room impassively for some time, then slowly shook his head up and down.

"I understand."

Sahaan stood, and with his cane clanking against the metal floor panels, made his way slowly up the stairs and out the door of Charles's chamber.

Charles surged up the spiral ramp of Redwing Spire, not a run or a jog, but the briskest of walks. When he arrived at the balcony café, he joined the queue straight away. While waiting in line, he pondered over what he'd read over the weekend. Porfini's *Debates* had certainly been intriguing. Was a person entitled to personal autonomy, or did they owe something to the community that had allowed them to thrive? What did a proper education consist of? Were mental and physical activity both equally important? Intriguing questions.

"Hi, Adam," Charles said to the cashier.

"Hey, how's your morning going?" With this he sent over the payment authorization for Charles's usual.

Charles validated the authorization. "Good. I'm excited. My band's playing later this week. It's our first time getting a gig downtown."

"That's great to hear. Good luck. Or is it, 'break a leg?'"

Adam laughed. "Either's fine. Thanks!"

Charles moved around across from the charger where Brad stood preparing a triple-watt shock.

"I finished *Debates*," Charles announced.

"Oh yeah? What'd you think?"

"Great stuff. Especially gets you thinking about the education system we've set up. We decided that we could offload physical maintenance to machines, but we just created all these other problems for ourselves. Overenergize yourself and bad things happen. And the expansion of memory hasn't helped us, either. It just allowed us to discover that the complexity of the material universe is that much more infinite."

"And we came up with all of that when making yourself better just meant exercise and reading." Brad held up one of his hands and turned it around in the air. "Makes you wonder, right?"

"If all this is really worth it."

Brad nodded. "Have you ever heard of Broderick Wayland?"

Charles shook his head.

"He's a writer in Eveling. Writes books that are *intended* to be scanned instead of downloaded. Do a search."

Charles searched.

"You'll have to page a bit," Brad added. "He doesn't usually make the first result set."

After scrolling through random entries for public record entries for Broderick Waylands on various continents, Charles finally happened on a network pub-portal for a Broderick Wayland in Eveling. A bit more searching, and Charles found Broderick's book, available for free:

Going Nowhere as Fast as Possible.

"Interesting title," Charles observed.

"I think you might like it."

"Thanks!"

"By the way, I finished *Treatise on Justice.*"

"And?"

"Makes you wonder whether or not we've over-complicated our legal system, huh?"

"Well, there is that, but I think you could also make the argument that we had to scale up the complexity when we made ourselves more complex. We over-complicated ourselves first." Charles glanced just then at the café queue, which had grown to a full eight people. "Well, I'd better head off to work. Thanks for the recommendation! I'll let you know what I think of Wayland. Sounds like a good one."

"See ya, Charles."

Charles plugged the voltage into his arm port and began down the Spire. A contemporary author concerned about the effects of induced evolution? Who'd have thought that possible? But it would have to wait until the weekend. Before him lay five long days of guiding a team in the collection of data about sub-atomic particle behavior. He released a sigh. Talk about going nowhere fast.

An idea struck him—he recalled the discovery he'd made that he dared not share with anyone. But it was out of the question. Just thinking about it was dangerous, especially in an open-web area like downtown Redwing. He pushed the thoughts aside and turned to his work calendar. Yes, it would be a busy week indeed.

Back on the surface, Sahaan set his handheld to block all

incoming calls but left his data connection active. The web had exploded with activity.

The first major theme he noticed amongst the posts were scenes in Portal City, mostly of vacant intersections and looted storefronts. Video footage of the containment facility was also popular. The nanite barrier surrounding it shimmered. That shimmer was the effect of nanite warfare, the Reclamation's defenders versus the Pinnacle's evolvers. So long as the Reclamation's nanites remained numerous enough to hold off their opponents, they would be fine—so long as the power held, so long as the Pinnacle nanites didn't receive a software update that would allow them to break the stalemate...

The second major theme was of people in other cities hoarding food and constructing nanite-resistant shelters of their own design. Sahaan shook his head. Those would do little good in the case of a full-on breach.

News reports varied depending on the political affiliation of the station doing the broadcasting.

Guardian networks had all but announced the apocalypse. They now had incontrovertible proof of the existence of nanite-bodied who desired to breach the Reclamation's walls (never mind Catherine's description of all the other groups), and the dangerous Reconciliation government had allowed one visitor to explode into nanites and were making no motions to extradite the other one. In fact, Senior Consul Sahaan Ekeer was still talking to the visitor, for whatever good that would do!

Reconciliation networks had taken Catherine's message as a clear indication that they had been right all along (never mind Catherine's description of the dangerous, radical parties still bent on the Reclamation's destruction). These stations were all but ignoring the situation in Portal City, and what little coverage they did give was to insinuate that those fleeing were behaving irrationally. Senior Consul Sahaan Ekeer's discussions with the visitor were the indicators of a rational government taking the proper steps to ensure a diplomatic solution to their problems.

At least he could get behind his own party's evaluation of how the country should act, even if he found their willful ignorance of certain key problems unnerving.

Sahaan dialed Lachel's number. She answered before the ring tone had even begun.

"How are you?" she asked.

"I'm fine. Healing. Feeling better all the time. Turns out I was right about Charles."

"I saw Catherine's message. What happens now?"

"We decide how to contact them."

"There's something you should know. Something that's not on the news."

"Oh?"

"Nishkap, Jaan, and I were on our way back from the store. There were people flooding out of the train station off of the trains from Adrine and Eline. They looked frightened, which makes sense. But there were also people arriving from the Bengine train. And they didn't look frightened. They looked angry, intimidating. We hurried past the station and back toward home. I didn't like how they looked, Sahaan. It worried me. And no one's mentioning anything about it on the news."

The Adrine and Eline train lines would have been carrying people from Portal City, but Bengine was a spoke city.

"Did they exit the train station?" Sahaan asked. "Did they actually come into Barine?"

"No, I don't think so. It looked like they were transferring."

"To the Adrine line?"

"Yes."

Shit. "How much food and water do you have?"

"Enough for about two weeks."

"Good. Stay inside. I'll come for you as soon as I'm able."

"Are you still talking to Charles?"

"He and I are taking a break right now, but I'd say overall there's been progress. Catherine's message seems to have jogged his memory."

"That's good. There's hope, then."

"There's definitely a reason to be hopeful. Take care."

"We will."

"Love you."

"Love you, too."

Sahaan dialed Bharo as quickly as he could.

"Heya. I'm almost ready to ask for discharge, so I'll be seeing you—"

"What do you know about spoke city residents boarding trains bound for Portal City?"

"Nothing." A pause. "Why?"

"Lachel tells me that she saw a group of angry Bengine residents change trains at Barine headed for Adrine."

It took Bharo only moments to walk through implications. "Shit. I'll phone the president."

"Think we can rally enough troops in the capital to keep the peace and prevent them from doing something stupid to the containment center?"

"If we act now, probably. I sure as hell hope so. I better get going. See you soon."

"See you then."

Sahaan ended the call and pocketed his handheld. He scanned the circle of military personnel around him, looking for a certain individual he'd seen before... There! He waved to Sergeant Major Semaag and began walking toward him. He was able to move faster now but still needed the cane. Semaag decided to pass the nanite defense perimeter and strode forward, meeting Sahaan halfway.

"Dr. Ekeer?"

"How many soldiers could you spare from here, Sergeant Major?"

"If I needed to, maybe two dozen. Why?"

"We need to leave enough here to keep Charles safe, but all the rest need to get to Portal City as quickly as possible."

"Is there an order from the president?"

"Consul Bharo is talking to him now. You should have it soon. If there's any preparation you need to do—"

"Understood."

"Thank you," Sahaan said, and returned to the stairwell while Semaag disappeared into the perimeter.

Sahaan stood over the narrow stairwell. It lay now directly beneath the sun, ablaze and brightly lit at this one point of the day. He had his own battle to fight, his own part to play. He descended, one step carefully after the other toward the door that led to the hallway and the hallways that led deeper and deeper, past disused and broken computers, ancient technologies of defense.

What was it all for? Had his ancestors fought in vain so that his generation could tear itself apart out of fear? No. He wouldn't let it happen.

Fear won't win, he repeated to himself. Not in me, not in Charles, not in Lachel and Jaan, not in Bharo, not in his country.

Fear won't win. It can't. Because that would truly be the end.

Charles walked up the short flight of concrete steps to a newly decorated storefront a few blocks down the street from his apartment. Just a few days before the building had been an abandoned lot, but yesterday, as he'd been walking home from work, he'd noticed a new building had gone up, the front bedecked with tables and small chairs underneath large umbrellas.

The sun shone down brightly, and Charles chose a chair beneath an umbrella. He worried only briefly about occupying a table before purchasing anything—only about half of them were occupied. At one sat a couple with a child, perhaps five years old, between them. An older couple sat across the way.

Charles folded his arms and thought back through *Going Nowhere as Fast as Possible*, collecting and organizing all his thoughts.

"Hey." The familiar voice broke Charles's reverie.

Charles stood up. "Hey, Brad. How you been?"

"Good, man."

They proceeded inside the cafe and entered the queue at the cash register.

"I finished *Going Nowhere*," Charles said. "My biggest question... He's cagey about it. Does he really have actual, physical books?"

Brad nodded.

"So, he can read?"

"I'm not sure, but that's my opinion."

"When the pre-Break authors talk about libraries, my imagination goes wild. I mean, imagine shelves and shelves of books. Imagine being able to sit quietly and just think about stuff."

"We had more time for that before, too."

"How do you mean?"

"It's the weekend now, right?"

"Sure."

"Did you know that the weekend used to be two full days long?"

Charles shook his head. "When did that happen?"

"Post-Break. Vestig forms of our organism required more rest—about eight hours of sleep every day. It wasn't possible to work people more than forty hours in a seven-day span without fatigue taking its natural toll and impacting the quality of their work. Thanks to these supposed improvements, a hundred-hour work week is now the norm."

"I would be able to scan so many books if I had a full two days every week. That would be phenomenal."

"Don't forget, you'd be more tired, too. People usually lost that time to just recovering from their work and taking care of their living spaces, which didn't automatically clean and repair themselves."

They reached the cashier and paused to order their voltages.

"So," Charles said, "I guess my biggest questions remain around what to do. Wayland laid out all my grievances with what we've done to ourselves. It was kind of cool to realize I'm not the only person who thinks about this stuff."

"Yeah, I looked you up on the web. You've got an interesting background."

"You mean the physics part, right?"

Brad nodded. They picked up their voltages from the counter, went to sit outside under one of the large umbrellas.

"What can I say? I like solving math problems. Always have. But I also love stories. I found I loved ancient stories, too, the really old ones, like *The Politics*, but some authors weren't available for direct download, and that's how I found out about scanning."

"Slower, less efficient, but the experience of imagining is so much more vivid." Brad grinned. "Think about what it would be like to read."

Charles shook his head. "I'll bet the vestigs have libraries."

"Who knows? Their culture could have become anything. Maybe they gave that up and went with optical scanning or direct download, too. You don't need to change the whole human genome for that, just some simple implants."

"Sure. What do you think has happened to the vestigs? Are they staunch militarists backed by their parallel universe friends, or are their walls just waiting for a gate crashing?"

"If you liked Wayland, then I think you know that there are, at least theoretically, other possibilities. Not that any of those are politically feasible."

"Like contact?"

Brad nodded. "We're making a lot of assumptions about what they're like, and that's based on what their ancestors were like, which was mostly based on the fact that we were trying to change them all into something they didn't want to become."

With his next statement, Charles added an encryption key to their conversation. "What if it were possible to get a person inside the walls? One of us. But, in order to do it, the technology would become available to everyone. Even the hard left."

Brad jammed the voltage into his arm port. His words came with the signed encryption key attached. "Difficult question. How would this person get in, anyway? Are we talking about reducing someone to pure-biological? There are a whole host of ethical issues there—"

"It wouldn't really be someone here going there... It's more like, a person would... come to be inside their walls. And we could give them the memories of someone here. That's easily enough done since we have the SMEI."

"SMEI?"

"The Standard Memory Engram Interface. It's how we make and share memes."

"I see. So, theoretically, this would be a kind of biological person inside their walls, but with the memories of someone here."

Charles shrugged. "Assuming pre-Break brains can handle SMEI data structures. There's no telling what they would or wouldn't remember. For all we know it could make them completely demented."

Brad nodded. "I see. But then, assuming that this hypothetical process becomes available to everyone, then a bad actor could use it construct any kind of organism, like one that replicates nanites with its cells, or self-destructs, or introduces viral agents, or any number of nasty things."

"Yeah. That's the conundrum."

Brad tapped his foot, his toes clanging against the bolts in the stone slabs of the patio. "Well, I'll give you this. It's a way cooler idea than the holographic messages that the Centrists are always going on about."

"Do you think that the risk is worth the potential reward?"

Brad pondered that over a moment. "I don't know. In our current political climate, it does seem quite risky. Just look at our president."

"It's impossible to tell what would happen. That's what makes it so hard—" He cut himself off, realizing he'd almost strayed out of the hypothetical.

Brad's next words came unencrypted. "What do you like best about being a physicist?"

"That's easy. Solving problems."

"Anything you don't like?"

"The arrogance of some. Of many."

Brad nodded. "If I could choose someone to be our ambassador to the vestigs, I think I'd choose you."

Charles chortled. "Really? Me?"

"Yup."

Charles plugged in his voltage. They'd talked a lot at the café Brad worked at, and now here outside of work, but what made Brad think that he'd be a good ambassador? Weird. Charles decided that if one day he did decide to act on Project Hermes, he'd find someone other than himself to be the memory template. His personality? It seemed potentially more dangerous than anything the leftists could dream up. And what would his memories achieve there? Solutions to physics problems? Knowledge of literature they already possessed? No, he would need to find a real diplomat to be the template.

"What else are you reading these days?" Charles tried.

"Lots." Brad grinned.

One of the most important skills Sahaan ever learned in politics was the ability to *appear* to make decisions definitively and effortlessly, even when his own thinking on the topic was fraught with indecision and doubt. He found himself in such a predicament now. If he stayed in Citrine with Charles, then he would not be able to help his administration with the impending political crisis in Portal City. However, if he left Citrine now, he could potentially do lasting damage to his relationship with Charles.

He walked the halls of the Citrine military bunker slowly, to give himself more time to go over everything he knew, think through all potential ramifications.

By the time he reached the door to Charles's room, he'd made his decision, and although he wasn't by any means certain that it was the right one, it was the one he would now stick to.

Charles lay on his bed, impassive. He remained there, even as Sahaan's cane clacked on the way down the stairwell. Sahaan sat in the chair at the table.

"Why did Stok do it?" Charles asked, looking at the ceiling, his tone stoic.

"Mostly he just wanted to go home. But the militia in Adrine, then it was just called A3, learned about Alterra's walls from him."

"We blame him." Charles turned himself, and sat with legs over the edge of the bed and making eye contact with Sahaan. "Even though it doesn't make any sense. But it's that moment in time. Everything seemed to be going fine. We were discovering amazing new things. We controlled the whole planet. Everything seemed like it was within our grasp. And then the walls showed up, and suddenly we didn't control the whole planet. And suddenly, sub-atomic quantum mapping got infinitely more complex and a hell of a lot duller, too. And the biosphere of perfect organisms we were working on... Well, Catherine already told you how that went. I— Or, the other Charles, rather, is a physicist. He got so massively bored with his work. Imagine, Sahaan, training for a specialized profession for over a decade, and then actually landing a job only to discover that your work consists of repeating the solution to '2+2' in a trillion different ways. So, yes, the other Charles and I, we can forgive you for this. And I understand why you didn't tell me at first, and I don't blame you. But most of the Pinnacle will not react in this way. Only the Centrists, and maybe not even all of them, will understand. They will only feel that Stok Thiksay is when everything started to go wrong."

"Thank you," Sahaan said. "For understanding and for explaining."

Charles took a deep breath in and closed his eyes momentarily. "How are you going to respond to Catherine's message?"

Sahaan pursed his lips. "Unfortunately, there's another situation we need to address first."

"Oh?"

"An internal problem. In Portal City."

"I see. So then, you're—?"

"I've decided to go back to Portal City, yes. Bharo will be here tomorrow morning."

"Is there anything I can do to help?"

"If you remember anything about the Pinnacle that I urgently need to know, wave at those cameras," Sahaan pointed at the ceiling, "and tell whoever arrives. They'll get me the message."

"The memories are getting better now. Though it's so odd to know that it's not my life. It seems to me as though I was there, especially as the memories get clearer."

Sahaan stood. "I have to get going."

Charles nodded. "Take care of yourself."

"I will."

Sahaan retreated up the stairs and out of the bunker wondering if he'd made the correct choice. There was a good chance that he wouldn't be in time or able to help the Portal City situation, but he had to try if he could. He could also miss some crucial revelation from Charles. But he had made up his mind, and he had to project decisiveness and certainty, though his own mind was not even close to made up.

When he'd gone far beyond the encampment perimeter, he dialed a cab. He was walking much more easily now, he realized. He almost didn't need the cane. He asked the cab driver to take him to the train station and watched Citrine pass by as the cab sped down nearly empty streets.

Just under two weeks ago, he'd seen this same city through the windows of a cab on his way to give a speech, one intended to bring people together. And now here they were ready to explode at each other.

Sahaan shook his head, and hoped his decided path was the correct one.

Charles had only been on an airplane three times before in his life. All three times had been for academic conferences when he'd been in graduate school, activities which he had gladly dropped once professional life had supplanted academia. He supposed this trip was a conference of sorts, albeit a much different one than any he'd attended in the past.

He looked out the window of his plane, watching the water below. From this height, it appeared a flat, static surface. So much water, stretching in all directions. It was comforting that this view, at least, had been untouched by humans and their nanite sculpting technology. It was, however, hard to ignore the glittering sparks of blue that passed through the air in the plane's wake, an effect of the quantum slipstream technology that allowed the plane to exceed the speed of sound without creating sonic cacophony. Their trains utilized the same technology. Whole continents could be traversed in a matter of hours. One of the early wonders of deeper sub-atomic investigation. But now all the wonders were gone, and a physicist's job was to complete a catalogue that insisted on belching up three new mysteries for every element they managed to completely document.

"We're beginning our descent into Eveling," the computer pilot broadcast to each passenger's mind. "The local time is ten-twenty-seven. We will be landing at eleven-fifteen. It is partly cloudy and eighteen degrees in Eveling. Please sit back and enjoy the rest of the trip."

Charles decided to take the computer's advice. He lay

his head back against the headrest and closed his eyes. He tried to imagine what a person waking up inside the vestigzone would experience. They wouldn't be able to call out for help over wireless. They would have neither wireless communication adapter nor receivers. They would have organs called a mouth, vocal cords, and ears. They would have to call out to others by vibrating air with their vocal cords. How would he make sure such a person could speak the vestig's language? He could fill the ambassador's mind with their writing (plenty of that remained in the Pinnacle's archives), but how to give the ambassador the ability to speak it?

Still too many problems and too much risk.

He felt the plane start to descend, and when he looked out his window, he now found land passing below his eyes. Everywhere he looked, the same reddish-brown earth splotched with tufts of silver. The silver spread out in every direction, a writhing, serpentine mass.

The blue sparks became more scarce, then disappeared completely, and the plane's speed decreased noticeably.

Charles took a deep breath and closed his eyes once more, remaining that way until he felt the plane bounce against the anti-grav runway and slow to a crawl. Once the plane had taxied and parked, Charles gathered up his things and exited into the airport.

He made his way through the terminal, and since he didn't have any luggage, made his way directly out onto the frontage road.

"I've arrived," Charles called out over the network.

"Welcome to Eveling," Broderick Wayland replied. "Are you feeling decharged from the flight?"

"I could use a charge," Charles admitted.

"I know a good place." This message came with physical coordinates and a web reference for a restaurant attached. "Meet you there at three?"

"Sounds good. See you then."

Charles looked up the coordinates of his hotel and took off toward it. Best to freshen up first. It wasn't every day you got to meet the source of your inspiration.

The train from Citrine to Adamantine was eerily vacant. Only two other passengers were in the entire car, a mother and her infant daughter, sitting up front.

Sahaan found himself constantly refreshing the news feeds on his handheld, looking for some indication that the news had picked up the movements Lachel had noticed. Sahaan wondered if a contingent from Citrine was headed toward the capital as well. If so, they had taken a train prior to his. And despite having put in a message to the Hilltop Suite that he would reach the capital by dusk, he had heard nothing in reply. Bharo had messaged that he was preparing for a morning departure to Citrine.

Under normal circumstances, Sahaan would have gladly taken such an opportunity for a mental break, but he found himself wracked with worry. He simply could not take his mind off of the congregation that Lachel had seen and its implications. He wished he could be in the capital now.

In the distant past, his ancestors had possessed the technology of flight, but with the wall's effective vertical range not reaching higher than about ten stories, such modes of travel had been impractical since the war. It didn't stop him, however, from wishing for a thirty-minute flight between Citrine and Portal City.

At the Adamantine train station, he switched platforms so as to board the next train heading through Adrine to Portal City. A train arrived within ten minutes, and he boarded, noting this one also, was nearly deserted, containing only a man in a suit and tie and a young woman carrying a backpack, probably still in school.

Both exited in Adrine twenty minutes later, leaving Sahaan alone in the train car.

Sahaan stood up, walked to each end of his train car and peered into each of the adjacent cars in turn. Both were also vacant.

As he walked back to his seat, his phone dinged. Then again. Before he had even sat down, a flurry of activity appeared on his feed.

First—satellite video of mobs of people gathering at the edge of the containment center; military and police equipped with riot gear gathered at their periphery.

Second—satellite video of a similar mob forming around the Alterran portal facility; military and police with riot gear were attempting to reach those few attempting to hold the barricade.

Third—messages from the Hilltop Suite notifying all staff of an upcoming presidential broadcast.

Fourth—government state of emergency notifications.

And then a new notification, a video feed, streaming directly from the largest news broadcaster in the Reclamation.

President Aavee appeared on Sahaan's handheld, his form projected oversized atop the containment area facility.

"Citizens of the Reclamation," the president announced. "We find ourselves in the midst of extraordinary circumstances. One hundred and twenty-one years ago, we were victorious in securing our land against a formidable enemy. But the time of war has been long over, and an envoy of that former enemy has reached out to us, extending the possibility of peaceful coexistence."

The president was interrupted by shouting from the crowd, which grew ever louder. It was hard to hear, especially over the handheld, what individual voices were saying, but Sahaan did catch a few tidbits such as, "we're being invaded," "down with the Seditious party," and "kill the invaders."

"I ask you now to return to your homes. It is not possible to open the Alterran portal at this time. My government is working on a plan to return those trapped inside the containment area to their original human forms—"

A lot happened all at once in the moments that followed. Someone shouted "kill them," and fired an energy weapon at the containment field.

"Do not fire at the containment center!" President Aavee ordered. "You will only damage our defensive network!"

Indeed, the shimmering containment field wobbled where bolts of energy hit it. Only a few at first, and then more.

And then Aavee, looking sadder, older, and more disappointed than Sahaan had ever seen him, said, "Troops are authorized to use any means necessary to neutralize those who threaten our containment field." And his hologram flickered away to nothing.

Sahaan gulped and gasped simultaneously.

The satellite imagery erupted into a veritable warzone of beams of light, some impacting officers, some impacting civilians, and many more being absorbed into the shimmering field. All at once, that field blobbed outward, expanding into and through a contingent of soldiers fighting hand-to-hand with civilians. Another blob emerged from that one, then another blob out the other side. The containment field continued expanding in fits and bursts, eating up buildings, streetcars, people, anything and everything succumbed. And it didn't stop, rather the blobbing expansions came faster, picking up speed and engulfing whole city blocks at a time. Screaming people, tripped people, injured people all were overtaken by the field and absorbed. Before too long, the field wasn't absorbing any gunfire, as all of the shooters had been absorbed into the zone, and still the zone expanded. The footage became a side-by-side view with the portal, where scared citizens had completely burst through the police and military barricades and were now hurtling themselves through the portal to Alterra. And still, on the other half of Sahaan's screen, the expansion continued, the hazy white field spilling down streets and engulfing building after building, until— the Hilltop Suite! The blobs marched up the hill crashing through the parliament building's west wing, then spilling over to eat up the middle and east wing, too. On it went, up the hill, all the way to the Suite, where it bulged again, engulfing the north half of the structure.

And there it stopped.

Sahaan gulped. His breath came fast, and his heart felt as if it might pound out of his chest.

The locomotive, oblivious to the calamity, continued

on its course unperturbed, carrying Sahaan toward the disaster zone.

The news anchor remained silent, and the satellite image shifted to a single view, a full topology of Portal City, the new boundaries of the containment zone clearly outlined. It now encompassed nearly a quarter of the city, from the northwest city limits to the Hilltop Suite. The portal remained outside the zone, lying a kilometer south of the Hilltop Suite.

Sahaan's handheld rang, interrupting the video feed. How much time had passed since the horrific images from his handheld? Five minutes? Ten? He wasn't certain. From a glance at the handheld's clock, perhaps ten.

He answered the call.

"Hello." A young woman's jittery voice. "Is this Senior Consul Sahaan Ekeer?"

"Speaking."

"This is Assistant Communications Director Khatra Aapada." Sahaan remembered her. He'd introduced himself, and they'd spoken briefly about work-related matters on a handful of occasions since. "I appear to be the most senior member of staff remaining outside the containment zone. I've gotten everyone out of the Hilltop Suite, and we are headed southeast. Our destination is the meeting hall near the Alterran embassy. We'll set up a provisional government there."

"That's a good plan, Mrs. Aapada. I take it, then, that the president—"

"He is inside the containment zone, yes."

"And the Parliament Majority Leader?"

"We have not heard from him, and both parliament buildings were completely absorbed, sir."

The 'sir' clinched it, and Sahaan knew what her next words would be before they were even out of his hand-held speaker.

"I believe that makes you the acting president, sir."

"Yes," Sahaan said. "That is indeed the protocol."

Although Charles had grown up in Grandtown, a suburb of Redwing, he'd visited a handful of other cities. It was a thought he'd had before, but now, seeing Eveling, it only reinforced his sense of the homogeneity of all the Pinnacle's cities. The same prefabs had been used to construct everything, from train stations to storefronts to skyscrapers. Walking the streets of Eveling, Charles felt himself to be occupying a reorganized and somewhat smaller version of Redwing.

Did it have to be that way? He wasn't sure. At any rate, it didn't seem to bother most people. Brad had been the first person who seemed to notice the same things that Charles did. Whenever he'd broached the topic at work, he'd be confronted with befuddled stares and social awkwardness. Not that he'd tried much. He'd quickly developed a personal policy of his work relations remaining strictly about work.

At last he came upon the restaurant that Broderick had sent him. It had been duplicated from the same prefab as two restaurants near his workplace in Redwing, although this establishment had a different name and had chosen a different color scheme for the decor. But everything else: the chairs, tables, and layout of the furnishings were an exact copy.

"Charles?"

He turned around to find himself facing a man perhaps five to ten years older than himself, slightly taller, and imposingly broad frame. But his smile proved disarming, and Charles smiled back. "Broderick! I'm Charles Mayworth. Great to meet you."

"Likewise."

A waiter approached, and Broderick asked them to look up a reservation under his name. Shortly thereafter, they found themselves seated at a table with a north-facing view of the Bekel plains and a small, spiky offshoot of the Nakash mountain range.

"It's great to finally meet you," Broderick said.

"Same here."

"Are you still thinking of writing an interpretation of *The Politics*?"

"I'm still going back and forth on that. No one would scan it. And I'd probably end up just repeating others anyway."

"You should write it. Someone has to keep the torch of wisdom burning."

"Torch of wisdom?"

"A very old metaphor for a very old human problem. It may seem as though we have entered a dark age for intellectual inquiry, but if you read enough Kenek, Rema, Xelas, and the other ancients, then you'll see that getting too worked up in what's best *practically* rather than *actually* is a human failing that far predates the Break. Though the Break certainly didn't help it any."

"But it's caused all these problems."

"That's true, but think also about what good it's done. Are you familiar with the concept of disease?"

"Sure."

"It is very different for vestigs. For example, search for

the term 'cancer.'"

Charles did as instructed, and within moments he'd absorbed the synopsis of all relevant data on the many permutations of the disease. Charles gulped twisted up his face, revolted. "And this can just... happen to any of them?"

"And now think of what it must have been like to contract this disease before public medicine, before the various therapies you've just learned of. And us? We just correct the offending code. Done. Do not blithely discount these advances."

Charles couldn't believe what he was hearing. "But deceleration, everything you've written..."

"It's all true. I think that biological forms of the vestigs offer a deeper, fuller human experience than ours, even if it is more fragile and more fraught."

"And what do you think of communication with them?"

Broderick initiated encryption of their conversation. "It needs to happen."

Charles took a quick glance around the restaurant. "Is it safe to talk about this here?"

"Encrypted, it is safe enough."

"Brad and I wouldn't think twice about talking about such things in Redwing."

"Redwing is far from the vestigs' walls. Here in Eveling, the topic cannot be discussed as lightly."

Charles nodded. "Why does it need to happen, though? We could go on as we have been."

"No. That's exactly why everyone is moving toward the extremes of the political field."

Charles quirked an eyebrow. That the political arena

was growing more tendentious, that the extreme parties were growing and the moderate ones shrinking, was all common knowledge. But no one had publicly presumed to analyze *why* that was occurring.

"You like stories, Charles. I can tell that from our letters. When you scan a lot of stories, you can start to compare them. Once you've compared enough of them, you can start to analyze them, and once you've done enough analysis, you can start to tell the true ones from the false ones, false in the sense that they are distorting reality rather than making it clearer.

"Now, here's the thing. Everyone, everywhere, is telling themselves stories all the time, without even realizing it. An example is the extreme left. The story they are convinced is true is that the vestigs behind the walls are dangerous barbarians with weapons of mass destruction, their fingers poised over the ignition buttons. You and I know that this is likely a false story. But to the people who believe this, it *is* reality. They have no framework with which to make a better evaluation.

"The reason we need to contact the vestigs is that, if we did, we would all finally have real data about what their intentions are, and we could all stop guessing. I worry that, if we become too extreme, then even real data wouldn't matter anymore. The crazy stories would simply become reality. No amount of contradictory information has ever dissuaded the true zealot from his crusade."

"Crusade?"

"Search it."

Charles did. Then he checked that the encryption was still active. "But contacting them could also disrupt them. What if they're telling themselves crazy stories, too, and all it would take is a message to send them into chaos?"

"Yes. That is a risk. But then they would merely be proving our hard left-h parties correct, and that would make for a very bleak future of Asura."

Charles pondered that for a time. "Do you know how to *read*, not scan, but really read?"

Broderick smiled and unencrypted their conversation. "Yes."

"So, when you read, can you really hear the words' pronunciations in your mind? You could synthesize speech if you needed to?"

"I used a scan of a very old book out of the University of Nightbridge. It's a very technical document from an ancient field of the academy called linguistics. It was a comparison of acoustic and digital encodings of meaning. Part of it contained a synopsis of the phonetics of the vestigs' language."

"Two hundred years..." Charles's shoulders slouched. "Then, the pronunciations of the words have probably all changed."

"It's possible, but my understanding is that it takes language much longer to change, especially in societies with a public education system, and it's extremely unlikely that they've given that one up."

Charles perked up. "Is this research you could share?"

"Certainly," Broderick said.

The waiter returned and asked for their order just then. At that moment, Charles couldn't have been more glad he'd made this trip. He'd found just what he'd been looking for.

Sahaan stepped into a room that felt like a parallel reality version of the meeting hall he remembered. It contained all the familiar decor, the flags on the wall, Alterra's and Asura's side by side. But the rest... an intern with disheveled hair talked frantically into her handheld. A young man wearing a headset sat at the far end of the conference room furiously typing on his computer, and on and on. All in all, perhaps some forty of the Hilltop Suite staff were here, all busy, some sweating, others jittery.

"Mr. President?" Assistant Director Khatra Aapada stood at his side.

"Mrs. Aapada. What's our status?"

"Yes, sir. First, the containment field. It is, thankfully, stable. However, the emergency generators in all twelve cities are now active, and it is only with their combined output that the containment field is stable. However, we estimate that we will run out of fuel first at the Enerine reactor in ninety-seven days, at which point the containment zone will begin to expand again. Second, is our military capacity, which has yet to be determined. We have not been able to contact any members of Central Command. We are continuing to try to find out who is still in charge at the portal, but it sounds like most, if not all, of the senior officers were near the containment zone. We are working on getting estimates of how much of the military remains and where they are. Since we ordered the military to divert as many troops as possible to Portal City, we expect casualties to be quite high. And finally, civilian casualties. Now, I've been told that these numbers are a guess at best, and we won't be able to tell for sure unless we can get our nanites into the containment zone—"

"The number, Mrs. Aapada."

"We estimate between 7,000 and 18,000 civilians were absorbed into the containment zone."

Sahaan bit his lip. Mrs. Aapada herself had only barely been able to speak the words. Her voice came out raspy and her words clipped. Deep inside, Sahaan wanted to shriek out, his rage near blinding. But he kept that down, deep down. If the Reclamation was to have a future, he now had to be the best human he could possibly be. There was no one else left.

"Understood. Have we talked to the media?"

"Portal One Studio is now inside the containment zone, sir." They were the Reclamation's most watched broadcaster. "They are off the air. The others are only showing satellite footage of the capital, at least for the time being."

"Let's get in contact with them. It will show them that we have a plan and we're on top of the situation. I'm going to draft a speech. Tell them I would like it broadcast to every city."

"I'll get right on that, sir."

"And I want regular updates on the military situation. We'll need every last surviving soldier. Oh, and one more thing, see if someone can get ahold of Bharo Meharab. He should be in the Adamantine Central Hospital. He'll want to come here, but I want him out in Citrine instead, as he and I had originally planned."

"Understood, sir."

Mrs. Aapada ran off.

Sahaan looked around the large room. As he recalled,

there were a few offices somewhere behind the central meeting chamber. He now needed to focus on what he would tell his country.

"Hey, Brad?"

"Hey, Charles! It's been a while. How have you been?"

"Well, all right..."

"Sounds like maybe not so great."

"I need someone to talk to, and I wasn't sure who I could reach out to. I was hoping we could talk."

"Sure, man. Sure thing. What's going on?"

"I'm about to make a decision. A big one. I was able to avoid it for a while. It was impractical. So, it was easy to dismiss it— What kind of encryption is this?"

"Best you don't ask. Suffice to say, only me and a few people know the decoder for this one. ... You still there?"

"Yeah. Yeah. I guess, I was just saying that it was easy to ignore this problem when it was only a pipe dream, something that wasn't even practical, anyway. But I've solved all the problems. It's just pushing a button now, but I don't know if I can make this decision for so many people. In my work, we have these big bureaucracies, and, sure, they stifle individuals from going off and doing their own thing, but most of the time that's good. And maybe my case is like that. Maybe there are a lot of other people who know way more than I do about the situation, and there's a good reason why they haven't acted."

"No one knows any more about the vestigs than you or I."

"Brad, it's best if you don't guess at what—"

"I knew three years ago when you were first hinting at it."

"I don't want anyone else responsible for this."

"So you can carry it all alone? Clearly that's bothering you. How did it happen, anyway?"

"Brad..."

"I trust this encryption, if that's what you're worried about. It can't be broken. Not in our lifetimes, anyway."

"... One of the sub-atomic particles I catalogued early in my career, it was the one that makes the vestigs' walls work."

"No fucking way."

"I kept it to myself. I documented it as inert for the official records and kept the real observations to myself. You now have the power to end my career, by the way."

"How does that translate to getting a person inside their walls, though?"

"I did my own tests, made some samples of iron with the quantum properties induced. They're pretty resilient. The quantum field can absorb a lot of energy, but there's a point at which the matter changes. And you can use the orientation of the incoming energy to move the particles of the wall around. And that means—"

"Holy fuck." Brad let out a laugh. "You're going to turn their walls *into* a person?"

"Yeah. That's the idea, anyway."

"So, once you do this, can the left overrun their walls?"

"No, I don't think so. Doing this doesn't allow anyone to find the sub-atomic particle in question. But it would allow them to repeat the process of changing a wall."

"Right, like we talked about before."

"Yeah."

"Well, let's look at our options. We can do nothing

with this information, in which case, the parties get more extreme, and more insane, until one day someone does decide to attack the vestigs somehow. Or we can use it, in which case we get a person inside their borders who can talk to them, tell them about us, about *all* of us, and also the potential that one of our groups will repeat the process."

"And I'll go to jail."

"Assuming they trace it back to you."

"They will."

"Let me help with that part."

"Brad—"

"You asked for my help."

"I did."

"So let me help."

"Okay. Sure. Last logistical problem."

"Shoot."

"We need a template for the memories and personality."

Brad sighed. "I already told you the answer to that, too."

"C'mon. Seriously? He's going to need to talk politics, not physics."

"Damn it, Charles. What was the very first book you told me about?"

"Reading a three-thousand-year-old research paper called *The Politics* is a bit different from brokering international peace, don't you think?"

"Maybe. Or maybe you're just the right mix of passion, intelligence, and patience."

"..."

"Charles?"

"Thank you."

"See. Any of my other friends would be screaming back at me by now."

Charles chortled. "Fine."

"So, what has to be done next?"

"Nothing."

"Nothing?"

"Nothing. I already executed the program."

"You wrote a computer program that can transform a wall on another continent into a person?"

"Yeah."

"Techies..."

"Go to hell."

"After you, my friend."

A knock on his door. Was it his door? Sahaan supposed it was. He was the president, after all. But this did not feel like his room. In his brief survey, he had discovered stuffed into the room's shelves and desk drawers a million bits of paraphernalia from so many decades' past negotiations between Alterra and the Reclamation. It certainly did not feel like 'his' room.

Another knock.

"Come in," Sahaan said.

A man pulled the door cautiously open, still bumping it into a stack of boxes, regardless. He slid into the room and stood up straight. Sahaan recognized him as the ambassador of Alterra, a Mr. Rajaad Ot.

"Hello, Mr. Ot."

"President Ekeer."

Would that ever cease to feel weird? "What can I do for you?"

"First of all, let me say that your staff are handling the situation remarkably well, given the circumstances."

"Thank you, Mr. Ot."

"I was wondering if I might be permitted to send my report through the portal today, despite..." He merely let the sentence hang.

"That will be fine. I'll write you something for the officers stationed there."

"Might I also know, Mr. President, since I must make recommendations to my government, whether or not the containment field is stable?"

"All indications are that it is now perfectly stable."

"I see. But its southeast edge is now less than a kilometer from the portal."

"It is."

"And how long can your generators keep it stable? Is it a matter of weeks, days, hours?"

"*Months*, Mr. Ot."

"I see. Still, I think it best to inform you that my recommendation to my government is that we construct walls around our portal. As a precaution."

Sahaan took a deep breath to calm himself. "That seems prudent. I would probably do the same thing in your position. Do you expect any political difficulties on Alterra?"

"On the contrary, I expect they will want to know what they can do to help."

"Thank you, Mr. Ot. I will keep that in mind."

"Thank you, Mr. President." Mr. Ot pulled the door open as far as he could, once again banging it into the stack of boxes, and slid out the door.

Sahaan shook his head and returned his attention to

his speech.

"Sahaan?"

"Hi, Lachel."

"Oh, Sahaan. Is it true?"

"Depends what it is."

"That you're the acting president."

"Yes, that's true."

"And is the containment zone really stable again?"

"Yes."

"Good. That's good. How are you holding up? I wish we could be there with you."

"You and Jaan stay in Barine. Please."

"It makes sense. You're right, of course. What are you going to do?"

"I was actually calling you about that. I'm preparing a speech. It's going to be... Well, it will be *something*, that's for sure."

"You'll outline a plan for the containment field, I'm sure."

"Yes."

"And a path forward for reconciliation with the nanite-bodied. With the Pinnacle."

"Yes, that too."

"Shouldn't that do?"

"I don't think so."

"Oh?"

"I'm going to use an old trick. A very old one. Politicians have been using it for centuries, probably longer. And I'm not sure how I feel about it."

"What trick is that?"

"Use an emergency to push through policy changes

that are badly needed but were held up during the expansive bureaucracy of peacetime."

"What kind of changes?"

"You'll see in the speech. I wanted to tell you in advance, though, that I have listened to you, and your reasons for loving the Reconciliation Party the way you do. And I want to keep all those good things. I don't want those to go away. There are just... elements that have to change. And we've run out of time. We can't avoid changing them anymore. ... Lachel?"

"I love you so much."

"I love you, too. Tell Jaan I'll come out to Barine as soon as I can. And I haven't forgotten that I owe him a voidball game."

"Break a leg."

"Love you. Goodbye."

"Bye."

"Good evening, fellow citizens of the Reclamation. I am speaking to you from the temporary government headquarters in Portal City. This has been a difficult night for all of us, most especially those of us with a loved one trapped inside the containment zone.

"As many of you have seen already, a group of citizens fired energy weapons into the containment zone earlier this evening. While their intent was to damage the evolver nanites inside the containment zone, their weapons fire instead damaged our own containment nanites, causing the containment field to partially collapse and expand in all directions.

"The containment field is now stable. Let me repeat that. The containment field is now stable. Its continued

234

stability is now dependent on two factors. First, the containment field must absorb no further disruptive forces. Second, the expansion of the field has increased its energy requirement. We now require the emergency generators of all Reclamation cities to remain active until the current emergency has been resolved.

"I wish to make this last point perfectly clear. If Bengine's reactor fails, then Adamantine falls. If Citrine's reactor fails, then Besserine falls. If Eline's reactor fails, then Cynine falls. Each and every one of us must do our part to ensure that the power flow to the capital remains uninterrupted. We stand or fall together.

"Now, to the matter of resolving the current emergency.

"First, it may surprise many of you, especially citizens of Enerine, Exenine, Bengine, Citrine, and Cynine, to hear me say this, but our first resolve must be increased attention to our walls. The nanite-bodied, whose nation we have learned is called the Pinnacle, possess a technology by which they can transmute our wallslabs into people. As we have heard from their holographic ambassador, some of these people will be friendly, others hostile. There is no way to tell until they arrive. My government will be doing everything in its power to stop these visitations until such time as visitors to our country can arrive authorized and cleared through a practice of customs and border inspection, similar to the policy we maintain with our allies on Alterra.

"Second, in addition to being broadcast throughout the Reclamation, from this moment forward, this speech is also being broadcast into every major city of the Pinnacle. It is simultaneously a call to action for our citizens to ensure our continued safety and wellbeing, and also a response to the message sent early this morning by the Pinnacle ambassador Catherine.

"To the citizens of the Pinnacle, I have this message. The government of Reclamation aligns itself ideologically with your center. We too dream of the world you describe, the one where we live in harmony, the one without walls. However, we also recognize the very real political necessity of those walls in the here and now, and we will not dismantle them until such means have been discovered for us to ensure our continued existence in the bio-material form of our choosing, which is decidedly this one. We offer those on your three right political axes the future possibilities of open but controlled travel between our states, trade of our flora, and the opportunity for individuals to become like us and join our society, if that is what they want. To those on your three left political axes, if we are attacked, we will defend ourselves with every last ounce of strength, every last weapon at our disposal, and every last nanite program we can type out. Our friends on the parallel world Alterra are indeed strong, and the current emergency has only bolstered our alliance.

"However, we do not want to resort to weapons, or to merely trade with you from behind our walls. The path we *want* is the one described by Catherine. That is what we will work toward, despite the limitations imposed by the practicalities of both the left and the right.

"Citizens of the Reclamation, tomorrow you will vote for a new president, who is to take office in one month's time. You will vote either Reconciliation or Guardian, and I urge you to vote with both your hearts and minds

236

for whichever candidate you think most capable.

"It occurred to me, however, as I drafted this speech, that the path I am laying forward for us, is neither a path of 'reconciliation' nor a purely 'guarded' posture. It is a path of both. I dislike the idea of choosing one or the other of two policies, which are both crucial to our survival. For the duration of my time as president, I will not be representing the Reconciliation Party. Rather, I represent Cooperation. Call that a party, if you wish, though at present it has a membership of merely one. If there is one thing you take away from my speech, let it be this: Dazine does not survive without Exenine. Adrine does not survive without Citrine. And the same for every other city. We stand or fall together.

"Thank you, and good night. Rest well, for we have much work ahead of us."

"Mr. President?"

A shake of his shoulder.

Sahaan jolted awake out of a dreamless sleep. His head was slumped in his arms atop his desk in the small office with the piles of boxes partially obstructing the door. He sat up straight and blinked a few times.

"Mrs. Aapada." Sahaan's view came into focus. "What time is it, Mrs. Aapada?"

"Eight, Mr. President."

"Has there been any communication from the Pinnacle?"

"No, sir."

"And the staff?"

"Busy, sir. Well, about two-thirds of them to be precise. I divided everyone into three groups. They're taking turns getting four hours of sleep each. But I make sure each discipline is represented in each group, so we won't be lacking a skill set at any point."

"Good work, Mrs. Aapada. I think the military has a term, a field promotion. How would you like to be my acting Vice President?"

"I would be honored, Mr. President."

"You're doing an excellent job. Now, which of these three groups are you in?"

"I hadn't assigned myself to one."

"Well, as acting president and acting vice president, we need to cover for each other. I've gotten my four hours of sleep, so now it's your turn. What do I need to take care of during that time?"

"Yes, sir. The communications team is monitoring for any sign of a signal, and also preparing for the media briefing at ten. We've decided to have it in front of the View Seven building, since all the usual venues are... unavailable. There's the military liaison who should be arriving back from the portal soon with an update. If he's not back within an hour or two, we'll want to get someone in communications on that too, make sure the situation there isn't degrading. And the science division has their hands full. Definitely keep an eye on them. They're still monitoring the containment field, of course. The acting science director, a young man by the name of Vigy, he said he's concerned about the power requirements, and he's preparing some new models. I think that's all the major items."

"Thank you, Mrs. Aapada." Sahaan moved to the door. "Time for you to take a break now. That's an order."

She hesitated for a moment uncomfortably before the

238

door. "May I... perhaps use this room, sir. My apartment, it was near the Hilltop Suite."

"Of course."

"Thank you, Mr. President."

Sahaan exited the office, walked down the short hall, and entered into the main diplomatic meeting space turned office of the Ekeer presidency. He almost allowed himself a small grin at the ridiculousness of it all, when he noticed that the entirety of the staff had huddled in one corner of the room.

Sahaan approached the group. "What's going on?"

The entire group stood upright, moved away from the center of the enclosure of people, to reveal a young man with brown hair, glasses and freckles gazing into a holographic computer display. No one spoke.

"I asked a question," Sahaan said.

The man at the computer screen gulped, cleared his throat, stood and looked at Sahaan. "They've replied. Sort of."

"Sort of?"

"It's just data," a woman near him said.

"Data for what?"

"Tell him about the header," the woman said.

"Mr. President," the young man began, "I could be misinterpreting this, so it's really not ready."

Sahaan lowered his head and gazed down at the young man. "What do you believe it to say, at this moment?"

"We think it's schematics. For a communication device. A real-time communication device."

Sahaan nodded. "Communications team, science team. This is now your top priority. Everyone else, back to your assignments, please."

The crowd dispersed to other desks.

"If it is schematics," Sahaan said. "Can we verify the device isn't dangerous?"

"It looks like they've gone out of their way to send us schematics rather than a computer program for nanite assembly. It will take us a bit longer to build one, but I think we'll be able to verify the safety fairly easily."

"Could they transfer a program into the containment zone with this?"

The man shook his head. "I don't think so."

"I want us to be absolutely certain."

"Yes, Mr. President."

Sahaan looked around him. Everywhere around him people were typing at computers, talking into handhelds, or conversing with one another. The room felt alive with energy, but he himself felt spent. And for the first time since leaving the hospital, his left side felt worse rather than better. He would have to push through. For Lachel and Jaan, for the people trapped in the containment center, for the entire Reclamation. All his responsibility now. From here on out, there would be no second chances for any wrong decisions.

For the next four hours, Sahaan dealt with all the paraphernalia of minor problems that cropped up and needed solving. The other news agencies contacted them with a complaint that View Seven was being singled out for favoritism, and Sahaan had the venue moved to a neutral location, an intersection in the business district now abandoned. The science team's research adjuncts also needed help gaining access to a number of online systems, which only senior staff were normally allowed to access.

Before Sahaan knew it, Mrs. Aapada strode into their makeshift office, looking fully rested and ready to go, despite the fact that she must still have been exhausted. Sahaan gave her a rundown of their situation, primarily with regards to the science team's discovery.

"They're still at it," Sahaan nodded toward the scientists, all of them poring over their monitors.

"I'm sure they'll make absolutely certain it's safe first."

"Naturally."

"How do you think they'll respond to your message? The Pinnacle, I mean."

She'd intuited his great fear. "My hope is that they will want to discuss the terms of a non-aggression treaty. Can you take things from here?"

"Absolutely, Mr. President."

"Thank you." Sahaan retreated into his office, closed the door gently, sat down in his chair, and leaned back into it as far as it would go. His side was killing him. And was he sweating? Damn it. Of all the times...

He dialed Mrs. Aapada's handheld.

"Yes, Mr. President?"

"I need you to find me a doctor. Please do not tell any of the staff."

"Yes, sir. Right away."

He set the handheld down on his desk and put his head in his hands. He told himself that we would pick the handheld up again if he felt lightheaded or woozy, or anything else. The pain in his side flared, and he leaned back again. Far from picking up his handheld, he drifted off into a morass of pain. Somewhere in his head, he registered himself slumping against the desk, then part of him hit the floor, but after that, there was merely nothing.

Sahaan awoke prone, horizontal, an oddly familiar face filling his entire field of vision.

"Mr. President?" Dr. Darshak asked.

"Yes?"

"Good to see you again."

"Good to see you, too. You're in Portal City?"

"You've been unconscious for some time. Please don't try to get up."

"Is Mrs. Aapada—?"

"I'm here." Mrs. Aapada's voice was nearby, but he could not see her.

"I need a status update."

"Mr. President." Dr. Darshak exhaled. "You've worsened your condition by driving your body to exhaustion. You need to rest."

"No," Sahaan said. "Absolutely not. Do we have the device, Mrs. Aapada? And is the doctor cleared?"

"To the extent that we can reproduce the procedure, he is cleared. We have the device ready to go, but we have been waiting for you, sir. I should say, we have figured out how to route their communications protocol through our own computers. The scientists think it should be even safer than building the device outlined in their schematics."

"Good. Then we can do it from my office." Sahaan recognized the ceiling and walls. He was still in his small office in the back of the meeting hall.

"I don't recommend that," Dr. Darshak said.

"Is my life in danger?" Sahaan asked.

"Not now, but if you continue to exert yourself—"

"Can I sit up?"

"Only if you do so carefully. Let me help. Mrs. Aapada?"

With the two of them at his side, they first raised his torso, so he was sitting on the floor, then helped him rise to a stance, hobble on weak legs to his desk, where he fell more than sat into his reclining chair there.

"We'll do it here," Sahaan said to Mrs. Aapada. "Can you have them prepare that?"

"Right away." No sooner had she said the words than she was out the door.

Dr. Darshak crossed his arms and leaned back against the wall.

"Thank you, doctor," Sahaan said softly. "I have to be strong around all of them." He nodded toward the door. "And even her. In a way, especially her. She'll have a long and fruitful career after this. But only if we can make productive contact." A pain shot through his side and he winced.

The doctor shook his head. "You need a proper recovery. In a hospital."

"I need to do this."

"Can't you leave it to her?"

"No. I sent them the invitation to talk. It has to be me."

Dr. Darshak bit his lip. "Any responsibilities that you can give up you give to her. And you let me know immediately if your symptoms get worse."

"I will."

An awkward silence descended upon the room, but fortunately, Mrs. Aapada returned just a few minutes later with the brown-haired scientist Sahaan had spoken to earlier that day.

"One more thing," Mrs. Aapada said, while the scientist began setting up a computer on Sahaan's desk. "It's one in the afternoon. The polling has started."

Sahaan nodded and even managed a small smile. "This will certainly be an election cycle for the history books."

"All ready, Mr. President," the scientist said. "When you're ready, just hit this button."

"And then I'll be connected to them?"

"If they're receiving, yes."

"Well, let's get started then." Sahaan tapped the holographic button in front of him. It expanded into a window showing two horizontal lines. "Hello?" Sahaan said. The left line burst into a waveform. The right line remained a line.

"Hello?" Sahaan tried again. "This is Sahaan Ekeer, President of the Reclamation."

Nothing. They waited for ten, maybe twenty seconds. No sound emanated from the computer. Sahaan looked at the scientist with a raised eyebrow. The young man leaned in toward the computer hands reaching toward the keyboard—

"Hello." The voice was monotone and androgynous, giving the impression of ancient voice synthesizer technology. "This is... This is Charles. I am a... a citizen of the Pinnacle. Please forgive me. I am translating. I am doing my best. Catherine's message was prepared."

"Is this... your own voice?" Sahaan asked.

"We do not have voices. One hundred and six years ago the mouth and voice box were removed from our species. They were no longer necessary. It was decided."

"It's good to talk to you, Charles. Thank you for making this communication possible. Please tell me, what has been the reaction in the Pinnacle to my message?" Sahaan asked.

"Argument. Debate. The leftwards parties, they are afraid. Some want to talk, though. They still worry about the portal universe. The right is eager to talk. So we can talk."

"I appreciate the opportunity. And I have a proposal for the Pinnacle."

"Yes?"

"I would like you to tell me if you believe it will be viable. If the Pinnacle will accept the proposal."

"I am listening."

"I am proposing an agreement called a non-aggression treaty. It will have stipulations. Things that each side must agree to. Do you understand so far?"

"Yes."

"The Reclamation will agree to the following three things. Number one. We will select twenty-five different floral organisms from the parallel universe and send them to you. Number two. We will make a selection of pre-war history and literature available to you. Number three. We will agree not to expand our wall system for a period of no less than ten years, with provisions to extend that time frame. Any questions?"

"No, President Sahaan Ekeer. That is clear. Please continue."

"In return, the Pinnacle will agree to the following three things. Number one. Visitations in the form of walls transforming into people must cease completely for a period of no less than ten years. Number two. The Pinnacle will provide access to a selection of your history and literature of the last one hundred and twenty years. Number three. The Pinnacle will provide us with a means to *un*-evolve the Reclamation citizens who were transformed by Samantha's nanites."

Silence.

"Charles?"

"Numbers one and two are easy. Number three... It will be difficult here."

"My number three will be difficult for me as well."

"Your Charles... Has he told you yet what my job is? Does he remember at all?"

"He has said that you're a physicist."

"I *was* a physicist."

"You are not anymore?"

"I broke our law."

"I don't understand."

"I sent you Charles."

Sahaan had to blink a few times as he processed that. "But, is this discussion authorized?"

"Yes. This new position is part of my... There's no word. Let's call it parole."

"I see."

"Can I speak to Charles?"

"I'm afraid he's in another city. But I assure you he's quite well."

"I would like to be able to speak to him. Tell me, have you shown him a library?"

"Not yet. I'll be sure to find a way to do that."

"I have digressed, President Sahaan Ekeer. I apologize. I will deliver your proposal to my government, and they will discuss it."

"Thank you, Charles."

"President Sahaan Ekeer?"

"Yes?"

"Your speech to my country. It was more memorable than your country's previous communications. You have given the impression of a strong country, united and determined. It is commendable."

"Thank you, Charles. I hope we get to learn more about the Pinnacle in the near future."

"I hope so, too. Goodbye."

"Goodbye, Charles."

Dr. Darshak stood leaning against the door frame, his arms crossed. "I presume you'll need to be available when he responds."

"Yes," Sahaan said. He slid his computer down the desk to the young scientist, who was clearly eager to begin analyzing whatever data it had collected from the call with Charles.

"And then after that can we get you to a hospital so that you can heal properly?"

"I suppose it depends on what the reply is."

At that moment, acting Vice President Aapada took a call on her handheld and excused herself into the hallway.

"I can oblige one more call, perhaps even a few. But this cannot go on for days. You need better medical attention that I can provide for you here."

"And our country needs to survive this crisis. This is bigger than just my life now—"

Khatra Aapada stepped back through the doorway and walked to the side of Sahaan's desk where the scientist sat busily typing at the computer.

"Pull up View Seven on there. Quickly."

The scientist hesitated only a moment before

"What's going on?" Sahaan asked.

Aapada nodded toward the computer monitor, which the scientist was now spinning around for the whole room to see.

An anchor sat behind a stylized graphic design with the words: "Guardian, Reconciliation— Cooperation?"

The anchor sat poised, affecting a concerned and deliberate countenance. "A rough estimate at this time is that the Cooperation party has received eighteen percent of the vote. It is important to note that, at this juncture, only twenty-nine of a total of two hundred forty-seven districts have reported their ballots, and so this may still be only a temporary aberration. However, imagine that Cooperation write-ins were to receive a majority of the vote. The party has no officials, no established procedures, no council of delegates, none of the political infrastructure required in order to allow it to function. Presumably, President Ekeer would be the obvious choice to carry our government into the next term, but who would be his vice president? Who would compose his cabinet? We will continue to bring you live election coverage as the votes are confirmed. Again, at this time, the standings are Guardian 42%, Reconciliation 41%, Cooperation 18%." Aapada reached down to the computer keyboard and stopped the video.

Sahaan was awestruck. He had simply needed people to set aside their political differences long enough to keep the generators running. But, of course, people weren't that simple. They'd heard him. His message had come through loud and clear, and now... He looked at Dr. Darshak and had the sudden memory of telling him in the train, just two days ago, that politicians should be able to count on the political apparatus to correct the consequences of their decisions in the long term. Well, this was quite decidedly short term.

"We leave this alone," Sahaan decided. "It's tomorrow's problem. I added the Cooperation bit to keep us unified in our defense of the power grid and the containment zone. If I walk that back now, the results could be disastrous. If 'Cooperation' wins the election, we can deal with that in a month." He glanced at Aapada. "What do you think?"

"I agree. As you say, at least people have unified to protect the walls and the power stations. The election is a secondary priority."

"Good," Sahaan said.

The computer monitor began oscillating a waveform pattern and emitted a ringing noise not unlike a bell.

"That would be the Pinnacle," the scientist said.

Sahaan took a moment to collect himself, then nodded to the scientist, who pushed a button on the computer and pushed the device toward Sahaan.

"This is President Sahaan Ekeer of the Reclamation," he said.

"This is Charles."

"Hello again. How can I help you?"

"My government has issued a response to your proposal."

"Your government is expedient."

"I was going to apologize for the delay. This particular decision caused much debate."

"I see. What is the response?"

"To items one and two of the Pinnacle's terms, there is

no debate. Those two terms are accepted completely. We need to discuss the... means of the third. The Pinnacle is not willing to share with you the nanite programs which are capable of... changing one of us into one of you."

"I see. Is there a counter-proposal?"

"The Pinnacle realizes this is a crucial term for the Reclamation. We would like to let the provision stand, with a modification. One of us will administer the execution of the nanite program that will change your citizens back. I should be clearer. The proposal is that I will enter the Reclamation, go to the containment zone, and restore your citizens to their original forms. I will also reprogram all Pinnacle nanites to return with me to my country."

Sahaan nodded. "We will need some time to discuss this. We do not operate on your time scale. We will need at least an hour."

"I understand. I will make that clear to my country."

"I will be in touch soon."

"Goodbye."

"Goodbye." Sahaan ended the call.

"Absolutely not," Darshak said.

Sahaan looked at Aapada, who wore the same bemused smirk on her face that Sahaan had. It was a frightening prospect, but imagine if it worked. A Pinnacle citizen walking through the Reclamation, *restoring* humans to their original form. It would be a powerful symbol. It might even be powerful enough to push past the fear that war had ingrained upon Reclamation hearts and minds.

"You're considering it..." The doctor looked between them, aghast.

"The only question," Sahaan said, "is whether or not

we can be reasonably certain that we can keep ourselves safe."

Sahaan gave Khatra instructions to find the most senior remaining military advisor and member of the Engineering Corp as quickly as possible and bring them to his office. Khatra nodded and was out the door without another word.

"Why are they so opposed to just giving us the program?" Dr. Darshak asked.

Sahaan was poised to answer, but the scientist poked his head up from the computer. "Probably because it would let us do to them what they've been doing to us for the last two centuries."

"It would allow us to weaponize that program," Sahaan said. "Given their position, it's a reasonable request."

"*Reasonable?*" The doctor frowned. "What's to prevent them from overrunning the Reclamation once they're inside? They could explode just like Samantha, and this time it won't be inside a containment zone."

The scientist sighed and pushed down the screen of his computer, apparently deciding to fully join the conversation. "I heard that the request is for just one of them. This Charles. Assuming it is just one person, then we have weapons that we know can kill them and inoculations that we know can prevent transformation, correct?"

"Well, yes."

"Sounds as though we could probably manage, as long as we can give Charles a large enough escort." The scientist turned to Sahaan. "How's he supposed to get inside, anyway?"

"That's why I need an Engineering Corp representative," Sahaan said. "I need to know all the possible risks and precautionary measures that can be put in place if we intentionally open up a path through the walls."

"May I be frank, Mr. President?" The doctor asked, eyes wide.

"Certainly."

"This sounds like a plan that will end the Reclamation."

"We have two other options," Sahaan said. "First, we could continue to wait, hoping that another option presents itself within three months, at which point our power will run out and we will be overrun by the nanites inside the containment zone. And then there's the other alternative. Dr. Gyaan, would you please elaborate for the doctor the plan you described to Vice President Aapada?"

"Sure," Gyaan said. "The basic idea is to compress the containment zone into nothing. Right now, our nanites are just holding back the Pinnacle's nanites and preventing them from expanding any further. If we increase their replication rate, we believe we can actually push them back."

"Why on earth aren't we doing that?" Dr. Darshak asked.

"Imagine," Sahaan said, "what one of our citizens inside the zone would experience."

"The shrinking wall would tear apart their bodies when it touched them," Dr. Gyaan said. "It would kill everyone in the containment zone."

Dr. Darshak stood, silently staring at the wall behind the president.

"That remains our plan of last resort," Sahaan said.

"We need to see if we can make the logistics of Charles's plan work before we forfeit the lives of fifteen thousand of our own citizens."

Dr. Darshak nodded, still frowning, but saying nothing. Dr. Gyaan re-activated his computer screen.

Sahaan recalled just then that there was one more thing he needed to do. Sahaan pulled out his handheld and dialed Bharo.

"Hello, Mr. President. You've caught me on a rare excursion to the surface... Do I call you Mr. President now?" Bharo's voice intoned.

Sahaan smiled. "I didn't make the rules. Sure."

"How are you holding up?"

"Pretty well, thanks to the good doctor here. How is Charles holding up?"

"Much better. He's remembering more and more all the time. He's heard about the containment zone incident and he wants to know what he can do to help."

"Great," Sahaan said. "I want you to talk to the military and find out whether or not they're confident that they can safely transport him to my office in Portal City."

"Oh. Okay. Sure. What do you want him to do when he gets there?"

"I'm going to introduce him to his counterpart in the Pinnacle. The man his memories are templated from."

Before too much longer, Khatra Aapada returned with both a man and woman, each of them filing into Sahaan's now very crowded makeshift office.

The man was perhaps Sahaan's age. He wore a military uniform, with medals indicating him to be a Master Sergeant. He also wore a pair of glasses with large, black frames. He stood poised, his eyes scanning everyone and everything in Sahaan's office. Sahaan got the impression he typically sized up situations this way, quickly and perhaps even effortlessly.

The woman wore blue overalls and a brown-grey heather work shirt, the standard garb of the Engineering Corp. Their insignia were woven into the strap of their overalls. Hers had four stripes. A division leader, then. Her gaze was erratic. She looked as though perhaps she might be claustrophobic.

Khatra stepped forward. "Master Sergeant Anush and Supervisor Jeenya, Mr. President."

Sahaan introduced himself. "Forgive me for not standing. My doctor has advised me to remain seated." He shook their hands, then nodded toward the doctor. "This is Dr. Darshak. And also, Dr. Vigy Gyaan, our science advisor. I'll cut right to it. We've established communication with the Pinnacle. They've agreed to undo the damage Samantha caused, but only on the condition that one of them is allowed to enter the Reclamation and run the nanite programs himself. What I need from the both of you are the answers to two questions. First, can we provide a military escort capable of neutralizing a nanite-bodied if he proves hostile? Second, we will need to provide a gap in the wall through which he can pass. What can we do to prevent any unwanted visitors from entering the Reclamation?"

Jeenya's eyes had grown intense and gained extraordinary focus. She looked as though she had something to say, and so Sahaan nodded to her.

"We have a protocol for this planned out," Jeenya said. "It's just a thought experiment meant for undergrads. I can't believe we'll actually have a practical use for it. The idea is to make an airlock out of the walls, except it's not an *air*lock but a *nanite*lock. We put some of the walls on rollers so that we can quickly open and close a breach. But instead of that breach opening into the Reclamation, it just opens into another ring of walls, which has another open-and-close section on its opposite side. We leave that one closed until we're certain we don't have any unwanted guests inside the airlock."

"How long would it take to set up such an airlock?"

"About two days. And under the current situation, let's make that three. We'd have to call in a favor from Alterra. With the visitations and Citrine-Adamantine wallroad explosion, we've only got two backup wall slabs left."

"Will they have enough?" Khatra asked.

Jeenya nodded. "They should. They were pretty well stocked, last time I checked."

Sahaan turned to Master Sergeant Anush. "And the military situation?"

"We could do this only if we reduced the portal to its minimum functional capacity, which I don't like. I fear another civilian rush on the portal."

Dr. Darshak adjusted himself against the door frame. "How many soldiers are you thinking?"

Anush turned to Sahaan. "We would escort him from this airlock to the Portal City containment zone, and then back to the airlock, correct?"

Sahaan nodded.

"Let's say seventy."

The doctor nodded. "About two days to get them all inoculated."

"And," Anush added, "we will need to pull our quantum-disruptive armaments out of storage and make sure they still work. But that will take a day at most."

"Well," Sahaan said. "It sounds like we have a plan. We just need to set a location for this airlock. Presumably at the point where we can minimize the length of Charles's journey to the capital."

"The wall between Barine and Exenine," Jeenya said. "That would be best. The *closest* wall, strictly speaking, is in the Enerine suburbs, but it's also heavily populated. The stretch of land from Barine to Exenine is mostly un-inhabited." She turned to the Master Sergeant. "How does that plan sound?"

Anush nodded. "Easier to secure if there are fewer people. I agree."

"Choose a precise location, and send that to this office within the next thirty minutes. I will tell Charles to be there in five days. That should give us enough time to make the appropriate preparation." Sahaan paused. "I never imagined I would be doing this, but here I am. Here we are. About to have a nanite-bodied visitor to the Reclamation. If he is genuine, I want this to work. If he is not, then I want us at least to be safe. If you think of any other contingency plans or safety procedures, you are authorized to implement them. Thank you."

The members of the room began filing out, except for Dr. Darshak who moved behind Sahaan. Sahaan turned his head and saw that he was tinkering with the thermostat. Probably for the best. Sahaan had been starting to sweat. He was also was starting to feel a bit lightheaded.

Dr. Darshak moved back around to the front of the desk, watching the door. When the last person had left, he raised an eyebrow and said, "I need to get you to the hospital now."

"I need to tell Charles."

"Let someone else do it."

"I will tell Charles."

A deep sigh, in and out. "Okay. But I'm having them prepare—"

"I need to walk out of here myself, doctor. Can you make that happen?"

"Mr. President—"

"Can you make that happen?"

A slouch of the shoulders. "There will need to be an ambulance outside. But I suppose I can give you some painkillers and we can try."

"Thank you, doctor. It's the visibility of this thing. It's very sensitive."

"I understand."

Sahaan turned to the computer and opened up the feed for View Seven while Darshak tapped at his handheld, presumably ordering said ambulance.

"Since we need to wait for Jeenya to tell us the coordinates," Sahaan said.

The news announcer had become very animated. "At this time, we have one-hundred and eighty-six districts reporting. Cooperation write-ins now total 37 percent of the vote, giving them a lead over the two traditional parties. Guardian is at 30 percent and Reconciliation at 33. With the race this close, anything could happen as the remaining districts report in. Those who have voted Cooperation are now arriving at the power facilities en masse and volunteering their time, claiming themselves to be 'cooperationists,' both in support of wall defense and communication with the nanite-bodied. We talked with one such individual earlier today—"

Sahaan turned off the broadcast.

"Dr. Darshak?" Sahaan asked.

"How about we just talk until we hear from Jeenya?"

"That sounds like a better plan."

"Charles?"

"Hello, President Sahaan Ekeer."

"The Reclamation agrees to your terms. I am sending you the coordinates where we will open a gap in our walls for you to enter. Have you received those?"

"Yes. I have them."

"Will any nanites be coming through with you?"

"No. Only the nanites that compose my body. They will not leave my form, and no others will be coming through. They told me to tell you that we will be shutting down all non-essential programs on our side of your wall to make sure that only I go through."

"Thank you for that assurance. There is something else you should know. There will be a military force of seventy soldiers on this side. They will guide you to Portal City. This is for your own safety."

"I understand."

"There are a number of preparations on our side. We will need five days. Does that work for you?"

"It does."

"I will order our scientists to prepare the flora samples, as well. You can take those with you when you are done in the Reclamation."

"I understand."

A pause.

"Is there anything else, President Sahaan Ekeer?"

"... Charles, it is very possible that I will not get to meet you during your time here, though I would very much like to. The man who has your memories is a rare mix of both intelligence and empathy. He searches relentlessly for the knowledge he knows is locked inside him. He has represented the Pinnacle well."

Another silence.

"Charles?"

"Thank you, President Sahaan Ekeer. A friend will tell me that he 'told me so.' Does that make sense?"

Sahaan chuckled. "Yes, I think it does."

"I will be there in five days. At noon."

"At noon will work."

"Goodbye."

"Goodbye, Charles."

"At this time, we now have confirmation that two hundred and twenty-nine districts have confirmed their ballot totals. Guardian has 32% of the vote, Reconciliation 31%, and Cooperation 37%. At this point, even if no Cooperation votes were to arrive from remaining districts, Cooperation would still be the winning party.

"In a typical election cycle, the winning party would use the intervening month to nominate candidates to various political posts. It is unclear how in this election cycle we should proceed. Under normal circumstances, Parliament would be able to convene and ratify any appointments made on behalf of the new party, but the current emergency has made that impossible. At the present moment, only two MPs remain outside the containment zone, and one of those, MP Bada Kismat for Exenine, remains in critical condition at Portal City Central Hospital.

"The President's office has issued a statement that they will provide a list of appointments by the end of the week. It describes the present situation as 'extraordinary,' but says that the president's office is fully committed to upholding the constitution and our democratic procedures to the best of its ability.

"Stay tuned for our next segment. Earlier today, our reporters in Besserine, Cynine, and Adrine went to those cities' reactor facilities and talked to citizens who have volunteered to defend and monitor their respective cities' power supply to the capital..."

"Hello?"

"Hi, Charles. This is... Well, I've been calling myself Charles. I suppose I should stop."

"No, it's fine. It's fitting. I think that's the word."

"Seems right."

"Did you have trouble with their language? I was worried you'd have trouble with that."

"No. The language came fine. The memories were the most difficult part. Catherine's communication helped a lot, though."

"That's good. I'm glad. Have they treated you all right?"

"Yes! I mean, well, there was an incident with a train. But it wasn't Sahaan's fault."

"President Sahaan Ekeer?"

"That's right."

"You talked with the president?"

"For a full three days. And then more later. But recently I've been talking to Consul Bharo Meharab. He showed me around Portal City Central Library today. He also showed me a famous book. It's famous because Sahaan's grandmother read it because of him, and used it as inspiration for a speech. And then she inspired him to go into politics. I read it. I know what that must mean for you. Reading. Because you can only download data directly into your brain, or at best, run it through a scanning processor in your mind, which is kind of like reading but not the same."

"What did you think of reading, Charles?"

"I liked it. I think it's better than scanning. And you're never going to believe me when I tell you what book I read."

"Why's that?"

"Sahaan's inspiration, the book his grandmother read— it was *The Politics* by Kenek, the book that got you talking to Brad."

"..."

"Charles?"

"Yes. I'm sorry. That's amazing. Have you talked to Sahaan about *The Politics*?"

"Not yet. He's not available right now. But I'm going to see him soon."

"Say hello to him for me."

"I wanted to ask you one more thing."

"What's that?"

"I think... I want to go to the Pinnacle. Unless you tell me I shouldn't."

"You'll be very welcome here if you decide to come back. You... You understand what will happen to your body if you do that, right?"

"I do. And I remember enough now to know what

effect my memories will have when they're available in the Pinnacle's memetwork. They told me you'll be visiting the Reclamation in four days. Can I go back with you?"

"Yes."

"Okay. I'll try to read as many books as I can until then."

"Please do. I'll see you soon."

"See you soon."

Sahaan retained few memories of the first day following his surgery. There were exactly two things he recalled with clarity. The first was seeing Lachel and Jaan's faces when he first woke up. The second was Khatra Aapada telling him that the Cooperation Party had won the election. There were other tidbits in there. Khatra was preparing to evacuate Portal City of civilians completely in preparation for Charles's arrival. Dr. Darshak appeared to announce the operation had been a success. A number of the details of that conversation had not made it through the sedative, except for the look on the doctor's face when he'd said, "*if* you remain in bed this time."

The following days passed uneventfully. He received regular updates from Khatra on how the preparations were progressing. Sahaan watched the news from time to time but mostly talked to Lachel and Jaan.

Two days before Charles was to arrive, the Portal City evacuation order was announced. Lachel and Jaan were given an exception, as were Dr. Darshak and a number of other patients and medical staff. They were given strict instructions, however, to remain inside the hospital at all times on the day of Charles's arrival.

The next day proceeded much as the day before it. The news was now covering the Portal City evacuation and Khatra Aapada's address to the nation about the government's plan to let a nanite-bodied inside their borders. The response was not an uproar, but rather a dampening of the high spirits that had rallied citizens to support and defend their local energy centers. A few individuals made comments online about wishing they could take back their vote for Cooperation, but most of the country seemed to make the unconscious jump from a hesitant trust for Charles the visitor, who had never so much as lifted a finger against them, to Charles the nanite-bodied, who was offering to save the lives of twelve thousand three hundred citizens (the exact number of those inside the containment zone was, by this time, known).

The whole country sat, holding its breath, waiting to see what this new visitor would do. It was during this interim that Bharo showed up at the hospital, surrounded by five military officers, and also with Charles.

"Welcome to Portal City!" Sahaan said.

"Thank you, President Ekeer."

Sahaan let out a small, embarrassed laugh. From others, he could get used to that. He wasn't sure he ever would with Charles. "Did you get to visit a library, like you wanted to?"

"Yes. I've been to Portal City Central Library several times now. In the Pinnacle, no one reads. We download data directly. Anyone who wants to can know the contents of innumerable books in seconds. But no one has the experience anymore of imagining a sequence of events as their eyes scan over words. It's an experience I want to bring back to them."

"I see. Does that mean—?"

"I've decided to go back. With the other Charles."

"Do you know how you'll be regarded in the Pinnacle?"

"Charles tells me I'll be fine. I trust him."

Sahaan had to smirk at that. How odd to be able to have a conversation with a person whose memories you mostly shared.

"There are other things they'll experience, too. Crying. Eating. A myriad of other sensations that don't map to anything they know. It will be good for them, I think."

"They will... experience all this?"

"They have something called the memetwork. Experience can be recorded and shared. Either privately or publicly. I want to make my time here public. Anyone will be able to download my experience and live through my time here as though they were me... in their heads. If that makes sense."

"I think it does. You're decided then?"

"Yes. I'm sure."

"Good luck."

"There's one more thing I wanted to ask you about. When I went to the library the first time, I went instinctively for a particular book. In a way, it's the whole reason that Charles ended up deciding to bring me into existence. Bharo mentioned it's important to you, too. Kenek's *The Politics*."

Sahaan smiled widely. "Yes. My grandmother introduced me to that work. She was trying to unite the two parties."

"For him, it was fascinating. The Pinnacle made so many modifications to the human genome, and yet our

264

social organization still fell into familiar patterns, ones that Kenek described so clearly three thousand years ago. All we managed to do in that regard was amplify our human problems."

"It's similar to what we did. My grandmother realized, at the end of her life, that she'd been so busy trying to prove the other side wrong and her side right, that she'd lost sight of the fact that her brother was a human being, whose perspective was valuable."

Charles nodded. "It will take a very long time for each side to unlearn fear."

"It will," Sahaan admitted.

"Will you be seeing us off tomorrow?" Charles asked.

Sahaan glanced at Dr. Darshak. "I hope so. It remains to be seen."

The doctor released a sigh. He shook his head at Lachel, who eyed Sahaan warily.

"Well," Charles said. "In case I don't see you again, goodbye. And thank you for everything you did for me while I was here."

"Thank *you*, Charles. Goodbye, and good luck."

Charles stood, and left along with the soldiers and Bharo, who waved to Sahaan and his family on his way out.

On the day of Charles's arrival, the news began a non-stop satellite broadcast of the area outside the wall around the new airlock. Sahaan and his family watched from his hospital room, attention rapt. Even Dr. Darshak showed up and took a seat.

When the nanite-bodied Charles was spotted moving toward the airlock, the attention focused in on him. They watched him enter the airlock, the walls sliding back in place behind him. A large group of military personnel stood around him, all holding weapons of a make that Sahaan had only seen in history textbooks.

They stood motionless for some time. Perhaps too long, Sahaan thought. The scientists were probably just being thorough, he kept telling himself. Finally, the interior door of the airlock started to slide open, and the whole room exhaled. Charles had passed the first test, at least. No Pinnacle nanites had followed him in through the airlock gap.

As the walls slid open, the view switched from aerial to a ground-based location near the airlock's outer wall ring. A camera person must have been granted access to film the event. The walls rolled along their track, and Charles appeared, striding out through the gap in the walls, his body towering three additional meters over the heads of the soldiers surrounding him. His skin was a shimmering, metallic gray. His feet were haunched back like a quadruped's. His head was taller and longer, and he possessed nose, ears, and eyes—very human-looking eyes—but no mouth. The surface of his entire body was aflutter with orange holograms, appearing and disappearing across the surface of his frame too quickly to grasp at what any of them were, or to read them if they contained any kind of writing.

The ground had been marked out for him, a white line leading away through a field comprised mostly of tall grasses, a narrow corridor of which had been mowed down so that the white line would be visible. Charles followed the line without a moment's hesitation.

The camera followed him, and a few minutes later

they came to one of the largest semis Sahaan had ever seen, probably something military-grade. The soldiers ordered Charles into the bed of the trailer, and he complied. The trailer took off through the plains, and before too long, came to the edge of the Eline-Portal City highway, where it clambered up onto the pavement and then, having righted itself, took off toward the capital.

"When will he arrive?" Jaan asked.

"In an hour or two," Lachel said.

Commentary appeared on top of the video of Charles's now very uninteresting, silent ride in the back of a military tractor-trailer. Sahaan lay quietly, realizing that it was likely not just the entirety of the Reclamation watching these events. Catherine had said that Pinnacle nanites watched them from above, moving across the dome-shaped field created by the walls, watching. The entire planet was likely watching and waiting to see what would happen next.

Conversation in Sahaan's hospital room grew lighter. Even Dr. Darshak joined in, before starting a round of checking all of Sahaan's vitals.

"You're doing well," he said. "How do you feel?"

"Definitely better," Sahaan said. "Perhaps I could—?"

Darshak raised a hand. "We'll see."

Sahaan grumbled, and Lachel shot him a gaze.

When Charles's semi exited the highway into the city, the news grew much more active. The cameras followed the semi, with Charles's head sticking up comically out of the back, through the city, and around turns, until finally the white, shimmering containment boundary appeared. The light from it seemed brighter than ever, lighting up all its surroundings.

The semi stopped just ten or twelve meters from the boundary, and one of the walls along the bed of the semi was pulled down. Charles hopped down, his enormous feet cracking the pavement. He pulled one foot up, looked down at it, then seemed almost to wince. He proceeded with much more careful steps toward the boundary of the zone.

And here they were. The one moment Sahaan and Aapada couldn't have possibly prepared any contingency for. If Charles decided now not to neutralize the Pinnacle nanites, but to empower them in some way, to cause them to again expand, it would at the very least be bad; it could potentially be the end.

But he had to start somewhere. Trust always had to start with that leap of faith. If he could never trust at all, then they would remain perpetual enemies. Such an extraordinary risk. But for the lives of twelve thousand people? Yes. He would make the same decision again.

The soldiers held their firearms ready.

Charles grew closer to the containment zone field. His steps grew more careful, more hesitant, but still he drew closer.

He came to its edge.

He stepped through it, disappearing from view.

A gasp came through the news feed from the cameraperson.

"What's happening?" Lachel asked.

"Was he supposed to do that?" This from the doctor.

"He wasn't specific about the details," Sahaan said. "He merely said he would neutralize all the Pinnacle nanites and put our people back the way they were."

Unbearably long minutes passed. The news anchors

began reading off energy usage statistics for the containment field, amongst its other monitoring equipment.

"Wait!" The voice of one of the scientists on the news interrupted one of the anchors. "There's a fluctuation. Another one. Power requirements are dropping! Get a camera on it. Is the field itself shrinking?"

The view from the street returned. At first there didn't seem to be any change, but then Sahaan saw it, a water drain slowly peeling into view at the base of the field, a street lamp slowly appearing, then the side of a damaged car. Charles came into view, too, the field moving through and around him. He walked back toward the semi and merely hopped into it, shaking the vehicle as it did so, a blank, plain expression on his face as the containment field receded into the distance. People had now appeared, some two blocks away, lying on the ground, naked.

Aapada dialed her phone frantically and began speaking hurriedly with the Army Medical Corp liaison about the logistics of getting medical attention to the survivors.

"What happened to their clothes?" Jaan screwed up his face.

Lachel put a hand on his shoulder. "Until just now, they were all as big and as tall as Charles, honey."

"I want to go see him," Sahaan said, his gaze directly at Dr. Darshak.

The doctor looked at the machines hooked up to Sahaan, and winced, then sighed. "All right."

Sahaan got on his handheld to Bharo. "Tell them to hold until I get there."

"All right," Bharo said. "I'm still trying to get our Charles and the shipment of plants all ready to go, anyway."

Sahaan dressed, and then he, Dr. Darshak, and his family got slowly underway. The soldiers posted at the entrance to the hospital did not try to detain them.

Dr. Darshak retrieved his car from the parking garage and they piled in, Lachel looking up the location of Charles's semi and giving instructions to the doctor.

They arrived to see Bharo pull up in his own car, their Charles exiting out the passenger-side door of Bharo's car, and scientists carrying trays of plastic baubles emerging from the back seats.

Lachel helped Sahaan out of the car, and they all moved toward Bharo, then toward the semi. Pinnacle Charles stood up in the back of the semi when he saw them. The soldiers rolled down the grating in the side of the semi, and Charles stepped carefully down onto the pavement.

Sahaan looked up at him, looked up into his eyes, and smiled. Charles, he realized, couldn't smile, but there was a joy, a very human kind of joy, that Sahaan recognized in his eyes. He thought back to the stories he'd learned about his great-great-grandfather, about arriving on Asura and being hauled up into the air in the enormous hands of a person like Charles. He recalled his own instinctive fear of the breach in the Citrine park walls. He didn't want to be afraid anymore.

"Thank you," Sahaan said. He pressed his hands together and bowed slightly, a very ancient gesture of respect.

Charles pressed his hands together and bowed his tall head down.

Sahaan gestured for his family to come forward. "This is my wife Lachel, and my son Jaan."

"A pleasure to meet you," Lachel said.

Jaan repeated the phrase meekly.

Charles nodded, then climbed back into the semi, and waved to them, while it was being loaded.

"I'm glad you could be here." It was the voice of the boy who was definitely not a boy.

Sahaan turned. "Charles! You're going with him, then."

Charles nodded.

"I'm glad I could be here, too."

"Take care. I'll be in touch."

"I'll look forward to it."

Charles waved as well, then approached the semi, where a soldier had to pick him up and haul him into the back. The doors of the semi rolled up, its engine started, and it thundered away.

Pinnacle Charles watched them until they were out of sight, his head sticking up out over the walled bed of the semi. Sahaan wondered what untranslatable words were flowing through that mind. He would find out in a chat with Charles over the communication device some years later.

"I was thinking," Charles said, "how I would be able to share my memories of this too, of the Reclamation's president thanking me, of him using respectful gestures. I was thinking I would show them all that we don't have to be afraid of you or diminish you anymore. That we could respect you instead."

Epilogue

CHAIR: Good evening, and welcome to this evening's symposium. The topic for this evening is the events surrounding the first contact between the Reclamation and Pinnacle in 2916, a topic we have chosen since this year marks the bicentennial of the founding of the FSA. We have with us this evening Dr. Iti Haas of the University of Archway, Dr. Derek Sommers of the University of Redwing, and Dr. Adya Hyaan of the University of Adamantine. We'll start with Dr. Haas, who has recently completed his Ph.D. on Charles Mayworth and his role in first contact.

DR. HAAS: Good evening. Thank you for having me. I know that the goal is for us to have time for discussion at the end, so I'll be going over everything at a high level. Charles Mayworth left us an enormous wealth of written work both about his life leading up to first contact and everything that he learned from his walldoppel. I think we have probably all watched or downloaded those experiences at some point by now, since they've been so heavily integrated into secondary curricula. While it's widely known that Mayworth was a prolific writer, the sheer volume of material cannot really be appreciated until you task yourself with studying it. Even I was forced to scan a good chunk of it rather than read it due to the practical limitations of time, and the irony therein is certainly not lost on me. Charles Mayworth was of a political orientation at that time which had become critical of the changes that the Pinnacle had made to the human organism and their myriad unintended side-effects. Today we possess a well-trusted system of integrating a change into a sub-population who desires it and watching the effects over three generations before either ratifying the change for widespread use or mandating that it spread no further. In Charles's Pinnacle, no such system existed. The human genome was modified wherever and whenever it was deemed by any individual to potentially be better, and those changes were allowed to propagate uncontrolled throughout the entire population. The Nanophage was also still sixty years away, this being the computer program-biological hybrid virus that wiped out almost two-thirds of the population of the Pinnacle, and so this was also a time in which the general populace of the Pinnacle was largely unafraid of any negative effects of their changes. You can see perhaps hints of a growing concern when Charles writes about his early political influence. The failure to create hybrid technological-biological flora was certainly a damaging blow to Pinnacle psyche, and got some people, like him, thinking about what other negative impacts might be forthcoming, but at the time this was merely speculation. My big takeaway from studying Charles was the sheer tenacity he showed. One of the more interesting details is that he had been capable of enacting his plan to create a walldoppel for nearly twelve years before finally doing so. When he first discovered subatomic particle QF8634A92, he kept the discovery to himself. He formulated the plan for creating a walldoppel but did not act on it. Two things are striking about this. First, the friendship he struck up with Bradley Moore, who ultimately convinced him to pursue his plan. The other detail is that he paid for the energy to execute this plan out of his own pocket, wiping out nearly half of his life savings at the time in order to do so. This was someone deeply committed to his principles, and that impression is reinforced all the more throughout the written work he has left us.

CHAIR: Thank you, Dr. Haas. I have a number of questions, and I can see that our audience does, too, but again, let's hold those until the end. Dr. Derek Sommers is a senior fellow at the University of Redwing. He holds a doctorate in Alterra and Asuran history, and his most recent book is *Connected Worlds: The Long History of Cross-Societal Influence in Pre-FSA Societies*.

DR. SOMMERS: Thank you, and good evening. For this symposium, I'll focus on one section of my book in particular, part two, which is about the role of chance in the development of pre-FSA social configurations. Particularly, I began noticing a number of parallels between first contact in 2916 and the end of the Resistance Period leading up to 2804. Dr. Haas has already done me the favor of outlining how Charles Mayworth only proceeded with his plan to create the walldoppel after encouragement from his friend Bradley Moore. About their meeting, Charles writes, "It was pure luck. On a particularly lousy morning, I abandoned normal social inhibitions and admitted to a complete stranger my interest in a three-thousand-year-old political philosopher." This chance event culminated in decisions that changed the course of our entire civilizations, though they may have seemed innocuous at the time. A less well studied period of our history is the Resistance, most notably because there are a number of disagreements on what political structure exactly to assign the pre-Pinnacle technologically modified humans. My own position is somewhat irrelevant here, as I wish to focus attention instead on a topic less well studied, that of Resistance culture itself. Few know this today, but the walls of the Reclamation were actually an Alterran invention, not an Asuran one, and an accidental one at that. The portal that the first Alterrans arrived through had already been active for over thirty years, and they found that the iron deposits in the hill beneath the portal had already gained quantum repellent properties. A man named Stok Thiksay, whom I could talk about for just as long as Charles Mayworth, actually brought the walls through the portal to Asura with his husband (then boyfriend) Le Namgyal. Stok had spent a year on Asura alone. He had come through the portal to Asura as part of an ancient Alterran ritual of redemption, which no longer exists, although you can still see some of its trappings in the Alterran graduation ceremonies, especially those of the Alterran Institute. One of the most ironic things about this situation is that Stok Thiksay was not the first visitor from Alterra. The literature indicates that dozens, perhaps even hundreds of Alterran visitors preceded him, but all before him were immediately transformed by the evolver nanites which then covered Asura entirely. Stok survived and was able to tell the Asuran Resistance about the walls because he had illegally entered walled zones on Alterra and exposed himself to nanites running benign programs. Interacting with those nanites slowed the evolver nanites long enough for the Resistance to find and save Stok. Without *these* chance occurrences, there would not have been a Reclamation or, arguably, a Pinnacle either. There is some, admittedly divisive, speculation about whether or not the Pinnacle became an organized political entity as a reaction to the appearance of the walls on Asura, or whether they would have continued to maintain the form of political organization they had prior (again, I'd like to set the status of that configuration aside for the sake of this discussion). In both cases, Stok and Charles, we see individuals who possessed both determination and a strong sense of their principles. However, without the occurrence of *chance* events, we can hardly imagine the kind of societal dynamics we can see in our present-day society ever having come into existence.

CHAIR: Thank you, Dr. Sommers. Again, I would like to remind the audience that we will be holding questions until the end. I can already see some productive parallels for our first two speakers to address. But before we do that, let's give the floor to Dr. Adya Hyaan of the University of Adamantine, who has recently finished her doctoral dissertation on the changing relationship between humans and nanotechnology over the last four centuries.

DR. HYAAN: We are all familiar with the debate around the social dynamics of nanotechnological integration with human biology. A commonly held belief is that these debates are relatively new problems for us, the result of recent innovations in nanotechnology and biomedical research. It is also easy, when analyzing the past, to look upon past nanotechnological and genetic modifications with horror. I focused my paper on this social dynamic, and I argued that the dynamic itself has never really changed. To give a concrete example, if we take a look at the time of the Resistance, we had one group staunchly opposed to any biological modification, some even to the point of being opposed to technological advancement writ large, and another group willing to make absolutely any change. That is what it looks like to us *now*. But according to accounts of the people in those time periods, *their* own past was filled with people making terrible decisions about their health and well-being due to lack of technological expertise and general social recognition of the problems, their present had birthed miraculous new technologies capable of solving those problems, and, depending on who you asked, those technologies were either a vast cornucopia of gifts to humanity, which would keep on giving the more we invested in them, or, alternatively, a dangerous path to degeneration and the ultimate debasement of the species. Cast in those terms, does this sound like a past or a contemporary problem? It is interesting how this same paradigm persists across the past four centuries, its details always changing, the variance between the extremes always changing, but the fundamental dynamic remaining ever-present. To riff off Dr. Sommers's astute observation of the parallel between the end of the Resistance period and first contact, I would add a second parallel: both are examples of a culture moving from an extreme position regarding the relationship between humanity and technology to a more dynamic, nuanced position. In the case of the former, the shift was isolated to Alterra. In the case of the latter, the shift affected all three societies, ultimately culminating in the integration of two of them into the FSA. I analyze our current cultural climate as one in which we are moving once more toward extremes. Although we can hardly compare ourselves to extremes such as those found during the Resistance period, it is nonetheless concerning. It is also disconcerting to hear that perhaps the only thing that stands between us and a perpetual slide into more extreme positions is perhaps chance occurrence, and I'm curious to ask Dr. Sommers if there is anything we can actively do within our social and political institutions to resist that change. But perhaps that's a topic for another panel.

CHAIR: Thank you, Dr. Hyaan. Well, we certainly have an exciting foundation for questions. Where to go from here? Normally I would pose the first question to get things started, but this audience seems brimming with questions already. Let's start with you. Yes, you.